Jonathan sq

"You're safe here. The attacked you."

Panic screamed through her aching body. She knew she could trust *him*, but not all those other people— the police, the family. She couldn't fit them into the puzzle that was her life, no matter how hard she tried.

An awakening instinct warned her to hide her fear. Maybe the emptiness inside her would fill up with all the pieces she needed. Until then she was alone.

She balled both her hands into fists. She had to try to explain.

"I'm afraid because…because I can't remember anything. About myself. About my past."

She unfurled one fist, her fingers desperately searching out his as she willed him to understand.

"The only memory I have is you."

ABOUT THE AUTHOR

Lynn Leslie is the pen name of the dynamic writing team of sisters-in-law Sherrill "Lynn" Bodine and Elaine "Leslie" Sima. Both women have been writing for most of their lives and are avid researchers, a skill that is evident in all their novels.

Both women love to travel and are involved in various social-service groups in their communities. They also love to spend time with their families, who reside in the Chicago area.

Books by Lynn Leslie

HARLEQUIN SUPERROMANCE
485—DEFY THE NIGHT
566—COURAGE, MY LOVE
604—SINGAPORE FLING

HARLEQUIN INTRIGUE
129—STREET OF DREAMS
192—THE LAST GOOD-NIGHT
287—NIGHT OF THE NILE

HARLEQUIN AMERICAN ROMANCE
551—CRUISIN' MR. DIAMOND

THE OTHER AMANDA
Lynn Leslie

Harlequin Books

TORONTO • NEW YORK • LONDON
AMSTERDAM • PARIS • SYDNEY • HAMBURG
STOCKHOLM • ATHENS • TOKYO • MILAN
MADRID • WARSAW • BUDAPEST • AUCKLAND

ISBN 0-373-70735-5

THE OTHER AMANDA

Copyright © 1997 by Sherrill Bodine and Elaine Sima.

This edition published by arrangement with Harlequin Books S.A.

® and TM are trademarks of the publisher. Trademarks indicated with ® are registered in the United States Patent and Trademark Office, the Canadian Trade Marks Office and in other countries.

Printed in U.S.A.

To Dr. Marc Simeon Karlan.
Thank you for your expertise—
you gave us exactly what we needed!

With special thanks to Dr. Steven E. Rolhke and to
Sue and Norm Westerhold for all those great
weekends in northern Wisconsin.

PROLOGUE

ACROSS THE PARK the moon, like a giant red beach ball just above Lake Michigan, beckoned her into the night. Surely it would be cooler by the water. Here, under the Majestic Hotel marquee, the combination of good old Windy City summer humidity and hot lights made her skin feel clammy.

She flicked open her compact to examine her carefully made-up face. Blush highlighted her cheekbones, accentuating the hollows in her face. Her lips were pale and glossy but her eyes looked tired. And frightened. She stretched her lids so her mascaraed lashes nearly brushed her brows and smiled experimentally.

There, that looked better. No one but she would notice the tiny glimmer of anxiety that lingered.

Somehow, some way, she had to change her life.

Holding that thought, she dropped the compact back into her evening bag, waved at the doorman and started across the street toward the lake.

The park grass felt like a slippery cushion under her feet. She slowed her pace to avoid catching her heels. She couldn't be late for this appointment, but she didn't want to arrive with a run in her stockings or grass stains on her dress.

When she was halfway through the park, she noticed that the moon had risen high over the lake and dimmed to a pale glow. It seemed as if all the lights in the world had gone out. Where a moment before she had seen park benches and a children's playground to her left, everything now lay in shadow.

Suddenly, out of the darkness something hurled itself against her legs. A scream tore from her throat, and she swayed for balance before she realized it was a small white poodle dragging a leash.

Relief flooded through her. Abnormal relief. Overwhelming relief. She leaned over to pet the furry animal licking her leg, laughing nervously at the absurdity of her fears.

"Hi there, guy. Where's your owner?"

"Ralphie! Ralphie, stop jumping on the pretty lady!" An elderly woman, her face flushed, rushed up to grab the leash with trembling fingers. "I'm so sorry. The naughty boy got away from me again," she gasped.

"That's all right. No harm done." She straightened while watching the woman struggle to catch her breath. "Are you all right? Can I help you?"

"No, no. I'm fine now." The woman held up her hand, with Ralphie's leash wound tight around her palm. "I have him and I'm taking him straight home."

"Okay. Have a nice evening." She smiled and stepped back, anxious now to reach her destination.

"You, too. Be careful in the park, dear. It's getting dark."

She nodded and walked backward for several yards, watching the woman to make sure she would be all right. Ralphie and his owner disappeared behind some bushes. Beyond the darkness, lights flickered on through the trees like fireflies. Part of her wanted to follow the old woman and her dog out of the park, back toward those lights, but she knew she couldn't.

Sighing, she turned around slowly. She had to get this over with before she could take the woman's advice. She crossed a reservoir of darkness between the town lights behind her and the moon-painted lake before her. The sudden and complete silence made her feel very isolated. She might be the only person in the world.

Alone, in a dark, silent universe. Funny, how often she felt this way.

A rustle off to her left, like something or someone brushing against one of the low bushes shattered the quiet. Probably a raccoon, or maybe another dog, she reasoned. Yet a tingle of fear made her quicken her pace in spite of the treacherous grass.

A second sound rippled around her. Louder. Closer.

She froze in a puddle of shadow, knowing any movement would betray her presence. Then terror struck her like an icy fist to her chest. Someone was here in the darkness with her. She could feel someone watching her. There was nowhere to hide.

She whipped around in a panic, hurling herself back toward the street, back toward the lights, the old woman and the poodle. Her feet slid on the grass, her legs twisting under her as she fell to the ground. Clawing at the soaked earth, she tried to get away.

There was no sound, no warning. Pain exploded through her body, and she screamed when merciless feet kicked her onto her back and more monstrous pain pierced through her like a million knives stabbing at her flesh.

She threw her arms up over her face, trying to protect herself. She tasted blood in her mouth, smelled it on her hands before they fell useless to her side. Something inside her mind began to shut down as a dense black cloud swallowed her.

Without warning, a light filled what remained of her consciousness. Through the skin of her eyelids, she could feel its brightness, sense its warmth.

Irresistible.

She forced her eyes open. An angel looked at her. So this was how it felt to die.

CHAPTER ONE

DR. JONATHAN TAYLOR stepped out of Memorial Hospital into the sweltering summer night, the smell of acid from the steel mills in Gary assaulting his nostrils. In the distance he heard the whine of an ambulance racing toward the ER. Another siren, farther away, joined in. He was glad to be going home. Summer nights like this, when oppressive heat stacked pollution over the city, always drove people a little nuts. But none of it would be his problem until tomorrow. Grateful, he turned toward the staff parking lot.

"Wait, Jonathan! There's one coming in for us."

Damn!

"Bonnie, the skin graft on that five-year-old finished me. You didn't catch me." Only muscle-numbing exhaustion would have driven him to snap at his scrub nurse. What in hell was wrong with him tonight? He sucked in hot, acid-tinged air. "Masters can take it."

An ambulance screeched to a halt inches from him. The back doors flew open and two paramedics jumped out. He took a step back, clearing the way into the hospital, but then curiosity took over. He leaned forward.

Even with the ambu bag forcing air into her lungs, the woman on the gurney looked dusky from lack of oxygen. Coughing, spitting blood, she fought to move her head free of the restraining straps.

Deep inside him, something snapped. A sudden surge of adrenaline shot through his system. He was needed. He swung around, gave Bonnie a nod and shouted at the paramedic, "What have we got?"

"Mugging victim. Police found her in the park."

The trauma team swarmed toward the gurney, rushing the victim to the room set aside for life-threatening cases. Jonathan followed instinctively. The body on the gurney was starting to thrash violently as the victim struggled for breath.

"Get me the tracheotomy tray!" the resident on duty shouted over his shoulder.

The woman's dusky color changed to chalky white. She was choking on her own blood, fighting to breathe. Beneath her eyes, her face had caved in, cutting off her windpipe.

"She doesn't need a trach." Jonathan pushed through the trauma team. "Look at her irises."

The victim's irises were shrinking to pinpoints, her skin bleached out entirely. Jonathan knew he had to act. Inserting two fingers between her bloody lips, he pushed her palette up and forward.

Her thrashing and gasping stopped. The victim took in a sigh of air and opened her eyes. Her unfocused gaze searched, then locked onto his.

"You're safe now. I promise. I'm going to help you." Her eyes blinked, then refocused. "Stay with me." His harsh demand couldn't stop her blue eyes from closing again. He'd lost her to oblivion; probably just as well, from the look of her. Someone had beaten this woman to a bloody mess. How she'd endured this much he'd never understand. She was a survivor!

"Get a chin strap."

Bonnie handed it to him, as always, knowing what he needed without instruction.

Finished, he moved back to make room for the neuro team. Carl Johnson looked at him for confirmation.

"It's a craniofacial separation. God knows what else you'll find. I want to go in to reconstruct as soon as she's stable. Before the swelling prohibits."

Johnson nodded. "I'll let you know."

There were no cops in sight, and the ambulance had left on another run, so Jonathan headed to the locker room. He shed his faded jeans and red polo shirt for green scrubs, all the time wondering about the woman. He shook his head, brushing away the cruelty he'd seen. His adrenaline had kick-started him. All he needed now was to splash cold water on his face and down one cup of the bitter black muck the hospital called coffee to keep himself going. It was going to be a long night.

"Jonathan, I think you'd better see this."

He hadn't heard Bonnie come in. Something in her pale face made him grab the chart, but instead of looking at it, he stared at her. Bonnie was an old pro. Why was she so upset? She'd seen worse.

"What's going on? Dr. Johnson done?"

"Not yet." She put her hand out as if she might touch him, then stopped. "The victim is Randall Chambers's niece, Amanda Braithwaite. The police are in ER with her identification."

He heard her words. They crashed like clanging cymbals through his brain but their meaning wouldn't sink in. Because he'd been in the operating room for eight hours. Because he was hungry. Because he was impatient to do his job while he could make a difference. Because he didn't want to believe them.

"What?" He stared at the clipboard with the ER admittance chart a black blur. That woman with every facial bone pulled away from her skull so it hung like a bloody mask couldn't be *his* Amanda.

"It's Amanda Braithwaite," Bonnie repeated. "The police found her Medic Alert bracelet, her driver's license and..."

"All right! All right! I get the picture," he snarled, not wanting to understand, not wanting to believe.

Bonnie looked confused at his abrupt response, but she was smart enough to remain silent while he came to terms with his disbelief and anger. "Have you called her uncle?"

"No luck so far. Mr. Chambers is at that hospital administrators' conference in Dallas. We called his service and left a message. His wife wasn't home. We left a message for her to call the hospital immediately."

Amanda. Beautiful Amanda. Wild Amanda. Cruel Amanda.

He shut off that train of thought, knowing he was going to have to stop thinking of her as Amanda and start treating her as if she were any other patient. Otherwise he'd be useless to her.

"Where is she now?"

"Dr. Johnson ordered a CT scan and an MRI. They're finishing up now."

"Blood work done? Cross-matched?"

"Done. We have her records in the hospital computer. A positive. Penicillin allergy. Everything checks out."

The half-formed idea that someone had made a crazy mistake died a quick death. He relaxed his iron grip on the chart, took a deep breath, then thrust it back at Bonnie.

"Notify security that I need to get into Randall's office."

"What for?" She recoiled at his glare and clasped the clipboard to her chest like a shield. "Okay, Jonathan. Sorry I asked. You go up there, and I'll have security meet you."

Too impatient to wait for an elevator to the administration wing, Jonathan took the steps two at a time. The stairwell smelled of fresh paint, far removed from the life-and-death struggles going on below.

Amanda...

Light spilled into the hallway, where a security guard stood in the doorway of Randall Chambers's office. Jonathan nodded to him before pulling the door shut.

He scanned the bookshelves until he found the oval

silver frame. Sunlight streaked an eighteen-year-old Amanda's blond hair, and her blue eyes flashed in her tanned face as she smiled for the camera, one arm draped around her uncle Randall's shoulders.

Hers was a smile that wasn't easily forgotten. Jonathan hadn't seen it in the flesh for ten years. Not since the night he'd walked into his parents' lake house and found her in bed with someone else.

A sudden realization of how young he had been, Amanda even younger, took him aback. Arrogant and wild, they'd shared a summer romance full of great sex and lots of laughs. He hadn't even known he was halfway in love with her until that night. Then he'd been too hurt, his ego too bruised to deal with the consequences. He'd just walked away.

It had taken him a while to get over her, with the help of a luscious nursing student he vaguely remembered. He hadn't thought about Amanda in years. But now he needed those memories, this picture, as old as it was, to do what had to be done.

The door slammed against the wall. Startled, Jonathan looked up to find Carl Johnson looming in the entryway.

"Bonnie told me you were up here. The patient's being prepped for surgery. I found a subdural hematoma. She should make a full recovery—maybe some temporary memory loss—if no complications set in. As soon as I'm done, if she's stable, you can work your magic."

"ER trauma team find anything?" Jonathan asked

matter-of-factly. He kept his hands busy slipping the picture from its frame.

"Deep bruising at the throat and sprained wrists. She must have tried to fight the guy off."

"Was she raped?" The thought made him freeze.

"Nope. All her serious injuries are cranial. Some psycho. Maybe he was interrupted before he could finish."

"Let's go."

Jonathan's confidence built with every step he took toward the OR. Amanda wouldn't suffer for what she'd gone through tonight, he'd see to that. He was the best at what he did.

Johnson glanced at the picture he held. "Heard she was Randall Chambers's niece. That her? She was a babe."

"This is at least ten years old, but it's the best I've got unless Randall or his wife shows up." Jonathan's answer was clipped. He could hear stress edging every word.

So could Dr. Johnson, whose eyes narrowed with speculation. "She's lucky to be alive after a beating like that. I've never seen a worse craniofacial separation. You've got a night of it, buddy. Are you up for it? You were in the OR with the McKay burn for eight hours."

Some of Jonathan's youthful arrogance had never faded. It was part of what made him such an excellent plastic surgeon. "Don't worry. You do your job and I'll do mine. I'll give Amanda back her face."

SHE DRIFTED IN an endless black void. Cool, caressing darkness. She felt safe and comforted.

Safe.

The angel had said she was safe with him.

Suddenly vibrations of sound disturbed her sea of quiet and she stirred. He had asked her to stay with him. Had he come for her at last?

Another echo of sound reverberated through her. This time, an awareness, a *feeling*, ebbed to life at her center. She felt a pinpoint of heat in all her cold emptiness.

The sound gradually formed a pattern that beckoned her. It was *his* voice. She struggled toward it, but the pattern tightened into a knot of pain—pain pulsing through the darkness, engulfing her. She found she couldn't fight any longer. It was too excruciating to continue toward him. She had to escape from the pain. She turned to the darkness, and it took her, obliterating the sounds, a peaceful world where she could drift in oblivion.

She felt safe again.

THE VOICES RETURNED. This time she couldn't keep them at a distance.

A sob cut through her silent black world. Then a cry, as if someone were in pain, the rough edge of a strong voice—*his* voice. This time with his voice came comprehension.

"Dr. Johnson explained to you that Amanda is out of danger, barring any unforeseen complications. This semicoma is to be expected. It's aiding in her recovery. I feel safe in saying she'll wake up in the next few days.''

She trusted his voice. His strong, deep, comforting voice. He had helped her breathe, promised her she'd be safe. She sighed, a deep shuddering sigh of relief. If he said she would recover, recover she would.

''Do you have any questions?''

She clung to the sound of his voice. But to hold on to it she had to allow the other voices, the intruders, into her world.

''The poor dear. How she would hate all these awful bandages,'' a woman's voice complained.

''I still can't believe there's no brain damage after she had that seizure.'' A man, insistent and concerned.

''Are you certain she's all right, Jonathan?'' A soft, breathy whisper.

She fought against their doubts, fought to control the fears their words stirred inside her, where heat moved in slow circles, warming her.

''Randall, I explained to you that the subdural hematoma was successfully evacuated by Dr. Johnson. Posttraumatic seizures are common. They can occur up to two years after surgery. We're treating her with carbamazine for seizure prophylaxis.''

''Oh, my God! She just moved her hand. I swear I saw the fingers move on her right hand!''

''It was an involuntary reflex, Margaret. Perfectly normal. When I remove most of the bandages tomorrow, you'll be able to see the progress she's made in the last week.''

"The poor dear looks...so...awful." The cry gurgled into a deep sob. "I know she would so hate to...to be hideously scarred."

"Mother, you'll make yourself sick with all this crying. You heard Jonathan. She will recover. He is the best reconstructive surgeon in the city. Margaret, I think perhaps Mother should return home. All this is too much for her heart."

"Randall's right, Mother Chambers! I'll take you back up to The Lodge tomorrow. Randall will call you when Amanda wakes up."

The voices went silent. She began to fade into the depths of her black world. Some new instinct made her struggle, no longer content to welcome the emptiness. Searching through the darkness, fighting against oblivion, she sought one special voice.

And then, miraculously, he was there.

"Amanda, it's Jonathan Taylor, your doctor. I know you can hear me. You're safe and you're recovering. You'll still be a beautiful woman. Amanda, remember, I'm the best...."

She wanted to answer him, to tell him she understood. She tried to open her eyes, to let him see her comprehension, but the darkness rushed back, drowning her in cool oblivion.

THERE WAS A BRIGHT, blinding light. The darkness vanished, and with it her endless drifting. She opened her eyes. Where was she?

She found she couldn't move; she was alone, flat on her back, covered by a white sheet, surrounded by white: walls, ceiling, everything—white. She was in a whole new world. Heaven?

Where was her angel?

He would guide her through this new world. He would be her lifeline, her anchor in this unknown.

She drifted off into darkness once more, but this time it felt different.

When she opened her eyes again she realized she was lying in a hospital bed. Why? How had she gotten here? She couldn't remember. And she couldn't move, she was anchored to the bed in such a way that she couldn't even shift her head.

Why was she here? She lay there, flexing her fingers to prove to herself that she was alive, frustrated and fighting her stubborn memory.

She drew in a deep breath, trying to take stock of herself. She couldn't move, couldn't really see much, but she could feel. Something hard and cold pressed against her face. When she tried to lift one hand to explore it, she realized her left wrist was strapped down with a tube leading out of her arm. Her eyes followed the tube up to an IV bag hung on an aluminum stand. Cautiously she shifted her gaze to the right.

"Goodness, you're awake!"

The voice startled her. It belonged to a woman with a pale face dressed in a uniform jacket covered with butterflies. Her mind searched for a moment. Monarchs.

The nurse smiled. "How are you feeling?" she asked.

"Where is my angel?"

The smile disappeared. The nurse took her wrist and checked her over as if she were a specimen.

"Jonathan." Her voice was a soft whisper that sounded hollow to her. Strange. Not like Jonathan's voice.

"You mean you want to see Dr. Taylor?"

Instinctively she moved her head on the pillow, and that small effort caused an explosion behind her eyes.

"Don't try to move." The nurse's face started to fade. "Stay awake and I'll get the doctors for you."

The pain in her head began to settle. She was afraid to close her eyes, afraid the darkness would engulf her again. She was alone and afraid. If he didn't come soon, the whiteness might swallow her up and she'd disappear forever.

"Amanda. Amanda, can you hear me?"

She must have closed her eyes after all, for she found she had to open them to see him. The brightness dissolved in his dark hair, making it easier to see. His eyes were a mixture of blue and green and gold, just as she remembered. He was here at last. She wasn't alone.

She sighed. "I thought you were an angel."

The nurse laughed. "That's a new one."

He leaned over her so she wouldn't have to strain to see him. "How do you feel?"

"You are...the best, Jonathan."

The words made him smile. The nurse laughed out loud somewhere behind her, but she looked only at Jonathan. His smile was infectious, crinkling his eyes at the corners and slashing deep dimples in his cheeks. She wanted to share that smile, so she attempted one herself. Pain stabbed through her face.

"Hurts."

"Amanda, don't try to smile." His angel face hardened. Suddenly he was just a man. "You have a plate on your nose and wires in your jaw and in your mouth. Don't let that worry you. You're going to be fine."

"Why?" She suddenly realized it hurt to talk, but she had to know why. Why did she hurt?

He bent over her, and a wave of dark hair fell over his eyes. He tossed his head to clear the stray lock away. She could smell him; his masculinity permeated the scent of lime aftershave.

"I want you to rest now. Don't worry about anything."

"Can't close my...eyes." Every word she forced out through her lips brought pain. "The darkness..."

"No more darkness. I promise."

Despite her pain and fear, she believed him without question. She looked into his eyes, trusting that whatever he told her was true.

"You'll just sleep. And when you wake up, your aunt and uncle will be here."

Aunt and uncle? Pain centered at her temples in deep, hot throbs.

"You won't have to talk to the police about the night of the attack until you're feeling a lot better."

Police? Attack? She stared up at him, trying to hold back her rising panic. The throbbing in her head spread down her body. She didn't understand his words.

She knew so much about this world. She knew what a hospital was, what a doctor and a nurse did. She knew an aunt and uncle were members of a family. She understood those things. But police? Attack? She sensed that these words should make her afraid.

Jonathan was turning to go. He was going to leave her.

"Please."

But even he couldn't stem this rising tide of fear. It washed over her as she struggled with all this new information, trying to fit the pieces together.

The nurse came and looked at her. There was no comfort in her eyes.

She struggled against her doubts. Nothing fit. She believed him, but nothing he said made any sense. She tried to think of something else. There was nothing. Nothing in her mind. Her past was as dark as the oblivion she had drifted in for so long; black and empty and forever.

The only concrete images she could conjure up were of him—Jonathan.

"Please." She tried again.

"Amanda?" He turned back to her, just as she wanted him to. "Are you in pain?" His forehead creased, and the light disappeared from his eyes.

Physical pain she understood. It defined her whole being in this new world. It was meaningless compared to her rising terror.

She didn't have one tangible memory about herself.

About what had happened to her before she'd opened her eyes and saw Jonathan looking down at her.

Amanda. He called her that, so it must be her name.

But she couldn't remember what she *looked* like. Did she have dark hair like him or fair hair like the nurse? What color were her eyes?

She couldn't remember what she *was* like. Was she kind and good like Jonathan? If so, why would someone attack her? And someone must have. That much she understood. Had she made someone angry? How?

Who loved her?

Who hated her?

"I'm afraid." Her whisper tumbled out, turning into a sob that echoed against the stark white walls.

"Bonnie." The quiet word sent the nurse out of the room. She felt the bed shift as Jonathan sat beside her. He covered her right fist with one of his hands. It was large, with strong yet sensitive fingers. It felt warm and comforting.

"Amanda, I won't lie to you. There was severe damage to your face from the beating." His fingers tightened around her hand. "But I promise that when you're fully healed, you'll be as beautiful as ever." His eyes seemed to dissolve into a kaleidoscope of jeweled colors. They pierced through her, leaving behind a strange burning sensation in her chest.

"I'm not afraid about my face." How could she be? It would be a new face for her. She had no sense of how she looked.

"Then why are you afraid? Is it the attack in the park?"

Again he squeezed her hand. Now she understood he did it to make sure she believed what he said.

"You're safe here. The police will find the person who did this to you. He'll be punished, then you can put this all behind you."

Panic screamed through her aching body. First he reassured her, then he confused her. She knew she could trust him, but not all those other people, not all those other things. If he promised she would heal completely, she believed him. But the other things: the attack, the police, the family. These she didn't fully understand. She couldn't make them fit into the puzzle that was her life no matter how hard she tried.

An awakening instinct warned her to hide her fear. Maybe the emptiness inside her would fill up with all the pieces she needed. Until then she was alone.

Alone.

Somehow she knew she didn't want to be alone. Not anymore.

The only memory she possessed was of looking into Jonathan's eyes and being able to breathe, of finding comfort and reassurance. She clung to the recollection, balling both her hands into fists.

"I'm afraid because…because…I can't remember anything. About myself. About my past."

She unfurled one fist, her fingers desperately searching out his as she willed him to understand.

"The only memory I have is you."

CHAPTER TWO

SHOCK JOLTED THROUGH HIM like a current of electricity, wrapping itself around his veins and arteries, reaching into every part of his body. This was an Amanda he'd never known. Terror blazed out of her blue eyes—terror at the extent of her isolation and a vulnerability—that made her strangely appealing.

He lowered his voice to a gentle tone he rarely used and hardly recognized. "Tell me everything you can remember."

"You. All I remember is you." Her whisper broke into a sob. "I was...was struggling to breathe. Helpless. Alone. Dying." A deep sob shuddered through her. He felt it in her fingers as she gripped his hand. "Suddenly you were there, surrounded by a bright light, and the pain went away. You told me I was safe." She took a deep, shaking breath. "You told me that you'd...help me."

Her fingers trembled. Their weak plea compelled him to fold her hand between his palms, warming it.

What the hell had happened?

Both surgeries, his and Johnson's, had been wildly successful given the extent of her injuries. They'd agreed to induce a comatose state for one week to keep her quiet, to allow her time to heal. It shouldn't have affected her this way!

He'd hoped they were home free, that there'd be no complications. He'd hoped she would just be another case to him. The Amanda he remembered, all arrogant confidence, would recover quickly and just as quickly leave with her doting aunt and uncle. He would remain her doctor. A pleasant memory from her past. Not this. She was going to need a lot more help than he could give her.

"Please, Jonathan." Tears welled in her eyes, spilling over and spiking her lashes before gliding down her cheeks. She tried to raise a fist to scrub them away and winced with pain as the IV needle pressed into her skin. "Please...help me. I'm so scared."

Indecision, doubt in his ability as a surgeon had never troubled him, but this situation was clearly outside his realm of expertise. As gently as possible, he pulled away from her. It was time to be a professional.

"I'll get Dr. Johnson." He crossed to the door, turning at the last moment, compelled by feelings he'd thought long dead. "I meant what I said. You're safe here and I'll help you."

He found Bonnie hovering outside the door. "I've paged Dr. Johnson three times. He should be here soon."

"Yeah, thanks, Bonnie." He grinned sheepishly, knowing he'd been short-tempered and demanding lately. Amanda's case, Amanda herself, had thrown him a real curve, more than he wanted to admit, even to himself.

Waiting for Carl Johnson, he paced the corridor outside Amanda's room like an expectant father. This was Johnson's field; he'd know what to do. Even so, Jonathan didn't like this feeling of helplessness.

"Something has happened to Amanda. Tell me at once!" Randall's hoarse cry drew curious looks from nearby staff. They all knew Randall Chambers as a tower of strength who never got rattled.

"It's all right, Randall. Amanda's awake at last. I've just sent for Dr. Johnson to assess her status."

A smile of relief burst across Randall's ruddy face. "Thank God. And thank you, Jonathan." Randall leaned forward and clasped his shoulder in a fierce, emotional grip that surprised him. "I must phone Margaret right away. I can hardly believe that the one night we left for a few hours, Amanda woke up. Did she ask for us? May I see her?"

"Sorry. Not until Dr. Johnson clears it." Jonathan understood what Randall was going through, but he had to do what was best for his patient. "Go call your wife." There was no point in telling Randall about this new complication until he had all the information.

Jonathan stopped in midstride and muttered under his breath, "Where the hell are you, Carl?"

"Right here. Sorry, buddy. I was in surgery." Sighing, Johnson rubbed his neck above his sweat-stained green scrubs. "What's up?"

"Amanda Braithwaite is awake."

"Hey, that's great!" Johnson gave a bark of

pleased laughter. "All the neurological tests I've run the past week have been golden, just like I told you."

"Uh-huh. She has amnesia."

It took a full twenty seconds for Johnson to absorb Jonathan's curt announcement. Then he rolled his eyes. "Let's take a look at her."

She looked small, lost in an avalanche of white sheets and bandages. Jonathan resisted the urge to go to her and take her hand. What was happening to his professional detachment? He let Johnson take over, and stood back against the wall, trying not to respond to her fear as Carl pulled a chair close to the side of her bed.

"Hi, Amanda. I'm Dr. Carl Johnson. I performed surgery on you the night you were brought in. You're doing just great, but I want to help you some more. Let's have you stand beside the bed now." Johnson laughed low in his throat, as if he were sharing a private joke. "You know hospitals. We never let you rest."

Dr. Johnson gestured her up, not helping, yet close enough to catch her if she faltered. Jonathan couldn't keep himself from lunging forward to maneuver the IV pole out of her way, fighting to stay back when she struggled to keep her narrow white feet under her. This was Johnson's examination. He had to butt out.

"A little balance problem, Amanda?" Dr. Johnson's mouth curled reassuringly. "That's normal."

"Yes...I...I feel dizzy."

Dr. Johnson finally stepped forward and helped her back onto the bed. Over his shoulder, her eyes sought

Jonathan's approval. He smiled encouragingly but waited for Johnson's next move.

"Don't worry about it. We expect a little dizziness. Can you tell me about the night of the accident, Amanda?"

She looked confused. Finally she replied, "No. I...don't know anything about an accident."

"All right." Dr. Johnson made her answer seem perfectly natural. "Listen, what would you like for dinner? We want you to be happy here."

"I don't know what I like. I can't seem to remember. All I know is Jonathan."

Johnson threw him a look that made him squirm inside. "All right. Don't worry about it for now. Jonathan and I are going to go outside for a few minutes."

She huddled under the sheets, looking at Jonathan with tortured eyes. "You'll come back?"

"Yes. I promise." Shocked at the rough edge of emotion he heard in his voice, he pulled the door shut behind him forcefully. The automatic brake caught it, closed it gently, pushing the air into the corridor on a sigh, mirroring his own feelings.

Johnson frowned. "We've got problems. Better call in someone from the traumatic brain injury unit."

Jonathan braked his inappropriate emotions. They had no place in what had to be done. "I'll get Patrick Newman down here. He's the best psychiatrist in the state."

It didn't take Newman five minutes to respond.

They briefed him while he nodded. Jonathan had questions, but Pat waved him away.

"Let me do my job, fellas." He turned to enter the room as Jonathan stepped forward. "Alone."

IT WASN'T JONATHAN. She was disappointed, but tried not to show it. The stranger wore the same white coat over his clothes as Jonathan and Dr. Johnson, so he must be a doctor, too, she reasoned, feeling pleased with herself.

"Where's Jonathan?" she couldn't help asking. This doctor was different somehow. His eyes were...kind.

"Jonathan will be in soon. I'm Dr. Newman. Jonathan sent me to ask you some questions about your past."

"I don't know anything," she said, confused that they didn't understand her, or maybe they just didn't believe her. They could ask all the questions they wanted, it wouldn't help. Her past was a dark tunnel broken only by the bright light that had brought Jonathan to her.

"Do you know your name?"

His gentleness persuaded her to try again. Of course she should know her name! "Everyone calls me Amanda."

"How old are you, Amanda?"

She struggled. Panic, like a storm in her brain, threatened to send her out of control. "I...I don't know."

"Tell me something you do know." He ignored her panic, remaining calm and reassuring.

"Jonathan helped me. He was surrounded by…by a white light. Then the darkness came. And the voices."

He smiled down at her. "Good. Tell me about the voices."

"I heard Jonathan. And…and other voices."

"Did you recognize the other voices like you recognized Jonathan's?"

Her head pounded as she tried to find something in the darkness, just one tangible memory. "No. Please. This makes my head hurt."

"You did well, Amanda." Dr. Newman patted her arm.

"Can Jonathan come in now?" She felt alone and afraid without him. The dark emptiness in her head was terrifying.

"Yes. I'll send Jonathan to you."

She sighed. As nice as this doctor seemed, he wasn't Jonathan. She sank back into her pillow, willing the tension to recede.

IT SEEMED FOREVER to Jonathan before Pat Newman came out of Amanda's room. "Well, what's the verdict?"

"I need to do a whole range of tests over the next several days for a complete assessment. However, she appears to be suffering from autobiographical memory loss, atypical in these cases. However, it does occur." Newman seemed to evaluate him. "You're going to have to be very careful, Jonathan. She remembers nothing before *you* on the night she came into ER. She's developing a very strong attachment, which for the sake of her mental health we can't sever, but we can't let her grow too dependent on you. She wants to see you now, in fact."

Newman searched his face, all business. "Can you handle this?"

"Of course." Jonathan rubbed his face with both hands, trying to disguise his feelings. "I've dealt with the doctor-patient thing before."

Except his other patient hadn't been so terrified and so alone, or evoked such provocative memories. Every time he looked at Amanda, a knife twisted in his gut. Would the beautiful, sensual, headstrong woman he had once cared for ever return?

"Doctor Newman!" Margaret Chambers, with Randall in tow, headed toward them.

Jonathan looked to Newman for guidance.

"She's not ready to see them." Dr. Newman squared his shoulders. "They'll only confuse her more."

"You know Randall. He'll insist on it. C'mon. We'd better all talk to them." Carl moved purposefully down the corridor to intercept them.

"Pat, you help Carl stall as long as possible. I'll try to prepare Amanda."

She was lying still, her eyes wide, then her fingers began pleating the sheet. Careful not to get too close, trying to walk that thin line between doctor and friend, Jonathan stayed at the end of her bed.

"Jonathan!" she gasped, as if she'd been holding her breath until he returned. The soft trembling of her voice begged for reassurance. A tear trickled down one cheek.

"Amanda, everything will work itself out." He spoke briskly, professionally. "You don't have to be afraid. Dr. Johnson, Dr. Newman and the rest of the staff are here to help you. I'm only the plastic surgeon. To get you well, we'll need lots of help."

"I'm sorry." A deep sigh rippled through her body. "It's just that to me you're the only real thing in this world. To make any sense out of the rest of it, I have to have a…a lifeline. For me that's…you." With a quiet sob, she turned her face away.

Could he handle this? The power she offered him could have enormous consequences. Could he forget the past? Treat her like any other patient? Ruthlessly he switched off all the red lights flashing in his head.

"I understand, Amanda. But your family is here, and they're very anxious to see you. They've been here every day just waiting for you to wake up. I know you don't remember them, and they may seem a bit intimidating at first, but your aunt and uncle love you and want to help you."

She raised her head, frightened but determined, and very, very vulnerable.

He couldn't resist. "Don't worry, I'll stay with you. We'll do this together."

Her grateful response triggered something he thought had died a long time ago. Without warning, memories rushed over him. The taste of her mouth.

The feel of her body under his. The passionate abandon they'd shared that summer.

"I don't remember my family. Will they think I'm crazy?"

"You're definitely not crazy." Was that why she seemed so fragile? Why hadn't Newman reassured her? "There's nothing wrong with you that can't be fixed with a little time. Now close your eyes and rest."

Like a trusting child, she obeyed him, and that small action tore at his heart. Maybe, just maybe, he couldn't handle this after all. Pausing at her bedside, he critically assessed the healing process. He'd remove the gauze wrap tomorrow, the wires and metal plate next week. She'd have bruising and swelling to deal with for a time, and the hair would grow out where they'd shaved her. He was used to dealing with the transient consequences of traumatic reconstructive surgery. But repairing her memory, the essence of who she was, was out of his hands. He hoped to God that loss would be as temporary.

"I KNOW THE DIFFERENCE between semantic and episodic memory, Dr. Johnson. I was a nurse in this hospital before you were out of med school! So what does this have to do with my niece?"

Jonathan entered a conference room fraught with frustration. Apparently Carl Johnson had been trying to explain Amanda's condition to the Chambers with little success.

"You are deliberately keeping us from our own

flesh and blood. Do I need to call a lawyer?'' Margaret Chambers had the polished confidence of a beautiful, mature woman. A woman who was sorely tried at the moment. Randall sat with his head down, wringing his hands, apparently overcome with emotion.

Jonathan intervened. ''Your niece is resting, which is most important to her recovery. I'm sure Dr. Johnson and Dr. Newman are only trying to prepare you so you'll be able to assist in that recovery.''

Randall looked up, a hopeful light in his eye. ''It's not irreparable, then?''

''Actually, I think you'll be pleased. Carl did an excellent job with the hematoma, allowing me to operate before a lot of swelling set in. In fact, Margaret, her bone structure will be restored to the perfection of your own.'' He'd dealt with hysterical relatives before.

''We aren't deliberately keeping you from her, Mrs. Chambers.'' Pat Newman jumped into the fray. ''I'm her psychiatrist....''

''Yes. Yes.'' She shook her head dismissively. ''But why does she need a specialist in physical medicine and rehabilitation like you? What has happened since we were here last?''

Randall reached over to pat his wife's hand. ''Margaret, let the doctors explain.''

''She's awake—'' Dr. Johnson stared into Margaret's pale face ''—but Amanda is suffering from some memory loss.''

Margaret gasped and shrank against her husband.

Jonathan had the impression that the only thing holding her together was the strength in Randall's arms.

"Is it permanent?"

"Most probably not." Johnson looked as if he meant business. "However, for the moment, Dr. Newman believes her personal memories are completely gone."

"She doesn't remember *us?*" Shock registered on Randall's face.

"I don't believe she does, Mr. Chambers. I'm sorry."

Randall buried his head in his hands. "I can't believe this is happening."

Margaret waved away any attempt at reassurance. "Is this a complication from the surgery?"

The tone in her voice drew a quick response from Johnson. "No. All her neurological tests have been normal. I would have told you if I'd seen any indication of this."

"Autobiographical memory loss is highly unusual in this type of case. If, as Dr. Johnson feels, it is not caused by the neuro-trauma, it might have other causes. That's why I've been called in to consult." Pat Newman spoke quietly and confidently. "In many cases like this memory returns gradually over a month or two, but the patient never recovers the moments of the attack. We believe it's a defense mechanism to spare the recurrence of pain and suffering. In any case, I won't know without more testing." Newman stood, as if the whole problem were settled.

"I want to take her home to The Lodge as soon as

possible.'' Margaret insisted. ''She'll get better there. She loves the lake. Tell them, Randall!''

Pale-faced, Randall looked from his distraught wife to each doctor. ''I agree with Margaret. At The Lodge, my wife and I can attend to her every need. My mother, who adores her, will be there. All of her own things are there. Surely that will help to restore her memory?''

''Yes. You are correct. Those things will all be important in her recovery. However, she can't leave the hospital without some rehabilitation.'' Pat Newman glanced around the room.

''Amanda has badly sprained wrists and is experiencing dizziness. I need to do some more tests.'' Dr. Johnson, too, was adamant.

''Besides, she needs time to get to know you before you take her away. She'll be afraid to leave me and the hospital.'' Jonathan wanted to get his point across. Amanda couldn't be taken anywhere. Not yet.

Randall's head jerked up, ''What do you have to do with this, Jonathan?''

''Dr. Taylor saw her when she first came into ER. She was conscious and he spoke to her. He is all she remembers.'' Dr. Johnson's announcement caused a stunned silence in the room.

''She's very vulnerable right now. And frightened of everything and everyone but me.'' Jonathan tried another tack. ''It will be much easier on her if you go slowly.''

Pat Newman pulled his glasses out of his pocket and jammed them on impatiently. ''This needless wrangling isn't getting us anywhere. It's important that Amanda not have to deal with any additional stress right now."

"What do you have to say, Jonathan?" Randall's hoarse voice echoed in the room. "Will you have time to assist Dr. Newman and Dr. Johnson with Amanda, given your heavy caseload?"

"Can you help my niece?" Margaret's unwavering stare challenged him.

He gave one brief thought to his heavy schedule and dismissed it. "Amanda believes I can help her. That's half the battle." He turned to Newman. "As soon as Dr. Johnson agrees, she can move upstairs to rehab and your care. I can do my post-op anywhere."

Johnson nodded and glanced around at each of them. "Then it's agreed, Mr. and Mrs. Chambers? Dr. Newman will take over Amanda's care. You should visit her now with Dr. Taylor. We'll keep him informed, and he will give Amanda as much time as we feel is helpful for her complete recovery."

Time. That was the key. Time for Amanda to heal. Time for her memory to return. Time for him to learn to deal with the fact that she was back in his life, dependent on him. Could there ever be enough time for him to forget the memory of making love to his patient?

AMANDA HAD WAITED to open her eyes until after Jonathan left her room. With her movement so limited, she didn't have much range of vision. Still, anything was better than being alone in her empty mind.

Why couldn't she remember? She fought to stem the rising panic by reliving every moment with Jonathan. Only he was real, only his voice meant safety.

After a while, muffled voices from the hallway and the clatter of carts rolling past her door intruded on her solitude. Somewhere out there was a whole world for her to discover. Out there were the answers she needed, the knowledge that would set her free. She made a vow that it wouldn't always be like this. She would do whatever she needed to make a life for herself. Jonathan and all the other doctors in the world, the faceless people that were her family, might try to do their best for her, but it all came down to her.

She concentrated, trying to capture some feeling of what her aunt and uncle meant to her. Nothing.

No matter how she tried, she found nothing and no one. How could this be? She must know someone besides Jonathan. She might not know how old she was, but she sensed she was an adult. How could she have no memory of herself or anyone else and still remember all that she had learned in school?

That was it! School! She'd gone to...

A deep sob caught in her throat as she turned her face toward the sun filtering in through the blinds. She closed her eyes again. She wanted her memory, her life, back so much it burned like a fire inside her. She wanted to know, yet suddenly feared what she might learn.

She ignored the sound of her door opening. Maybe they'd just go away. She didn't want to see more strange faces; hear more questions she couldn't answer.

"Open your eyes, Amanda."

The one voice she couldn't ignore—Jonathan's. She opened her lids slowly, focusing only on him.

"I've brought your aunt Margaret and uncle Randall to see you. They want to visit a few minutes."

Here it was! What she feared, what she coveted: a link to reality. She controlled her trembling body and looked past him to the strangers.

The woman had beautiful blue eyes set in a slant above cheekbones dusted a rosy color, giving her a kind of exotic air. She seemed to glow in the soft light. Maybe it was the blond hair and all the gold jewelry she wore, wide hoops on her ears and a matching choker. Her yellow silk dress molded a well-cared-for body. There was a sense of wary concern in her eyes. Amanda didn't want to see into those eyes, so she shifted her gaze to the man.

He was shorter and broader than Jonathan. And older, with thick gray hair and deep smile lines around his brown eyes. He didn't look frightening at all, yet a new trembling started deep inside her.

She must know this man and woman in an intimate way if they were her family. She stared at them, trying to find something to stir the darkness in her mind, but there was nothing to help her.

She searched for something to say to them. Like a pinpoint of light, a memory broke through. She grasped it before it fled like all the others.

"Did Mother Chambers go back to The Lodge?"

"Amanda!" The man gasped as the woman rounded on Jonathan.

"You lied to us!" The fury her aunt turned on Jonathan stabbed into her. Hot, stinging tears burned her cheeks.

"My God, she does know us!" Her uncle lunged toward her.

She tried to put her hands up to stop him, shaking her head in confusion, the pain throbbing through her face adding to this waking nightmare.

"Please don't yell at Jonathan. I...I don't remember you. I heard you talking...before when...when I was asleep."

Her uncle seemed to turn to stone at her words. "Oh, my God, we are frightening you. Margaret, stop. Amanda is crying." He backed away slowly. "You really don't know me? Or your aunt Margaret?"

Margaret crumpled into the chair beside the bed. Randall went to her side and put his arms around her to support her.

She didn't want to hurt these people, but they made her nervous and afraid.

"Amanda needs to rest now." Jonathan turned to protect her.

"No! Darling, I'm so sorry." Her aunt broke away from her husband and sank down beside her on the bed. She smelled like flowers, and the hand that patted Amanda's arm was soft, the nails long and painted red. "I apologize to Jonathan. I've been so worried about you. Now that you're awake, we have some work to do.''

Smiling, Margaret ran her soft fingers up and down Amanda's hand. ''I'll bring your own things to you. Then you'll start remembering just like that!'' She snapped her fingers and laughed.

After a moment Amanda thought of what to say. ''That would be nice.'' Her answer must have been satisfactory, because Margaret nodded.

''I'll buy you a beautiful new bed jacket. You will like that, I know, my sweet girl.'' Randall leaned over, so close she could see every line in his tanned face. His hand grasped hers so tightly she almost cried out in pain.

''I think Amanda's had enough excitement for today.''

She couldn't help but feel glad that Jonathan's words caused her aunt and uncle to move away from her bed. She wanted them to leave, because fatigue pulled at every muscle in her body. Yet, in another way, she wanted them to stay, to give her answers to the myriad questions brewing in her mind.

One pounded like a hammer behind her eyes. ''Jonathan told me my name and who you are.'' One last time she swept through the dark caves and hollows in her brain. ''But where are my parents? Do I have brothers and sisters?''

Her aunt glanced at Jonathan, and Amanda saw him nod. Bending forward, Margaret again patted Amanda's hand.

''No, you were an only child. Your mother was my

older sister. She and your father, Bradley Braithwaite, drowned in a yachting accident in the Caribbean when you were twelve. That was seventeen years ago. Since then, you've lived with us and Randall's mother. We're your only family. Mother Chambers, Randall and I.''

"We love you very much, Amanda.'' Randall's voice sounded thick with emotion.

She didn't know what to say, what to feel. She stared up at Jonathan, and he nodded, as if he understood her confusion. "Amanda's tired. You have to go now.''

"We'll see you tomorrow, darling.'' Aunt Margaret waved to her from the doorway. "And if Mother Chambers is feeling better, I know she'll want to come, too.''

"She refused to go home until we could tell her you were awake.'' Randall blew her a kiss. "We will be back soon.''

"I'll be right there,'' Jonathan called as they slipped through the door. He turned to her. "Did seeing them spark anything?''

His chiseled face looked so stern and his eyes so intent she wanted to say or do something to lessen his distress. "They seem to be...nice people. But I don't remember them. I don't remember anything except you and the voices while I slept.''

He nodded. "Give it time. This has been a lot for one day. I know you must be tired. Would you like me to stay with you?''

Of course she wanted him to stay! Without him she

was alone in her dark, empty mind. But he was a doctor and must have other patients to look after. Being able to reason that through gave her the courage to move her head the tiniest bit on the pillow. "No."

"I'll see you tomorrow, then." He hesitated slightly at the door, and she held her breath, hoping he might stay anyway.

The door closed behind him, shutting out the strangers and the voices and the things she couldn't understand. She was alone.

Tomorrow loomed like a promise and a threat. She would find the pieces of her life and fit them together.

DEAD. *She should be dead and buried by now. Instead she was thriving under Jonathan Taylor's care. He went in and out of her room at all hours of the day, never keeping to a schedule, never giving an opportunity to finish the job.*

It had be taken care of, and soon. Before her memory returned.

CHAPTER THREE

SOMETIME DURING the night she struggled awake to find a dark shadow standing over her.

"What are you doing?"

Someone, gowned and masked, turned away from her IV bag. She couldn't make out which nurse was on duty, because it was so dark in the room. Always before the lights had only been dimmed so they didn't shine on her bed.

"I'm just checking," a muffled voice answered her. "Go back to sleep."

The next time she woke, the night nurse was standing just inside her door. "Good. You're awake."

"Is it morning already?" Her head felt fuzzy and it was difficult to focus.

"Two-thirty. I'm going to take the IV needles out and you'll get real food in the morning."

"But you were already here."

"No, dear. You were dreaming."

She felt so much better with the needles gone. Real time must have nothing to do with hospital procedure, she decided as she fell back to sleep, curling her arms protectively around her body.

Real food, at least liquids, arrived with a clatter of

metal trays. The orange juice tasted like heaven, even though it was awkward to drink. Actually, she hadn't realized until this moment that she hadn't been eating or drinking. She raised her hand to tentatively explore her face. Her head was still all but immobilized by the bandages. A metal plate covered her nose, extending over her cheekbones. She didn't want to think about the wires in her jaw, deliberately keeping her exploration away from that area. Actually, the less she thought about it, the better.

There was still a monitor attached to her chest, but having her arms free gave her a real sense of getting better. She sat up and immediately lay back down. Still dizzy, she would have to be very careful. She reached for her juice and sipped at it, savoring the sweetness on her tongue.

The doctors would be in soon. She smoothed the hospital gown, wondering just what she looked like to them, to him. She wanted to tell Jonathan... actually there was nothing to tell him, she just wanted to see him again.

She must have dozed, for when she opened her eyes again, a nurse was setting another tray on her bedside table. She lifted the silver food cover with a flourish, revealing a thin gruellike cereal. Even that looked good to Amanda's empty stomach, so she couldn't wait to try it. The nurse had elevated the bed, and without too much effort Amanda was eating. Her hands felt awkward, and as she manipulated the spoon, her right wrist throbbed with pain. She wondered about the heavy bandages there.

When she was feeling pleased that she had successfully fed herself, even if it had fatigued her a little, Jonathan walked in. A sharp jolt of joy, an awareness of him as a man echoed against something deep inside her.

She seized on that vaguely familiar feeling—at last, something tangible to grasp. She was almost afraid to question him about it, in case, it, too, slipped through her fingers.

"Jonathan, did we know each other? Before."

His eyes widened. But before he could answer, her aunt pushed through the door. "Of course you know Jonathan, Amanda!" Her arms were full of packages, one hand holding an enormous vase of red roses. "His family has a house across from us on Clear Water Lake. Here, darling. I brought you your favorite flowers. Aren't they beautiful?"

They were the color of blood, but Amanda nodded.

Margaret smiled and placed them on her bedside table. Amanda couldn't smell them. Didn't roses have a distinct perfume?

Jonathan distracted her by announcing, "I'm taking your bandages off today."

He was all business as his nurse, Bonnie, came in with a wrapped tray full of instruments. She swung a table into place and stood at Jonathan's side.

"This won't hurt." His voice was gentle but impersonal.

"I believe you," she whispered and closed her eyes while he slowly and carefully removed the tight wrap from around her head and throat.

Margaret's gasp caused her to open her eyes. Jonathan was studying her and nodding.

He continued to work, Bonnie handing him instruments before he could even ask.

"You should be pleased." Margaret sounded surprised. "Darling, only someone with your superior bone structure could look so gorgeous with the butcher job they've done on your hair. Let me get a mirror so you can see for yourself."

Panic exploded in her chest, making it difficult to breathe. As curious as she was, she wasn't ready to actually see her face.

"No. I don't think Amanda needs a mirror yet. We'll wait until I remove the plate and wires next week."

"Yes."

"Good girl." She felt pleased at Jonathan's nod of approval and strangely bereft when he left without another word. Margaret followed him as Bonnie silently cleaned up, then left herself.

She was afraid to touch her face, and kept her fingers clenched at her side. Finally her eyes closed of their own volition and she slept again. When she woke, Randall was sitting in a chair pulled close to the bed, studying her face.

"Finally you awaken, my sweet girl." Leaning forward, he laid his cheek on the pillow beside hers.

Shock made her blink at him. He was so close their mouths nearly touched.

"Do you remember how much I love you?" His whisper brushed over her face.

An odd, heavy feeling filled her chest. She didn't want to cause him any more pain but she couldn't give him the answer he wanted so desperately.

"No, Uncle Randall. I...I don't remember. But I...sense how much you and Aunt Margaret care for me," she added, hoping it would be enough to wipe the stricken look from his face.

A deep shudder ran through him as he squeezed his eyes shut. "My sweet, sweet girl, if only..."

The door swung open, startling him upright. Jonathan threw him a curious look. "I didn't know you were in here."

"I brought Amanda some of her things. And the gifts I promised her." His smile looked sad as he touched his lips to one of his fingers and then laid it on her cheek. "Open your things. Perhaps they will help you remember. I'll be back to see you later."

For the first time, she noticed a suitcase and two boxes at the end of her bed. The things Margaret had brought were stacked against the wall. So much generosity. Too much.

Jonathan lifted a pink satin nightgown trimmed in black lace out of the suitcase. "Go ahead. Maybe some of these things will seem familiar to you."

The satin gown and matching robe were beautiful but sparked no memory. All the lingerie bore labels that she couldn't exactly identify but knew were expensive. The gifts from Randall were identical bed jackets covered with lace and delicate beading, one powder blue, the other shell pink.

She didn't know what to think about all these beautiful things. Jonathan was no help, sprawled in the chair beside the bed, his long legs stretched out, crossed at the ankles, waiting for her reaction.

"Are Aunt Margaret and Uncle Randall rich?"

"They're comfortable." He laughed. "You, however, are very rich. The only heir to the Braithwaite fortune."

Fortune. She searched her mind but found no impression of how it felt to be wealthy.

"What are you thinking about now?" His voice had dropped to the gentle tone she preferred.

"About being...rich. Did I embrace it or shun it? Did it bring me happiness or sadness?"

The dimples in Jonathan's cheeks deepened as he smiled. "I think you enjoy every moment of being able to indulge your whims. Does any of that stuff bring anything to mind?"

"No." She raised her hands to her head, wishing she could force her memories out. "All I have up here are impressions and feelings."

"Tell me about them." He leaned forward eagerly. "Maybe there's something Dr. Newman can build on."

She rested back against the pile of pillows, searching for the right words. "The nurses make me feel warm and...cared for."

"Bonnie and her famous back rubs." His burst of laughter caused her mouth to curl a little at the corners. It felt safe to smile now. It didn't hurt as much.

"Dr. Johnson and Dr. Newman are concerned, but a little more detached. I'm comfortable with them."

"What about your aunt and uncle?" he asked, watching her intently.

Now she had to be careful. She trusted him, but didn't know how much he would tell them. "I...I sense how much they care for me. But they confuse me." She didn't add that they made her tense and cold inside. She swallowed to soothe her suddenly dry throat.

Ever observant, Jonathan handed her a glass of juice. "And me?" he prompted.

"With you, I feel this...this...urgency to be close. To keep you with me. Do you think that's because we knew each other before?" His eyes had gone dark, almost black. "Were we friends?"

He shifted uncomfortably in the chair. Alarmed, Amanda reached out her hand toward him. "Did I say something wrong? You asked what was inside my head."

"Yeah, I did, didn't I?" But his smile didn't light his eyes.

Suddenly the beeper at his belt went off. He silenced it and stood flexing his shoulders. "I've got to go back to work. We'll talk more about this later." At the door, he turned back to her. "I'm going to leave this door open. You need to see more of the world."

The world in the corridor didn't seem very friendly, though. The nurses rushed from room to room without even a wave. There was an overwhelming amount of noise. A woman in a pink smock pushed a cart full of flowers past her door. Men, women and a few children rushed by, all impatient to get somewhere. She'd forgotten all about this world. Actually, with her door closed, she had felt safe and protected. Obviously Jonathan thought she didn't need that barrier any longer. Well, if he wanted her to learn about the outside world, she would.

From the snatches of conversations she caught, she began to understand that all this commotion concerned other patients. People visited them, sent gifts and flowers. When anyone slowed near her door, she braced herself, but no one stopped that day.

The next brought Dr. Johnson with his tests, Dr. Newman with his kind eyes and gentle questions, and, of course, the nurses. She was beginning to know them all by name—Leslie, Donna and Chris. After dinner, soup and Jell-O, Chris came with orders that Amanda should go for a walk. They made it halfway to the nurses' station before Amanda became lightheaded. She could hardly make it back to her bed, even with the nurse's help.

Her aunt and uncle came and went several times, but they didn't bring Mother Chambers. She discovered her aunt had brought toiletries, cosmetics, perfume. All of her favorites, apparently, but nothing she recognized.

Always the best part of each day was when Jonathan appeared. He came in the morning, professionally. In the afternoon he'd stop by just to chat. Once in a while he'd stop in the evening. She had no idea how unusual this was until, on an afternoon walk with Leslie, she saw him from a distance and he waved.

"Is he a friend of yours?" The nurse turned her around carefully, for she still had an occasional bout of dizziness. "He spends a lot more time with you than any of his regular patients."

That gave her something to think about. So what if other patients' rooms were filled with flowers and cards and balloons, while hers was empty except for the bloodred roses and gifts from her aunt and uncle. Jonathan was her friend. Yet, as she fell asleep that night, she decided to ask him why she didn't have any other friends to send her flowers or cards.

As she began to understand time and grow impatient with the sameness of her days, she realized she felt much stronger. Now she was anxious to get rid of the plate and wires and see her own face. Maybe then her identity would return.

Even so, there was a certain security in the sameness of her days. Then everything changed. Jonathan didn't come in the morning. The time for his afternoon visit came and went. A dull ache throbbed through her, and she was tempted not to eat lunch. She even thought of asking for him when she realized he wasn't coming, but instinctively she knew that was wrong. She paged listlessly through one of the fashion magazines her aunt Margaret had brought.

Suddenly she heard his voice. He seemed to be arguing, but that didn't matter; he was coming to see her. The day was suddenly bright. She hardly noticed the other men with him—two strangers and both of her doctors.

One was a policeman—she recognized the blue

uniform from the television shows she sometimes watched to help pass time. The other had on a brown tweed jacket and trousers. His tie wasn't neat like Randall's, and Jonathan seemed upset with him.

Her aunt and uncle crowded in, too, standing by the door. Jonathan sat in his customary chair next to her bed. Dr. Newman and Dr. Johnson stood on the other side. The strangers took positions at the foot of her bed. She felt surrounded by confusion and huddled under the sheet in her new powder blue bed jacket, looking to Jonathan for guidance.

He smiled. "Amanda, everything's just fine."

Dr. Johnson nodded. "Amanda, this is Detective Savage and Officer Mahoney. They need to ask you some questions about the night you were attacked. We think you're strong enough to answer now."

Dr. Newman's kind eyes reassured her. Her family was there, and Jonathan; she had nothing to fear. But how could she answer questions about something she couldn't remember?

"We'd like to tell you what we've learned, Miss Braithwaite. Your doctors have told us you're sufferin' from a temporary memory loss, and I want you to know that we understand. Don't worry about forcin' yourself to remember anythin', okay?" The detective spoke very gently.

Jonathan nodded as if he approved of the man's technique, so she nodded, too.

The officer pulled out a small book, consulting it as he said, "The Majestic Hotel confirmed you made a reservation that night but never checked in. The doorman says he saw you standing under the marquee before you crossed the road and went into the park.''

Detective Savage loosened his tie so it hung part-way down his white shirt. There was a gravy stain midway down it, and she concentrated on that stain, afraid to look anywhere else. ''We'd sure like to know where you were goin' that night. Or where you were for the six weeks before.''

The silence stretched, echoing in the dark corridors of her mind. When she didn't answer, he continued, ''You apparently E-mailed a message to your uncle on 17 May that you were goin' shoppin' out of town. Did you go with someone?''

All the questions were too much. Tears welled in her eyes. She began to tremble.

''I can't remember anything,'' she whispered.

''Well, you did meet someone in the park.'' The detective leaned on the railing at the end of her bed. ''You caught a runaway poodle for an elderly woman walkin' her dog.''

''Amanda has a dog,'' her aunt interrupted. ''She's always been kind to animals.''

''Well, ma'am, that bit of kindness saved her life.''

Amanda looked at the policeman.

''The park is my beat. That poodle escaped his owner again and I caught him.'' Officer Mahoney coughed and his face grew as red as his close-cropped hair. ''That's when she told me you'd retrieved him earlier and that you might still be in the park. I didn't like the sound of that, so I decided to do my sweep of the park and lakefront earlier than usual.''

"Mahoney didn't see your assailant, but he must have frightened him off, because the guy left this behind." Detective Savage laid a ring on the bed. A golden ring with a sapphire the size of a nickel surrounded by diamonds.

Her aunt sobbed. "It was my sister's. Amanda's mother, Alice."

Alice. My mother's name was Alice. A clue, but one that conjured up no response. She felt nothing— no waves of sentiment about her mother or the ring. Her only reaction was vague shock at the size of the stones.

"If we knew why you were walkin' in that park, Miss Braithwaite, or who you were meetin', it would sure help our investigation."

She wanted to tell him that she didn't know, but she could only scream silently into the darkness of her memories. As always, there was no reply. She tilted back her head and, through a veil of confusion, found Jonathan studying her.

"That's enough!" he growled, staring first at Dr. Johnson and then at Dr. Newman.

Dr. Newman nodded. "Dr. Taylor is correct. Miss Braithwaite needs rest. Pressure to remember could impede her recovery."

"No more questions, today, gentlemen." Dr. Johnson ushered everyone out, including her family.

She was glad to see them leave. Her head was pounding, and waves of fatigue made her muscles feel like spaghetti, but she didn't want Jonathan to go. She held out her hand until he took it in his own warm, strong one.

"It's all right," he soothed her. "Don't think about it anymore. I want to talk to the officers, but I'll be back and we'll put the ring away." He stood and she reluctantly let go. He placed the ring in her hand and turned out the lights as he left.

She closed her eyes, feeling the ring's weight in her palm. Her mother's ring. But she couldn't think about a mother she couldn't remember.

Who could she have been meeting in that park? Had they been following her or would they have tried to hurt any woman on her own, as she must have been? Would they try again? When? Why?

Yet even with the little she knew, she instinctively felt that she wouldn't have gone into a park alone at night. That just wasn't safe. She wrapped her arms tightly around her body.

The door opened.

"Why was I alone in that park, Jonathan?" she blurted out, gulping back tears. "Why am I alone now? No one but Margaret and Randall visit me. No one has called or sent flowers. Not even a card." She looked at him and saw a strange expression, one that she couldn't interpret, on his face. "Why don't I have any friends, Jonathan? Am I such a terrible person? Is that why someone wanted to kill me?"

"Amanda." Her name was a groan on his lips.

He crossed the room and his arms closed around her. Strong, comforting arms that she couldn't resist. She buried her face against his chest and let her tears soak into his soft shirt, clinging to the only person she wanted or needed in this frightening new world. The only one who made her feel safe.

"Amanda, listen to me." He held her shoulders in his firm hands. "You are not alone. I'm here."

He was so close she could see a shadow of herself reflected in his eyes. Yet a sense of urgency made her press even closer against him.

"Amanda," his warm breath brushed her lips.

She could taste him. She felt him shudder.

Suddenly light and noise exploded into the room. Without looking at her, he stood and moved away from the bed. Goose bumps ran over her skin where his hands had been.

"Here's an orderly now. I came back to tell you Dr. Johnson has ordered that you be moved up to Dr. Newman's floor."

"That means you're getting better." The orderly winked at her as he helped her into a wheelchair.

The unsettled sensation in her stomach had nothing to do with the elevator ride. The orderly pushed her out into another long corridor, this one carpeted, with artwork on the walls. It was much quieter, almost as if she had entered a hotel. Even her room looked different, not like a hospital at all. There was a regular bed with a wooden headboard and a matching bedside table. A lamp filled a corner of the room with a soft glow. There were actually drapes at the window. This felt more like a home.

She asked to sit in the large wing chair. She wanted Jonathan to stay so she could talk to him, but he wouldn't look at her. Dr. Newman knocked before he entered. He had his glasses perched on his forehead. For some reason, she found that amusing.

"Welcome to the rehab floor, Amanda." He patted his pocket, looking for his glasses, then realized where they were. "Tomorrow we will be starting various forms of memory tests. Do you have any questions about that?"

"Yes." The questions pounding in her head needed to be answered. She stared up at Jonathan, wanting him to understand her fear and need.

"Won't the person who did this want to stop me from remembering who he is?"

CHAPTER FOUR

THE EMOTION GLITTERING in Amanda's eyes froze him, but Pat Newman leaned forward eagerly. He pounced, "Do you remember anything about the person who tried to hurt you?"

Jonathan watched her grow rigid, sweat forming on her brow, her hands clenching as she fought to remember. Then she closed her eyes and sighed.

"I can't even remember how old I am. That detective said I'd been gone six weeks before that night, but I've lost a whole lifetime...." She lifted one hand in a pathetic gesture that tore at Jonathan's heart. "Who hates me so much he would do this? Does someone want to kill me? Help me find out who I am. Give me back my life. *Please.*" She shut her eyes as tears slid down her cheeks.

"We will, Amanda. I promise." Jonathan folded his fingers over her hand in a soothing grip. "I won't let anything else happen to you."

Pat Newman cleared his throat and moved away from the bed diplomatically. Jonathan suddenly realized he'd gone far beyond the doctor-patient relationship he was trying so hard to maintain and released her hand. "You've had enough for now. Try to rest."

She smiled up at him with a slight curve of her mouth and winced as her skin pulled. He fought to maintain his objectivity, reluctantly following the other doctor into the corridor.

"Is something going on that I should know about, Jonathan?"

Even as he shook his head in denial Jonathan recalled the sensory tug he felt whenever he was near her. Her memories might be gone, but his were strong, heightened by her unexpected sweetness and vulnerability. He couldn't keep fooling himself, but he'd be damned if he was going to let Pat Newman inside his head.

Newman hesitated, studying him, then capitulated. "Good." Lowering his glasses to the end of his nose, he frowned. "She needs you to be completely objective. Tomorrow we start the real tests."

In the morning, Amanda insisted she felt strong enough to walk to the first battery of tests. Jonathan had cleared his schedule, driving Bonnie to distraction, so he could observe. He sat near the door so Amanda wouldn't be distracted. After one nervous glance at him, she turned to concentrate on Dr. Newman's questions. The determined set of her mouth touched something deep inside him; she was obviously frightened but persevered anyway.

The first test dealt with general knowledge. Pat showed her pictures of actors, politicians and sports figures from different time periods.

"Can you name these people for me, Amanda?" he asked.

A spark came to life in her eyes. "That man with the powdered wig is George Washington." Her smile blazed like a million-watt bulb. She didn't have to ask if she was right; she knew it. Jonathan felt as if he'd taken a shot of whiskey on an empty stomach.

He couldn't know for certain, but it seemed she did best with the historical group. The familiar faces of presidents since Jimmy Carter, and celebrities like Michael Jordan or Harrison Ford, were out of her reach. Her performance was exactly the same for the Famous Names Test.

He was amazed by how well she concentrated. He was getting tired just watching her efforts, but each time Pat asked if she'd like to call it a day, she insisted on continuing. The next tests, consisting of verbal and nonverbal priming tasks, were more difficult. She showed above average learning ability under trying conditions, further indicating that she hadn't suffered any brain damage.

By now, she'd been at it for several hours. Because he was watching so closely, Jonathan saw a faint trembling begin in her arms and legs and signaled Dr. Newman, who stood immediately, as if this were the natural place to stop.

"Thank you, Amanda. You did very well today."

"Did I?"

The strain around her eyes showed how hard she'd been trying.

"Yes!" Jonathan agreed. "Now it's time for a nap. I'll take you back to your room."

Her steps were unsteady, but she didn't seem to

realize she was walking at a snail's pace. He put his arm around her, only to steady her. Any doctor would have done the same thing, he told himself.

She rested her head on his shoulder. "I know the date the nation was born, but I don't know my own birthday."

This was dangerous territory. He should talk to Pat before he gave her any information, but he couldn't resist her. Despite his doubts, he answered. "It's August 9. You'll be thirty."

She thought about that for a moment. "How old are you, Jonathan?"

"Thirty-five."

"Did we play together as children at the lake?"

Far too dangerous to go down this path. "No, not as children," he answered truthfully.

"There you are darling!"

He was saved by Margaret. She and Randall were outside Amanda's door, obviously waiting for her to return. He felt a sharp stab of relief. Right now, she didn't need the baggage from *their* past.

"We thought we would be on time for your tests."

Randall appeared to have aged ten years in the past three weeks, Jonathan thought. He saw his hand tremble as it reached for Amanda and gave her a gentle hug. He also noticed her flinch at the touch.

"Is everything all right?" Jonathan asked.

"I'm just tired. I need to rest." She laughed, a genuine, carefree sound that transformed her bruised face. She looked straight into his eyes. "I'm beginning to sound like you."

Whatever barriers he'd thrown up developed a few more cracks. He pushed open her door and urged her inside. "Take a nap. Doctor's orders. We'll all be here when you wake up."

She waved and sank down onto her bed. He pulled the door closed as Margaret turned to him.

"Well, what happened with the tests?"

Randall slumped against the wall, as if standing had become too difficult for him.

"It would be best for Dr. Newman to fill you in, Margaret."

She turned on her heel and marched toward Pat's office without another word.

Jonathan searched Randall's tortured eyes. "I really believe Amanda will make a full recovery."

In slow motion, Randall moved away from the wall, the effort draining all the color from his face. "Thank you for everything. This has been a very trying time."

Jonathan watched him move. Randall's steps were clumsy, heavy, especially compared to the determined stride of his wife. He made a mental note to check the last time Randall had been in for a physical.

He found Detective Savage waiting for him outside his office.

"I need to ask you a few questions, Dr. Taylor."

Surprised to find him alone, Jonathan glanced around. "Your partner isn't with you today?"

"Oh, no, sir. Officer Mahoney isn't assigned to this investigation. I brought him along the other day hopin' Miss Braithwaite might recognize him, since he was first on the scene." He sat on the chair Jonathan indicated and stretched his legs. "She still has no memory of the night she was attacked?"

"No." Jonathan sank into his swivel chair behind a desk piled high with paperwork. Bonnie, he noted, had formed two piles, one marked Urgent, the other Urgenter. He smiled absently before looking at the detective, who was regarding him with a curious gaze.

"Amanda only remembers me in the ER, before her surgery. That's it—the rest of her past is a blank."

"Well, that's what I want to talk about." Relaxing, the detective loosened his tie. "After givin' the matter some thought and questionin' a few of your old friends, it became clear to me that you and Miss Braithwaite have had a prior relationship. I mean before the night you performed surgery on her."

Jonathan's stomach clenched in warning.

"Had you and Miss Braithwaite resumed the affair durin' the six weeks before she was attacked?"

He resented feeling as if he'd fallen into the middle of an old Columbo episode. "My relationship with Amanda Braithwaite has nothing to do with your investigation, Detective. Actually, I haven't seen or spoken with her for ten years."

Ignoring his icy tone, Savage continued as if he hadn't spoken. "So, you know where she was those six weeks?"

"Damn you..." Before he could issue his denial, a sharp knock on the door interrupted him.

Margaret paused on the threshold to stare at the detective. "I'm sorry. I didn't realize you were busy.'' Nonetheless, she shut the door behind her and joined them.

Both men stood, but Margaret refused to sit. She glared at the detective. ''I'm surprised to see you here. Have you learned anything more about Amanda's attacker?''

''No, ma'am, we haven't. I was hopin' your niece had regained some parts of her memory.''

''When that happens, we'll let you know. Is there anything more we can help you with?''

Perhaps Margaret's style wasn't to his taste, but right now he found her refreshing. The detective looked like a man ready to call it a draw.

''No, ma'am. But I'll be in touch.'' He nodded in Jonathan's direction. ''Thanks for your time. I'll get back to you.''

Margaret lifted her eyebrows in disdain as soon as he was gone. ''Do you think that man has been watching too many old detective movies?''

Relieved that he wasn't her target this time, Jonathan grinned. ''He's probably great at his job.''

''Well, I hope so!'' Dropping down into the chair the detective had vacated, Margaret heaved a deep sigh. ''I want to catch the monster who hurt Amanda. Which is why I stopped by.''

Her imperious anger was gone, replaced by a soft charm that almost disarmed him. ''I know I've been difficult to get along with. I'm sorry. Between Randall's falling apart and Mother Chambers's health, I've been going a little crazy. I want to thank you for everything you've done for Amanda. Dr. Newman thinks your presence is responsible for her progress with the tests. Can you tell me what's next, Jonathan?''

"She has to take it one day at a time. So do we." He turned the page on his calendar, although it was unnecessary. He knew what was there—it burned in big red letters behind his eyes. Tomorrow was the day he'd find out how well he'd done. "Tomorrow I remove Amanda's plate and the wires. She should look more normal and will see her face for the first time. Let's hope it helps her remember."

TODAY WAS THE BIG DAY. Jonathan had promised she could see herself for the first time. She'd look in the mirror and know who she was.

When no one was watching, she'd begun to explore her face, touching it tentatively with her fingertips. High cheekbones. A wide mouth—of course the wires could have something to do with that. Her ears felt small and fit flat to her head. She'd kept her fingers away from the plate over her nose.

Sometimes she wondered why she hadn't cheated, trying to see her reflection in the bathroom mirror. But Jonathan had seemed to think she should wait, so she had. His warning hadn't kept her from exploring her head, though. On one side her hair was stubble, on the other silky and about shoulder length. She'd pulled a piece forward so she could see it out of the corner of her eye. It looked light, almost without color. Her skin was fair, she could tell from her arms. Her fingers were long, the nails strong ovals.

But she didn't recognize any of it! And when she started to think like that, her head hurt. So finally she'd given up.

However, today was the day!

Whatever pill the nurse had given her made her feel as if she were floating. Jonathan and Bonnie worked in slow motion; his mouth moved so she knew he was talking, but she couldn't hear a word he said. Despite her best effort, she finally fell asleep.

After a while she sensed someone at her bedside, but she couldn't seem to open her eyes. Whoever it was stood over her for a long time.

"Jonathan," she muttered, trying to fight the heavy fatigue.

No one answered, yet she could feel someone lean closer, feel the heat from a body over hers.

She moaned. *Jonathan, where are you? Save me!*

A glass was held to her lips as someone lifted her head. No! Instinct made her shove the glass away as she struggled back to reality.

When she woke, she was alone and frightened. The dream had seemed so real.

When she touched her pillow it was *wet*. Not a dream! For a moment she panicked, but then she remembered Jonathan had been here to take the wires out. She felt as if she'd been set free. Her jaws and mouth were lighter, softer, more mobile. She reached for the hand mirror conspicuously propped on the table beside her bed. Her heart pounded against her ribs.

"No, darling! Not yet!"

She hadn't realized the door was open. Aunt Margaret swooped into the room, dragging a tall, thin man behind her.

"I've brought your favorite hairdresser, Marcus. After you take a nice, hot shower he's going to do something with your hair. Only then will I let you look in the mirror."

Good. She could put off the much anticipated, much dreaded moment. And when she finally saw herself, she would be glad to look her best. Amanda allowed herself to be led to the bathroom and thrust under the shower. She hadn't realized how she missed the feel of the water beating against her skin. She breathed in the delicate apricot scent of the soap and shampoo and decided this was going to be a very good day.

Aunt Margaret insisted she dress in a frilly pink nightgown and one of the lush bed jackets Randall had brought her. Marcus was waiting by a chair facing the window with what looked like an entire beauty shop of products at his feet.

"Sit, darling! Marcus is the miracle man."

She wondered what he would do—her head had obviously been shaved on one side. He massaged her head gently through the towel before running his fingers through her wet hair.

"I can do wonders with this, Mrs. Chambers, never fear."

Fear? A cold shiver ran through her. There was nothing to fear here in the hospital. Jonathan had promised her he would keep her safe.

A layer of hair fell into the towel across her lap. It

wasn't quite colorless, but very pale gold shot with silver; very intriguing and not at all what she expected.

Marcus leaned over her with the dryer. Hot air brushed her cheek and neck as he worked with the brush, pulling her hair over to one side. All the time he worked he talked; nothing consequential, he just droned on. She liked him, she decided. He didn't put pressure on her by demanding she remember or by asking her opinion. He just did his job.

At last he was finished. He stepped back, and Aunt Margaret walked around her. Amanda could sense that Marcus was holding his breath, and for some reason she did, too.

"This will do."

His thin face split in a self-satisfied grin. "I thought so. You can look now, Miss Braithwaite."

Her breath seemed trapped in her lungs as her aunt held out the mirror. Tentatively she took it, concentrating first on her hair: a snug cap of waves, soft and touchable. An ache started in her chest. It was time.

She looked.

The face she saw was pale. There were a few purplish green bruises along her jawline, but she noted the well-defined bone structure, the narrow nose, the soft, wide mouth. Blue eyes, like Aunt Margaret's.

A pleasant face. A strange face.

She knew they were waiting for her response. It wasn't that this face displeased her. It was simply new to her.

"The hair looks very nice. Thank you, Aunt Margaret. Marcus."

Marcus looked pleased. Her aunt Margaret smiled and patted her arm.

"There, there, darling. I know it's been quite a day for you. Get some rest."

It seemed as if people were always telling her to rest. After Margaret hustled Marcus out of her room, she was alone. She studied her face, trying to pull a memory out of the blank vault in her mind. Turning from side to side, she contemplated every angle. She opened the closet and stood looking at the full-length mirror. She had no memory of herself.

No identity at all.

This day, so long anticipated, was a disaster. She sat back in the chair by the window, the mirror still clutched in her hand. Outside, the world moved on, but she was stuck in here. She had no life. No friends. Nothing.

She allowed herself this one moment of self-pity before raising the mirror to look again. Something called to her from deep in those eyes. It told her to stop feeling so helpless. A powerful belief took root in her mind. She would discover each new thing as if she'd been reborn. She would put together the puzzle of her life. She wouldn't let this defeat her. And if she became a whole new person, that would be all right, too.

Slowly she lowered the mirror to her lap and looked up. Jonathan was staring at her from the doorway. Dry-mouthed, she waited for his assessment.

"What do you think?" His voice was cool and steady, supremely confident.

"It's...okay."

"Okay isn't good enough."

Oddly nervous, she waited for him to cross the room to her. What was it about him that drew her so?

He was handsome and brave and good. He'd taken care of her. But she knew he must take care of the rest of his patients, too. She held her breath, waiting for the inevitable comparison between how she looked now and how she had looked before.

"It's time for more tests with Dr. Newman."

He surprised her. Wanting to touch him, she held out her hand. He took it, pulling her gently to her feet.

"What do you think?" She couldn't keep from asking.

"I think you are coming along very nicely."

Their steps matched as they paced down the hall. But this time Jonathan didn't place his arm around her shoulders to steady her. And although Jonathan stayed with her in Dr. Newman's office, she knew something was different between them. Her life had already been divided into *before* the attack and *after*. Now there was a new partition. *Before* she saw her face and *after*. The thought worried her so much she lost track of what Dr. Newman was asking.

"I'm sorry. I didn't hear you."

He peered at her over the top of his glasses. "I'm going to read some passages to you. Try to remember so you can repeat them back to me."

Somehow, between yesterday and today, this had become easier. Some paragraphs made her sad. Others made her smile. The last was a little longer, a story about a cat and two dogs finding their way back home. She laughed.

"That's what I need. A way to find my home."

The look that passed between Dr. Newman and Jonathan stopped the laugh in her throat.

"Did I say something wrong?" She twisted around, seeking Jonathan's face.

He shook his head.

"On the contrary. You did remarkably well, Amanda," Dr. Newman reassured her. "However, we have more tests tomorrow. A few days ago, I asked your aunt and uncle to bring in some more of your favorite things. We'll take a look at them."

"You did well today, Amanda." Hands jammed in his white coat, Jonathan paced back down the hall beside her. "After you see your things tomorrow, everything will start falling into place."

"If that happens, Jonathan, I'll remember our old friendship. I'd like that."

She watched him stiffen. He didn't actually move away from her, but she could feel that he had withdrawn emotionally. All her burgeoning instincts clamored that she not lose him; he was still the master piece of her puzzle.

"All you need to remember is that I'm one of your doctors. And we're all here to help you." His voice sounded strangely flat.

Nothing could stop this new fire inside her. "You

saved my life, Jonathan. That makes you more than just one of my doctors."

They'd reached her door now and he pushed it open, refusing to respond. An old woman was silhouetted against the window. Her black hat and dress held a sheen of green. They looked fragile, as if they might crumble to dust if Amanda touched them. The face, haloed by a mound of white hair gathered up into a knot, had pale, translucent skin, offset by snapping green eyes and a small mouth shaped like a bow.

"My dear child, you look as beautiful as ever." The woman advanced to feather a kiss across Amanda's cheek.

The lips felt dry and powdery. She breathed in the scent of lavender.

This was another voice from the dark time. "Mother Chambers?" Her tentative question caused rosy color to rush into the woman's skin.

"I knew you would recognize me, my dear. That's why I endured the trip here to bring your treasures to you." Her hand gripped Amanda's for support. "My dear, dear child. I've come to take you home to The Lodge, where you belong."

CHAPTER FIVE

I'VE COME to take you home to The Lodge, where you belong. The words seemed to come from far, far away. The old woman—her grandmother, she supposed—looked kind, smelled somehow familiar, but was a complete stranger. She tried to penetrate the dark cloud in her mind.

Her grandmother slipped into a chair with a faint sigh.

"I'm sorry, but I'm not ready to go anywhere yet." Reaching behind her, she groped for Jonathan's hand. When she couldn't reach him, panic exploded through her. She whirled. "Jonathan?" For one frantic second she thought he was abandoning her, but then he stepped forward to take her outstretched hand.

"It's all right." The feel of his strong fingers steadied the wild thud of her heart. He led her to her bed and gestured for her to sit.

Randall pushed open the door, strode in confidently and stopped, blinking in surprise. "Mother?"

That gave her a moment to think. For some reason, she liked the idea of having a grandmother. And this obviously fragile woman had come to take care of her. But how could she go away with someone she didn't know? How could she leave Jonathan?

By now Randall had backed into the hall and summoned his wife.

"What's going on here?" Margaret seemed as surprised to see her mother-in-law as Randall.

"We're discussing Amanda's recovery."

Jonathan stood between her and her family, a protective barrier. "Mrs. Chambers would like to take Amanda to the lake, but she still has rehab for her balance problem and her sprained wrists. Besides, Dr. Newman hasn't completed his evaluation yet."

Reacting at the same moment, Margaret and Randall spoke together:

"She should be where we can care for her!"

"Jonathan, surely you can see why this should be done."

"*Silence.*" The black ebony cane appeared out of nowhere to strike against the foot of her bed. Its handle was a beautifully carved cat's face whose jeweled eyes, exactly the green of the old woman's, seemed to be winking at her.

Her aunt and uncle drew together protectively. Jonathan stepped away from her to confront the tiny autocrat.

"My boy, you know full well I seldom venture from The Lodge. Only my deep love for Amanda precipitated my visit. Amanda has been gone from me too long." The lined hands clenched around the cat's head. "I will not leave without her." The force of her will blazed from her eyes, and suddenly Amanda realized that she, too, had the strength to learn all she needed to put her life back together.

She didn't wait for Jonathan to respond; she could do this herself. "I will leave when I feel ready, Mother Chambers."

The air seemed sucked from the room. They all stared at her.

"That's my Amanda!" Suddenly, blue veins showed through Mother Chamber's translucent skin. "But you sound different to me. Why is her voice so throaty, Jonathan?"

"Her throat was bruised in the attack."

"It's the medication, Mother." Again, Margaret and Randall spoke at the same time.

Jonathan turned to her and examined her face in that detached manner that made her want to look away. "Actually the slight huskiness in her voice can be attributed to both explanations. It will disappear with time."

"Time is a commodity of which I have precious little left." The cane thudded against the floor, its vibrations reaching out to encircle Amanda. "How may we hasten her rehabilitation?"

"Mother, we must do what is best for Amanda." Randall walked to her bedside and laid a heavy hand on her shoulder. He squeezed it slightly, giving her an encouraging smile. "When is Dr. Newman planning to have Amanda look at her things?"

"Tomorrow."

She glanced up at the curt rasp of Jonathan's voice.

"Perhaps he could fit it into his schedule today. If you feel up to it, Amanda?" Margaret clearly wished to placate her mother-in-law.

The kindness these strangers had shown her, the concern evident on their faces couldn't be denied. "Yes, I'm up for anything that will help me remember."

Abruptly she felt weighed down as if her body were absorbing all the tension in the room. Her wrists ached, her jaw felt numb, pain arced between her shoulder blades. As much as these people cared for her, they confused her.

"Jonathan, would you ask Dr. Newman if we can do it today?"

His face hardened as if he guessed her feelings. "If that's what you want. I'll be back."

"He always was a good boy." Mother Chambers sighed, her tiny mouth curling at the corners. "I watched both his parents grow up. And him, too, from the day he was born, you know." As if she were remembering, she closed her eyes. After a moment she took a long, deep breath, "I apologize, my dear. Of course you don't recall trivial matters. If only you could remember more. My dear, if I knew why you deserted us all those weeks ago, perhaps I could understand how this happened." A tear streaked down her parchment cheek.

A chill crept over Amanda. Everyone appeared to be leaning toward her, taking up all her space, studying her with curious eyes. She gripped the bed's headboard, praying for strength.

"Today I will remember."

Where had that come from? Who had said it? She

fought against a swirling tide that threatened to engulf her.

"Dr. Newman will see you now."

Jonathan. Jonathan stood in the doorway. The room stopped spinning as she concentrated on his presence. She could breathe again.

"That's wonderful!"

Margaret held out a satchel needlepointed with huge pink cabbage roses and took her place on Amanda's left. Randall stood on her right. An honor guard—escorting her to distinction or disgrace?

"I will accompany Amanda," Randall declared.

"And I!" Margaret added with a sharp edge to her voice.

Amanda felt trapped. "Please. I need to do this alone."

They looked confused as she stepped out from between them, but they didn't try to stop her. She left them to follow Jonathan back down the corridor.

When they were alone, she glanced up at him. "Are you still angry, Jonathan?"

He shook his head, avoiding her eyes. "I'm not angry. Your family has always been hard to handle." His voice was cool now, wary. "Sorry if that sounds too personal."

"But we were personally involved—Aunt Margaret said so." She felt a stirring of urgency as caution clouded his face. "Just how well do we know each other?"

"We'll talk about that later." He stopped and

pushed open the office door, allowing her to enter first.

He had withdrawn again. A hot flush tingled along her skin. She couldn't stop herself from whispering, "Maybe this time I'll remember everything. Including us."

Dr. Newman smiled his usual smile, adjusted his glasses and cleared his throat. Without any preliminaries, he held out a rectangular velvet jewelry box. She lifted the lid slowly. An overwhelming blaze of diamonds and emeralds caused her to suck in her breath.

"Are they real?"

"What do you think?" Dr. Newman's eyes looked huge behind his glasses. "Can you tell me anything about this necklace?"

"It's lovely." She tried to catch a glimpse of Jonathan so she could gauge his reaction as she lifted the necklace from the box. Nestled inside was a pair of matching earrings. "I don't *remember* this jewelry. But I can appreciate its beauty and how valuable it must be."

The stones were cold. The light refracted a miniature prism from the gems. She ran a finger over one earring, trying to picture how it would look on her— how this whole set must have looked on her at one time. She couldn't imagine owning anything as valuable as this. Very carefully she placed the pieces back in the box and laid it on the desk.

"What else is in that bag?"

The doctor handed her a silver-framed photograph.

A beautiful golden retriever seemed to be smiling at her.

"He's wonderful." Clutching the photo to her chest, she turned toward Jonathan. "What's his name?"

He glanced at Pat Newman. "*Her* name is Lady," he finally replied. "You've had her for years. Do you remember what a great dog she is?"

Jonathan moved toward her. As far as she was concerned, half her battle was won. There was a familiarity about the dog. Perhaps not about Lady in particular, but animals meant something to her.

"I like pets."

"Do you like this dog?" Dr. Newman asked. "How do you feel about this dog?"

She stared into Lady's soft brown eyes. "Yes. I like this dog."

Looking pleased, Dr. Newman took that photo away and replaced it with a man's gold pocket watch. It felt heavy but not familiar. She turned it over to read the inscription on the back. "To my beloved son, Cecil, on his twenty-first birthday."

"Who did this belong to?" she asked with a little shake of her head.

The silence made her realize they'd hoped she would be able to answer that question herself. She placed the watch on the desk. "I don't recognize it."

"It belonged to your grandfather." Jonathan said, when Dr. Newman remained silent.

"Go ahead, Jonathan," he urged. "Tell her the rest."

Jonathan looked uncomfortable. "Your father gave it to you right before your parents went on a sailing expedition." He hesitated. "Their last trip. They drowned."

"I'm sorry." He was so ill at ease she felt she should comfort him. She couldn't remember her parents. She understood that this information should make her sad, but it didn't.

"The watch meant a great deal to you."

There was nothing she could do but shake her head. Dr. Newman held out a diamond tiara. She knew immediately that these stones were as fake as the others were real.

"This is costume jewelry."

Dr. Newman leaned closer. "What makes you say that, Amanda?"

"This doesn't look as...nice as the other things." She searched for the right words. "This looks cheap." Confused by the contrasting jewelry, she looked at Jonathan. What kind of woman was she anyway? "I wouldn't wear this, would I?"

At last he smiled, a genuine smile that lit the little flames in his eyes. "This is from the first contest you won. Homecoming queen, I think."

Contest? She tried to understand this new glimpse of herself. So far she'd focused all her attention on the black hole in her mind. For the first time, she thought about her body, becoming aware of how full her breasts felt beneath her silky gown and how the material fell smoothly over her thighs. Did she have the kind of body that garnered titles and tiaras? Was she the type that needed them to validate her life? Was that why she had no friends?

Suddenly conscious that she was naked under her gown, she tightened the ribbons holding her bed jacket together. "I don't remember that. Is there anything else?"

The large gold scarab hanging from a gold chain evoked no memory, yet something about it made her trace the carving with her finger.

"This is…" It came like a bolt of light through the darkness. "This is Egyptian! I've always wanted to go to Egypt." That clear knowledge brought her to her feet. "I *know* this. I know something."

Laughing through her tears, she threw her arms around Jonathan. "I *remember* wanting to go to Egypt."

She felt his heartbeat, strong and steady against her breasts as he held her. "You've been to Egypt, Amanda." He said it gently, trying not to dampen her enthusiasm.

"*No!* I remember…"

"You may very well remember being in Egypt."

"No." She turned to Dr. Newman.

"Yes, Amanda." Jonathan gripped her shoulders from behind. "You've been to Egypt. You went with Randall when he attended an international hospital council in Cairo two years ago. He bought this scarab for you then."

Even Jonathan couldn't convince her. She didn't want to believe she was wrong, because for a precious few seconds she had felt her memories at her finger-tips.

Then the blackness closed in again. She couldn't remember anything. Defeat pulled at every inch of her. Unable to stop herself, she sagged backward, allowing Jonathan to absorb her weight.

"I'm tired. I want to go back to my room now, Jonathan." She disliked herself for using weakness to get through to him, but she couldn't resist leaning on him, having his arm around her as she walked back to her room. What kind of woman was she? What kind of woman would use anything to achieve her desire?

He stopped about fifteen feet from her door. "This was a breakthrough, Amanda. I know now in time everything will come back to you."

Her muscles were tight with a growing tension. She tilted her head back to watch his eyes. "I want to stay here, in the hospital, until I remember everything. Will you make the others understand that? Please, Jonathan. You said it yourself—they are hard to handle. I don't have the strength to fight them."

"Tomorrow you might feel differently. When you're not so tired, we'll talk about this. For now, leave everything to me."

True to his word, he deflected all of her family's eager questions. In a shorter time than she thought possible, she was once again sitting alone in her room. Only the faint scent of lavender lingered.

Who was Amanda Braithwaite? At last she had the first piece to the puzzle. She wasn't certain what all these pieces would add up to—if she would like Amanda or not—but she knew she had to go forward. A glow drew her to the window. A red sunset—red sky at night, sailor's delight. Had her father taught her that? A movement in the parking lot below attracted her attention. Margaret was helping Mother Chambers into a long, black car while Jonathan and Randall stood talking. She wished she could hear what he was saying.

But tomorrow he would be back to help her, she knew that. Trusted in that. Needed that. The reason she didn't want to leave the hospital became perfectly clear, adding to the puzzle that was Amanda. She didn't want to leave Dr. Jonathan Taylor.

JONATHAN'S NECK prickled with heat—someone was watching. He turned and squinted at the hospital, where the reflected sun made the glass melt together in a red-gold glow. He didn't really need to see—he knew it was Amanda.

Today had been hard on her. He could admit that the need to protect her exceeded his professional detachment. He knew he was flirting with unethical behavior, but there was nothing else he could do as long as she depended on him. This, after all, was Amanda.

He knew he needed some company, so from his car he phoned Carl Johnson to meet him for dinner.

Jake's was a favorite spot with the hospital crowd, noisy and crowded with great northern Italian cuisine. Johnson's incessant shop talk turned out to be exactly what Jonathan needed to keep his mind occupied.

Over Johnson's shoulder he watched a couple embrace in the shadows. He looked away immediately, stung by an odd dart of envy. Ten years ago, that could have been Amanda and him.

"I'll be removing Amanda's wrist bandages tomorrow and releasing her. From neuro-care, anyway."

"How did you know I was thinking about Amanda?"

Johnson blinked at his sharp question. "Hey, buddy, what's the problem? Pat Newman mentioned you were edgy about this case. Maybe I should have listened to him."

The waiter set a snifter of brandy in front of him. Deliberately Jonathan cupped it with his palms, considering his response. "I never knew he had such a big mouth. What else did he say?"

"We had a consult before I left the hospital." Johnson shrugged. "Neurological evaluation shows no cause for continued dominant retrograde amnesia. There's no doubt the severe concussion caused it. But, according to her test results, Pat thinks it could be psychological now. Let me give you some good advice, buddy. You gotta be careful with this one. Give up this case before it causes you big problems."

Problems! He'd known *that* from the beginning. Only Bonnie knew the facts about his prior relationship with Amanda, and she would never gossip. He'd thought he could control his feelings—it had been so long ago—but the attraction seemed to be growing more powerful, even though he'd tried to back off.

He was playing with fire, personally and professionally. Obviously, everyone knew something was going on between them.

Far from distracting him, Johnson had made him even more aware of his problems, and Jonathan spent a restless night trying to decide what to do next. When he arrived at the hospital in the morning, he found Pat Newman had scheduled a conference with the Chambers family.

The three of them sat in a tight semicircle, facing Pat's desk. He couldn't help but think that the Chambers, secluded on their private island in the middle of Clear Water Lake, were just as exclusive here in the big city. They had power and they knew how to use it.

Amanda had been the first to pierce that wall of privacy as she raced her motorboat back and forth from the island to the town dock. She wore the skimpiest bikini possible, and half the guys in town used to hang around the shore when she water-skied just hoping she'd fall and lose part of her suit. But she never did. With her hair streaming out behind her, in those tiny scraps of material, she had mastered the art of claiming the attention of every male from thirteen to sixty-five.

She had caught *his* attention, all right. And he'd been damned cocky because she'd chosen him that summer. He'd gotten burned and he'd learned the hard way—hadn't he?

Dr. Newman cleared his throat. "Amanda is an intelligent woman. Selective amnesia is very unusual in this type of case. Both Dr. Johnson and I believe it will dissipate in the next two to three months. There's really nothing more we can do for her here.''

"So long?" Penelope Chambers looked every one of her eighty-three years. "I want my Amanda back before it is too late.''

"Mrs. Chambers, Amanda's subconscious personality is still there and accessible, even though her conscious personality is gone.'' He lowered his voice, trying to be kind. "Remember she's going to throw up barriers when you pressure her. She doesn't recall loving you. But that doesn't mean that she can't learn to love you now.''

While Newman spoke, Penelope started to cry softly. Randall reached over and patted his mother's hand absently, as if his thoughts were far, far away. Only Margaret seemed able to digest the information.

"I think we should take her home. Now!''

At last Randall found his voice, echoing his wife's sentiment. "I would think familiar surroundings would hasten her recovery.''

Dr. Newman nodded. "I agree. However, I would like to hear what Dr. Taylor thinks.''

The moment of truth was at hand. Professional detachment warred with his instincts. In the end, he said simply, "I think we should allow Amanda to decide.''

AFTER SHE'D FINISHED with the physical therapist, Amanda insisted that her door be left open. She felt less alone when she could watch others in the hallway. Strange that Jonathan hadn't come today, she told herself, trying to keep her disappointment at bay. Usually one or more of her family had visited by this time, too.

Dr. Johnson came at last and removed her wrist bandages. Still no Jonathan.

Detective Savage walked past her door. She wasn't certain she wanted to talk to him. He brought back the fear and the pain, both of which she was trying to put far behind her. He walked by again. Once, twice. Finally she called out to him.

As he entered her room, she crossed her arms over her chest. He shuffled closer and smiled. Her first thought was that today his tie looked clean, and it hung straight over a crisp white shirt. When he didn't say anything, she blurted out, "I still can't remember anything about…that night."

"I know, Miss Braithwaite." Looking slightly chagrined, he searched in his pocket. "I just wanted to give you my card for when you do remember."

He placed the card on her palm, and she covered it with her fingers. "I wish I knew who did this. I…I think about it a lot."

"Well, miss, I'm afraid it's a crazy world we live in." She saw kindness in his eyes for the first time. "You might just have been in the wrong place at the wrong time."

Seeing her confusion, he shuffled even closer. "You don't remember yet that people get mugged in this city every day. It was probably just your money they wanted. Nothin' to do with you at all." Backing toward the door, he grinned at her. "You rest easy. I'm on the job."

Actually, he was much nicer than she remembered. She smiled at him and waved before lying back against the pillows to absorb what he'd just said. She squinted, hardly noticing how the skin pulled less and less as she healed.

A deep instinct born in the darkness had made her keep this, her blackest fear, a secret even from Jonathan. Okay. She'd accept what the detective said. Maybe no one hated her so much he wanted her dead.

"A penny for your thoughts, my dear." Mother Chambers banged her cane against the door.

Amanda bolted upright to help the elderly woman to a chair. "I was wondering when someone would come."

"Thank you, my dear." Her thin hand kept Amanda at her side. Her soft tears brought Amanda to her knees on the carpet beside the chair.

"Mother Chambers, I wish I could help you. I just don't know how."

"I know, my dearest one." She stroked Amanda's cap of hair tenderly. "When you came to us, you so quickly became the granddaughter I yearned for. I'm an eighty-three-year-old woman with a heart condition. Each day is a gift to me. Is it selfish of me to want you to be a part of every day I have left?"

Tears choked Amanda's throat. She might not remember this woman's love for her, but she could feel and see the emotion trembling through her fragile body. She wept for what had been lost to them both.

"My dear, dear Amanda." With shaking fingers, Penelope Chambers cupped Amanda's hot face. "You cannot stay in this room and wait for the world to come to you. You must go out and seize the world if you want it back."

She realized with a shock that one part of her agreed. This dear woman—her grandmother—was right. She'd been protecting herself, hanging on to Jonathan for too long. She had enough pieces of the puzzle to know that whoever she was now, she hadn't been a shrinking violet before.

After several long, painful minutes, she found her voice. "Could you please ask Jonathan to come to my room? I need to talk to him before I make a decision."

Her grandmother heaved herself up out of the chair and walked away with a much lighter step. Amanda knew she'd already made up her mind—the truth couldn't be denied.

Staring out the window, she waited for the only person who could stop her. She sensed Jonathan's presence before she heard him. She looked up and saw him reflected in the glass. He stood tall and straight; his face looked carved in stone.

She didn't turn toward him. "If I return to The Lodge, does that mean I won't ever see you again?"

His face lost its arrogance, and his mouth softened. She realized he didn't know she could see his reflection.

"I'll need to do some post-op follow-up in the next few weeks. I usually spend my weekends at the lake."

Smiling in relief, she turned to touch his arm, an intimacy that came naturally to her. "Do you think I will remember sooner if I'm surrounded by my own things?"

"Yeah, I do, Amanda." His voice was hushed, resigned.

She couldn't remember what had happened between them in the past, but she could understand this moment. He was going to miss her as much as she would miss him. Suddenly all was right with her world.

"It's all right, Jonathan." Trying to reassure him, she laughed. "If you spend weekends at the lake, that means I'll see you on Friday night. Right?"

Dimples pitted his cheeks, and he smiled back at her. "Yeah, I guess that means I'll be seeing you on Friday."

THE GREAT DOCTOR would never know how he'd revealed himself. He was in love with her. But now, he had to let her go. She'd be outside his protection, away from the rules and regulations of the hospital. She'd be vulnerable. Accessible.

And as long as she remembered nothing of that night, there was no urgency. This time the job would be finished. Before she could put the pieces together and figure the puzzle out.

CHAPTER SIX

THE BOAT WAS POLISHED teak and shining brass. It was so large it cut through the water without any discernible motion. From the deck, the wind whipped through her cropped hair as she studied the island. Her home.

A necklace of rocks and sand stretching along the shore wound around an unbroken stand of trees. It looked beautiful. Peaceful. But not familiar. She ducked her head and shut her eyelids, slowly running her fingers over the Medic Alert bracelet Jonathan insisted she put on when she left the hospital. It stated that she was allergic to penicillin. She remembered the detective saying it had been found on that fateful night that seemed so long ago.

The boat changed speed. Randall throttled down to ease into a vacant boat slip on an enormous white wooden pier. There was a pontoon boat docked on one side and a swift-looking motorboat on the other. She must have watched her uncle do this a million times, but today it was new and fascinating. The boat just nosed into its place as if it belonged there.

An old man with a gray ponytail caught the prow and snaked a rope around a cleat. His speed and the strength in his arms belied his grizzled hair and weathered face. She found herself fascinated by his eyes—light gray, like his hair, and almost opaque. Those eyes seemed to bore into her. She shivered, a strange reaction on this warm summer day. Unconsciously she wrapped her arms around her body, shielding herself.

"Don't be frightened, my dear." Mother Chambers patted her arm. "It is only Joseph Potter. He has been on the island with me for more than thirty years. He's always been your friend."

"Come along, Amanda! Step here on the side so Joe can help you out," her aunt said briskly.

She took his outstretched hand.

"Welcome home, Miss Amanda."

She hadn't expected his voice to be so soft, with a singsong quality. Nor had she expected his smile to be so sweet. Suddenly his eyes didn't look so frightening after all.

"I'm happy to be back, Joseph."

"We are certainly happy to have her back." Randall strode up from behind and engulfed her in a bear hug, almost overwhelming her with aftershave. When he stepped away to help lift his mother onto the dock, Amanda drew in a deep breath of pungent evergreen.

"Come along now!" Margaret led the way. A path had been cut through the dense wood. It was neatly trimmed and cleared.

Her shoes crunched on the path; behind her Penelope Chambers's cane ground heavily into the crushed rock. Worried that the walk might be too much for her, Amanda stopped and turned back.

"Continue on, my dear." Penelope waved her forward. "We are almost there."

A curve in the path hid Margaret from view. Amanda hurried to catch up with her. In front of her loomed a house that looked older than time, older than the trees standing sentinel around it.

This wasn't the house she'd conjured up in her mind when everyone had talked of The Lodge. The image of a white clapboard house with large windows facing the lake must be another place. She had so hoped it had been a true memory.

This huge pile of gray moss-covered stone with narrow leaded-glass windows and twin towers rising to the sky didn't strike any chord of recognition. However, it did leave her slightly awestruck. The Lodge was huge! It could be a hotel. She wasn't quite sure what to think.

"The towers are something, aren't they?" Margaret came out the front door and tilted her head in the direction of Amanda's gaze. "From the widow's walk you can see over the trees and lake all the way into town."

Dizzy from staring up at them, she shivered. "It's so big."

"It's your home, Amanda." A smile breezed across Margaret's face. "Let's go inside."

The perfume of roses and lilies hung heavily in the warm air of the entrance hall. The house seemed welcoming and comfortable, if a bit formal. There was a lush oriental carpet under her feet. On the far wall, a rose marble fireplace blazed—no doubt the source of the heat. An elaborately carved oak staircase wound up two stories, and on either side, tall double doors obscured the rest of the first floor. She had no idea what she would find behind those doors or where her bedroom might be.

Then she noticed something strange. The light seemed to constantly flicker. Ornate brass sconces followed the curve of the stairway, and above her head were myriad glass globes in a brightly polished chandelier.

"What kind of lights are these?"

"Gas, my dear." Mother Chambers sighed deeply. When Amanda turned around, Randall was helping her into a massive chair with carved arms and legs ending in claw feet. "I have maintained The Lodge exactly as my grandfather built it."

The note of pride in her voice couldn't be missed. It made Amanda smile. "It's very beautiful."

Of all her family, only Mother Chambers seemed to understand that her words meant she didn't recognize her home.

"Do not worry your head about it, my dear," she continued. "Give yourself time. After that trip, surely you must be as tired as I am. Your aunt Margaret will show you to your bedroom."

"Thank you. I'd like that." She followed her aunt's rigid back up the oriental runner that covered the polished stairs.

At the first landing Margaret leaned toward her and

whispered, "Don't worry. We do have modern plumbing. And you won't remember, but I had electricity put in the upstairs study years ago so you could watch television. There's a phone in Randall's office, and we have cellular phones, of course. We just don't talk about such things in front of Mother Chambers."

For the first time she felt as if she shared a secret with someone other than Jonathan. She began to relax. She put a tentative hand on her aunt's arm. "I'll be careful what I say, I promise."

On the second floor, there were more closed doors. At the end of the wide hall, her aunt stopped at a dark door, with a curved top and grapevines carved along the edges.

"This is your room." When there was no reaction, Margaret added, "I'll let you go in alone. I know I'd prefer that myself."

That growing sense of kinship made her feel more comfortable. "Thank you for understanding. But why is my door so different from the others?"

"Because we wanted you to have the best room when you came to us." A barrier lifted from Margaret's face—her eyes were glassy with tears and her lower lip trembled. "You were so young. Frightened. And you missed your mother so much."

She was stung by Margaret's grief, a grief from so long ago. Her memories were gone, yet she needed to say something. "It was kind of you to take me in."

"Kind? I loved my sister! I would have done anything for her!" Margaret blinked and slapped at her wet cheeks. "You certainly don't need this display now. Rest. I'll call you when dinner is served."

Her aunt turned and left before she could even push the heavy door open. Her heart pounded in her chest. Could this be the moment? Would she recognize this, her sanctum?

It was just another strange room.

Sucking in a disheartened breath, she realized this room was scented, too. Roses. Red roses everywhere. They were the only things in the room she recognized.

She didn't like them, but what could she do? Her family was trying to make her feel welcome. They couldn't know that somehow her injury had altered her taste in flowers.

The bedroom was large with mahogany paneling halfway up the walls. Above it, a pretty yellow floral wallpaper reached all the way to carved moldings at the high ceiling. A tester bed with lace hangings stood against the opposite wall. A mirrored dresser was flanked by tall, lace-covered windows on the wall to her right. On it, a silver tray held a monogrammed brush and mirror. A crystal bowl displayed more roses. On the other wall there were built-in bookcases, crammed with books and impersonal knickknacks surrounding a white marble fireplace. More roses on the mantel. A desk faced the bed.

It wasn't her room. There were no photographs, no mementos to give her a peek into her lost life. She sat on the bed, disappointed, searching for one familiar detail. Nothing brought a pinpoint of light into her dark, empty mind.

She reached for one of the heart-shaped lace pillows, hugging it tightly to her breasts. She didn't remember ever seeing these pillows before, but she liked them; and right now she needed something for comfort. She sat for a while, lost somewhere deep inside herself.

Then an open door caught her attention. Situated beyond the dressing table, it was irresistible. She crossed the room to find an enormous black-and-white-tiled bathroom with a deep claw-footed tub. There was a wicker étagère full of bottles: bath oils, lotions, every type of cosmetic, dusting powder, at least eight bottles of perfume. Were these all hers? Or had her aunt bought them for her homecoming?

She opened and smelled them all. Strangely enough, she only liked the one that had a tinge of spice.

The lure of a bubble bath was too much to resist, though. She found the matching bath salts and poured in enough to surround herself with scented steam. Slipping out of the white flats and the black-and-white linen shift Margaret had brought to the hospital for her to wear home, she noticed again the flimsy silk underwear. She knew it was expensive, but it wasn't really her taste. And it didn't seem to fit right. The bra flattened her breasts and it was a relief to get it off.

Automatically she turned to lock the door to the bedroom. She paused, a shiver crawling along her naked body. Why did it seem right to turn the brass knob? Why would she feel the need to lock doors in her own home, surrounded by her family?

No answer came to mind. She turned away, deliberately leaving the door unlocked. She must learn not to give in to unsubstantiated fears she didn't understand. One day at a time. That was what she'd promised herself the first time she looked at her face. She must never never lose sight of that. Not until she held her own life in her own hands again.

The hot water went a long way toward soothing her. She soaked, luxuriating in being able to pamper herself. It couldn't last. There was so much to learn, so much she could discover on this island. If only Jonathan was here to guide her through the process....

Without warning, the need to talk to him about her feelings crashed over her like a wave.

Wrapped in a huge white towel, she went in search of clean clothes. She found more underwear in a drawer. These bras also felt too tight, so she gave up and chose a black tank top and bikini briefs. Finally she found the closet through a door in the bathroom she'd thought was an entry from the hall. It was the size of a small bedroom, filled from floor to ceiling with rack after rack of clothes, shelves of hatboxes and rows of shoe boxes.

She reached for a khaki pantsuit. The pants gaped at her waist, but she'd probably lost a lot of weight in the hospital. The jacket hung loose everywhere except across her breasts. Too impatient to sort through shoes, she slipped on the white flats that she knew fit her. She ran the silver brush through her hair, fluffing

it without really looking at it. She still couldn't use
makeup so there was no point in fussing about her
face. Most of the bruising was gone, although a few
tinges of yellow lingered along her jawline.

She opened the door to the hall and stopped short.
Margaret had mentioned a phone. She figured the office would be downstairs, but the only way she was
going to find it was to go looking for it.

No one was around. The house was silent, feeling
almost deserted. Which way should she go? She
chose the doors on her right. They slid effortlessly
open to reveal a dining room large enough to seat
seventy-five. A brass-and-glass chandelier larger than
the one in the hall gleamed brightly over a table already set for dinner at one end. A clatter of dishes
came from a door open at the other end of the room.

She knew Randall's office wouldn't be near the
kitchen. She backed out, closed the doors and crossed
the hall. A fire roared in the black marble fireplace
that dominated the room. It looked like something
from another time. Like the pictures Dr. Newman had
showed her. All this crimson velvet and mahogany
made her feel as if it could swallow her up. The furniture, heavy and carved with claw feet, sat on an
ancient oriental rug patterned with burgundy and blue.
Large oil paintings covered the walls, all hung by
velvet ropes suspended from the crown molding. The
windows were heavily draped, shutting out the sunlight.

How could she ever have forgotten a room like
this? It was straight out of a gothic novel. How did

she know that? She could feel her pulse pound as she tried to find the answer in her mind.

As she moved through to the next room, she could see it was a smaller version of the first, except this fireplace was white marble and the decor was definitely daintier. A table under the window held a silver tea set that gleamed faintly in the dim light.

She might not remember these rooms, but their effect on her was overwhelming. The house seemed to close around her, suffocating her with its grandeur and opulence. She felt a need to escape, to bring in the cool evergreen-laced air from outside. She pushed through the next set of doors, anxious to escape.

The library, at last! The old-fashioned rotary-dial telephone sat on a rolltop desk of mammoth proportions. She picked up the receiver, the sound of the dial tone at once familiar and reassuring. Abruptly she realized she didn't know the hospital's number; there was no way to reach Jonathan.

Fear clawed at her insides. A dark panic overwhelmed her. Unreasonable, but nevertheless unconquerable. She scanned the desktop for a phone book. Randall worked at the hospital. Surely he would have the number somewhere.

She pawed through folders and stacks of papers, finding unpaid bills for flowers, canning equipment, horse tack, gasoline. She shook her head. None of this made any sense at all. But in her confused state, her only goal was to reach Jonathan. She picked up a curious bill that made her stop to read it again, thinking she had misunderstood. Why would anyone need hundreds of pounds of ice blocks?

"You look so right, here at home."

She jumped. Randall's whisper at her ear and his touch on her cheek startled her, and she batted his hand away.

"Don't touch me!" She began to tremble. The confused and hurt look on his face made her cover her mouth with her hands.

"I'm so sorry," she gasped through shaking fingers. "I...I don't know why I did that."

"I do." He had never looked kinder, or more miserable. "I frightened you. What were you looking at with such interest?"

He gathered all the papers and stacked them neatly back into their folder. "Mother insists on doing everything the way it has been done for a hundred years. I am behind on the accounts." His eyes were like pools of pain as they watched her. "Since your disappearance, I've let everything go. Will you keep this a secret for me?"

At this particular moment she would have promised him anything to assuage her guilt. "Of course I will. I didn't mean to snoop around your papers, Uncle Randall. I was just looking for Jonathan's number at the hospital."

"Here you are, Amanda! I've been looking everywhere for you." Margaret floated toward them, her long cream silk skirt flowing around her legs. She had dressed for dinner. Suddenly Amanda wished she'd spent more time looking through the closet for something to wear.

"What are you two doing in here?"

"Amanda wishes to call Jonathan at the hospital."

Suddenly the room seemed full of people. Mother Chambers stood inside the door with her cane braced in front of her. "I see you found them, Margaret. I have brought Amanda her dog."

She gestured, and Joe stepped forward, holding a golden retriever by the collar. The picture hadn't done justice to Lady's beautiful red-gold color. A surge of affection made her sink to her knees and hold out her hand. "Come, Lady."

The dog raced to her, burying its face in her jacket, sniffing at her. She whined but didn't lick Amanda's face.

"Hi there, girl." Amanda ran her hands through Lady's thick fur as her tail thumped against the floor.

"She's glad to see you. Sit, Lady!" At Margaret's command, the dog fell back on her haunches and stared up expectantly.

"Are you ready for dinner, my dear?"

This time she didn't push Randall's hand away as he reached down to help her to her feet. "I...I would like to call Jonathan first."

Mother Chambers's chin rose a notch. "I consider it appropriate for you to inform him of your safe arrival. Randall will place the call for you. We will await you in the front parlor."

After Randall dialed and dutifully handed her the phone, everyone followed Mother Chambers out.

Even Lady trotted away at her heels. Now the room seemed too quiet.

"Memorial Hospital. How may I help you?"

For a second she couldn't find her voice. "Dr. Jonathan Taylor, please." She could feel her heart pounding against her ribs, its echo beating at her temples as she waited.

"Dr. Taylor."

The sound of his deep voice, strong and reassuring, the voice that had called her out of the endless black void, was her haven in this unfamiliar world. She could hardly speak for the emotion choking her throat. "Hi. It's me. I'm here. And I miss you."

THE SOUND OF Amanda's voice and the uncomplicated honesty of her words loosened the knot of uncertainty that had twisted inside Jonathan since she left.

"Hello, Amanda. How was your trip home?" He shot a guarded look at his colleagues across the desk.

Carl Johnson had the sensitivity to walk to the window and pretend not to listen. Pat Newman, of course, sat rooted in his chair, watching Jonathan's every move, listening to every word.

"How could I ever have forgotten this house? It's...awesome."

He smiled at the amazement in her voice. He'd been worried about her reaction to that antiquated pile of stone. The place had scared the hell out of him as a kid.

"Yeah, it's amazing how well Penelope Chambers

has preserved it all.'' Constrained by his audience, he chose his words with care. "How are you feeling?"

"Lonely. There are so many questions I want to ask you. Nothing seems familiar. When are you coming?"

He'd never heard this wistful quality in her voice before. In all his memories of her, during their happy, wild months together, and even after, she'd always seemed totally in control and totally self-contained.

"I'm taking Friday off, so I'll be there in the late morning."

"Great. I can hardly wait."

An unbidden vision of Amanda standing naked in their secret place made him clear his throat. "I'll see you then. Goodbye."

He hung up the phone before he made a fool of himself. Ignoring Dr. Johnson's frown, he stared at Pat Newman. "She seems to be settling in just fine."

"Does she remember the place?"

"No. And it's hard to forget. All the kids on the lake named it the haunted house. Once I made the mistake of calling it that in front of my parents, and they took my waterskiing privileges away for a day. A disaster back then." He shrugged, trying to defuse Newman's intense scrutiny. "Penelope Chambers may be as eccentric as they come, but she's a grand old lady."

"Then why are you so concerned about Amanda that you're going up there early?"

He'd left himself wide open for that challenge. Laughing with what he hoped sounded like cool indifference, he shrugged. "Give me a break. I haven't had a long weekend in six months. I need it."

"Fine." Easing back in his chair, Newman grinned. "However, let me remind you that she is in the place best suited for her recovery and surrounded by people who love her. Don't get in the way of that."

DREAMS HAUNTED HER NIGHT: Jonathan searched through her enormous closet, unable to find her. Lady raced from the lake to the woods, whining and wagging her tail but never once stopping. Mother Chambers glided up and down the staircase in the flickering light, while Margaret and Randall hovered in the background to see that her every wish was carried out. Even Joe was there, his gentle smile expanding like that of the Cheshire cat.

She crawled around her bed, punching at the soft pillows to find a comfortable place for her head. Maybe it was something she'd eaten at the elaborate seven-course dinner. Or maybe it was the medication they all reminded her to take before going to bed, but it had never had this strong an effect on her in the hospital.

The dreams were so vivid she couldn't tell when they ended. She opened her eyes in the dark. Were the flickering shadows cast by the fire a dream, too?

Everything blended together in a kaleidoscope of pictures and people trying to find a proper place in her head. She saw four silhouettes standing at the end of her bed. Was it real? Were her eyes open or was this another dream? Who was there? Her aunt Margaret and uncle Randall and Mother Chambers, of course. But who was the fourth? It must be Jonathan.

At last she sighed. The smooth pillow molded her cheek. She felt safe now. Only two more days and Jonathan would be here.

SHE WAS HERE at last! On the island—where she could be watched and heard. There were two whole days before the interfering doctor arrived. He would never guess that he had helped to provide the perfect means for her disposal, that the medicine meant to control her seizures would send her into oblivion at last.

CHAPTER SEVEN

AMANDA STOOD ON the widow's walk staring across the whitecaps at the little town of Clear Water. From this vantage point, boats looked like toys coming and going at the public dock. There was a sand beach, practically deserted, off to her left. Beyond it pretty houses stretched along the shoreline. She wondered which one belonged to Jonathan. She wondered if she would just know when he was there or if she would be able to see from here.

Tomorrow. Tomorrow he would be here. Tomorrow she could ask him about all her jumbled thoughts and questions.

Below her, movement caught her eye. Randall walked onto the dock and cast a fishing line into the water. On the lawn in the shade, her aunt and Mother Chambers were sipping iced tea as they relaxed in white wicker chairs. A most appealing scene. Along the shore, beyond the dock, Joe was snapping pictures, focusing on everything from a sailboat out on the lake to Lady, who came out of the woods and sat on the grass beside him.

It was an ordinary day on Clear Water Lake, no doubt. Peaceful, lazy. No doubt it was she who was off balance. Nothing *felt* right to her. She stepped closer to the railing, her sandals shuffling on her feet. Margaret had jokingly insisted she eat a second helping of chicken salad at lunch so her clothes wouldn't fall off her. Very few things in her closet fit the way she thought they should.

Nothing fit. These people, as kind as they were; this house, as lovely as it was—nothing fit. A wave of guilt cramped her stomach. She squeezed her eyes shut against the pain, gripping the rail tightly. *These* people were her family. It was clear in every gesture they made, in all their encouraging words that they loved her. And while a part of her wanted to embrace all they offered, another part hung back, afraid.

"Don't stand so close to the railing, Amanda!"

A yank on her arm made her stumble sideways. If she hadn't been holding on so tightly, she might have fallen. She gasped in fear.

"I'm sorry I startled you." She felt her aunt's strong fingers on her shoulders, steadying her. "I thought you heard me coming up the stairs. Mother saw you up here and was concerned."

Far below, she could see Mother Chambers peering up, her face shielded from the sun by her huge straw hat.

"Wave to her so she'll know you're all right."

She did as she was told. Pleased, Margaret moved beside her to the railing. "It's quite a view from here, isn't it?"

"Beautiful. Which house is Jonathan's?"

"The white one south of town. There."

She looked in the direction of Margaret's outstretched finger. She could just make out large windows facing the lake; maybe it was the house she'd conjured up in her head.

"Oh." She was silent for a moment. "I wish he was coming tonight."

Her aunt's throaty laughter caught her off guard. "Don't get a crush on your doctor. It's not allowed, you know." Her aunt deliberately turned her away from the view. "You'd better get changed for dinner. Mother has asked Joe to prepare all your favorite dishes. She thinks we need to fatten you up."

As if on cue, Joe whistled to the dog and disappeared behind the house. Joe of the cool, watchful eyes and gentle voice. His sweet smile was so endearing she almost felt more comfortable with him than her own family.

"Tell me about him."

"Joe? He's been here forever, according to Randall. His mother was the housekeeper before she died." She leaned closer, as if afraid someone might overhear, even though they were above the treetops. "Joe went off to college and got into the drug culture. Randall told me he did everything, supposedly to expand his mind. Peyote. LSD. Hashish. God knows what else. What a waste. I gather he was half dead by the time he wandered back here. Of course, Mother took him in. He's never left. All he does now is take care of The Lodge and snap pictures." She started down the steps. "Personally, I think the man fried his brain."

Margaret's hard attitude came as a surprise. Had she, Amanda, felt this way about Joe, too?

Margaret looked over her shoulder as Amanda started down after her. "You don't have to be concerned. He's harmless."

"I'm not afraid of him." It was true. Her feelings toward him were a mixture of pity and sadness. "I think he's...sweet."

"Good. Now let's get ready for dinner."

The winding, narrow staircase leading down to the second floor was lit by a single gaslight. The odor of mildew overpowered the scent of roses that permeated the rest of the house. When she finally reached the hallway below, a fresh breeze blew through the windows, opened front and back. She hadn't realized she'd been holding her breath until her chest throbbed.

Margaret disappeared down the hall, leaving Amanda with a new discovery. She didn't like close places, like the winding stair to the widow's walk. She didn't like musty, dusty smells. She didn't like to be crowded or ordered about as if she were a small child.

She *was* ungrateful and decided to keep that discovery to herself. She didn't want Jonathan to learn the worst about her.

Thoughts of Jonathan lifted her spirits again. She soaked in a tepid bubble bath before donning a pretty floral sundress, which hung on her slender frame. The ornate mantel clock showed she had fifteen minutes before she was expected in the dining room. Time enough to go through the routine the therapist had advised before she left the hospital.

She faced the oval freestanding mirror and exercised her wrists. Closing her eyes, she executed the balance moves the therapist had taught her. They were easier each time. She knew she was getting better; even the headaches had decreased. She stood for a moment with her eyes closed, playing a game with herself. This time when she opened them, she'd remember.

She opened her eyes. A stranger stared back at her.

Blinking wildly, she tried to clear her vision. An icy fear made her skin crawl. She looked around, but she was totally alone.

WHO? Who had she seen?

Was it a trick of the flickering gaslight; a prank of her own imagination that had somehow altered her own face?

She had definitely seen another face in the mirror. A face she didn't recognize, yet somehow knew.

She sat down, hard, on the side of the bed, trying to steady her breathing, and gazed at her beautiful room. She didn't deserve all this. She wasn't who these people thought she was. The dark fears she'd tried to hide from everyone came rushing back. Detective Savage had tried to reassure her. The doctors, the therapists...

She couldn't live this way anymore. Only Jonathan could help her deal with this sense of unreality. Only he truly understood her. He *knew* who she was. He could be trusted.

She threw open her door. It banged against the wall. Tearing down the steps, she didn't care if anyone heard her. This time she knew where to go—straight to the study.

Her hand trembled as she dialed his number. It rang and rang, seeming to take forever. This time she was ready when she heard the operator's voice.

"Dr. Jonathan Taylor. It's an emergency. Please hurry."

JONATHAN'S BEEPER went off at the same instant the guy behind him started blasting his horn. Where the hell was he supposed to go? He was on the Kennedy expressway, stopped dead in a typical Friday afternoon Chicago traffic jam. If that emergency at the hospital hadn't delayed him, he'd be at the lake by now!

He turned down the jazz CD that was meant to keep his temper in check and punched in his service's number. He inched the Jag forward.

"Taylor here."

The message made him curse his surroundings. Now, more than ever, he wished he'd gone ahead and finished his flight hours. He could be there so much sooner if he'd bought that Cessna. Instead he'd have to do the next best thing.

She picked up the phone on the first ring, her voice ragged and breathy. "Jonathan?"

He could hear the fear in her voice as clearly as the night she'd confessed she had no memory. But something else was there, too. Something new.

"Amanda, I'm on my way. What's wrong?"

"I saw...I saw someone else in the mirror. I think she looked familiar." He could hear her taking deep breaths. "I know this sounds crazy, but I don't feel right here. I don't belong here. Please hurry. I need you."

"I'm on my way, but I'm stuck in traffic. You know you're perfectly safe at The Lodge. Think it through, Amanda." He paused to let that sink in. "Where are your aunt and uncle?"

"Waiting for me in the dining room." She sounded calmer.

"Ah, the palatial stateroom, ready to host millions." He chuckled, trying desperately not to make it sound too forced. "I used to think that was the biggest room in the world. Go have your state dinner. Remember, you're surrounded by family, and they'll take care of you. Then get a good night's sleep. In the morning I'll be there bright and early. We'll talk through everything that's worrying you."

"Okay. I feel...better now. I probably shouldn't have bothered you."

He heard her sigh. Damn! No matter what his involvement, he never should have let her go so far from the hospital. This recovery was going to bog down if she continued to have these attacks of nerves.

"Bye."

The phone went dead but he continued to hold it, almost like a lifeline. After their relationship had ended he would have bet money that Amanda Braithwaite couldn't ever get to him again. He would never forget that kind of betrayal, the pain of disillusionment. Yet something he saw in her eyes and the almost innocent look on her face now, consumed him, even though he knew better. He wanted her all over again. Right now, the past didn't seem to make any difference.

He shook his head in denial as the car inched toward a tollbooth. What would be his best course of action? Finally, he decided to call Pat Newman. He threw the toll in, merged successfully and then dialed.

Pragmatic as ever, Newman had the answer. "She's suffering from reduplicative paranesia. Fairly common. She thinks she's been mistaken for someone else. Patients often feel the accident happened to someone else."

"If you expected this complication, why didn't you say so in the first place?" Anger made him slam on the brakes. He hoped the guy behind him was more alert than he.

"It's not that I expected it. It's just a normal progression for what Amanda's been going through." Newman's calm voice eased Jonathan's tension a little.

"How can I help her?"

"You must make her feel comfortable with her identity, comfortable with her life. She sounds as if she's going to need a lot of patience and reassurance. The process will take time."

"I understand." Suddenly the car in front of him zoomed ahead. "Gotta go, Pat. This traffic jam has finally opened up. I'll call you again if I need you."

With any luck, he might get to the lake in time to visit The Lodge tonight.

Ten miles later there was another wall of cars. He resigned himself to the inevitable. Amanda's face was healing nicely—just as he'd promised. Now he needed to help her get back the rest of her life, no matter what effect it had on his peace of mind.

AMANDA PUSHED HER dinner plate away, hoping no one would notice that her hands were trembling.

"Is there something wrong with your leg of lamb, my dear?"

She shook her head, even though the only way she could swallow the meat was by smothering it in mint jelly to kill the taste.

"No. I'm just not very hungry."

"If you don't start eating soon, you'll need to buy an entirely new wardrobe. I can see one of your famous shopping sprees coming on!"

Her aunt laughed and Amanda smiled, wanting, needing, to feel closer to these people. "We'll go together, Aunt Margaret."

She glimpsed a puzzled look on her uncle's face, but when he caught her watching him, the expression was replaced by a placid mask. She hated that—everything she said or did seemed to be wrong. She didn't know how to find her way through her confusion without making mistakes.

"Dessert will certainly tempt your appetite, my dear."

Joe silently removed her barely touched plate and

replaced it with a crystal bowl containing a chocolate and toffee mousse surrounded by huge, juicy strawberries. It literally melted in her mouth.

"It's delicious."

At last she'd done something right. Everyone smiled and Mother Chambers nodded, beaming.

"It has always been your favorite."

She certainly could believe that as she devoured every one of the strawberries and most of the mousse. Feeling Mother Chambers's watchful gaze on her, she scraped up the last bite.

"Good, Amanda. Now shall we take tea in the front parlor?"

"I need Amanda to sign a few papers in my office first, Mother." Randall pulled out her chair and laid his arm across her shoulders. "Come with me. We'll join the others later."

"Nonsense, Randall!" Margaret pushed to her feet. "I'll have Joe bring the tea to your office."

He tightened his arm around her as he pulled her closer. "It will be all right. I'll take care of everything."

His whisper confused her; she didn't understand what he expected. He led her into his office and shut the door behind them. The room was shadowed by the flames in the fireplace. He lit an oil lamp on the rolltop desk before turning to her.

"Amanda, I miss you so much." He leaned down and brushed her short hair with his lips.

The feel of his kiss sent a tremor racing along her skin. She stepped back, then covered her movement by reaching toward the fireplace and shivering. "It's cold in here. What do you want me to sign, Uncle Randall?"

In the shadowed room, she couldn't see the pain on his face, but she could feel it as clearly as she felt the heat against her fingertips.

"I have frightened you again. Please forgive me."

His voice sounded different to her. Not precisely angry, just not the supportive tone she was accustomed to. She hated this. Now it seemed she was becoming paranoid.

"No, I'm the one who is sorry."

The door flew open just as she reached out to touch his arm.

"It's too dark in here! You're going to blind yourself working in this light. Joe, light the wall sconces."

At Margaret's command, Joe placed the silver tea tray on a low table by the fire in front of a velvet settee. With his brisk step, he had the room brightened in a few moments.

"There, isn't that better?" Pleased, Margaret sat beside Mother Chambers on the settee. "Actually, it's very cozy in here. This is a good idea." She gestured to Amanda to sit across the table from them. "I'll pour." Amanda took the cup she offered. "I put two lumps in yours." She laughed, as if they shared a private joke.

Amanda found she liked her tea sweet. It satisfied a gnawing in her stomach. She was beginning to feel more normal when, without any warning, a giant yawn widened her eyes. "Excuse me. I'm suddenly exhausted."

"Of course you are, my dear. Finish with this busy-work, Randall, so Amanda can get her rest."

"Sign where I've indicated, Amanda."

When she hesitated over the three documents laid out across the desk, he smiled at her. "These are routine accounts you sign off on monthly. Would you like to read them?"

Consumed by guilt that she should be suspicious of someone who had been so good to her, she shook her head. She stared at the signature she'd scrawled across the line. She realized this was the first time she'd written her name, and it had taken some effort to do so.

For a heartbeat, the mask slipped off Randall's face. It took every ounce of her courage to force her question through tight lips. "It doesn't look the same, does it?"

"You're writing with a sprained wrist, Amanda. That is why it looks so shaky."

She lifted her gaze, not understanding the odd note in his voice, but there was no mistaking the concern in his eyes. She couldn't stop herself from blurting out her real feelings. "Sometimes...sometimes...I don't feel like your Amanda."

Once before in the hospital she'd felt this silence close in around her. Her aunt and uncle looked at each other; without a word they turned toward Mother Chambers. Silent tears coursed down her cheeks.

Amanda felt as if she'd driven a stake through the old woman's heart.

Margaret's sigh ended in a faint sob. "You poor darling. I'm sorry you're so confused. And you certainly don't need our emotional response to make it worse. Ever since you've been ill, I've thought so much about how I failed your mother by not protecting you from this horrible accident. How can I help you get back to normal? To accept us again? All of us would do anything for that."

More guilt. She wasn't ready for how it made her feel—suddenly very cold and alone. But Jonathan would be here soon to help her sort through all her mixed-up feelings. She controlled her confusion as she stared into her aunt's tear-streaked face.

"None of this is your fault, Aunt Margaret."

"Of course it isn't. Just as your confusion isn't your fault. My dear, this will all look better to you in the morning after a good night's sleep," Mother Chambers said gently. "Come, allow me to walk you to your room."

As much as she wanted to get to her room, she held back, matching the older woman's slow pace. These people confused her—they were so good to her, so kind, yet she didn't feel as if she knew them any better now than she had when she first came out of her coma. She dreaded being alone, feeling cut off from everyone and everything, but even with her family surrounding her, she felt like a stranger. In the eerie half-light of the hallway, she tried to imagine knowing Mother Chambers as a child. She tried to imagine the hurt she was causing. Certainly Mother Chambers looked fragile—vulnerable—despite her upright carriage and determination. Amanda paced beside her silently, desperately trying to think of something to say to ease the strain.

She smiled as best she could when they reached her door. "I'm sure you're right. Tomorrow everything will be better. Jonathan is coming."

"I know, child." She cupped Amanda's cheeks in her cool, dry hands. "You must always remember we love you, too. Joe has left herbal tea on your bedside table. Remember to take the medicine the doctor prescribed. Rest well."

She stood and watched until the older woman entered her own bedroom far down the hall, wishing she could remember this kind lady who loved her so much. It would be nice to have someone besides Jonathan to rely on.

She undressed, slipped on a white cotton nightgown, dutifully drank the tea and swallowed the pill beside it. She yawned again, overcome by a desire to fling herself down on the bed. Instead, she walked to the window and looked out into the darkness. She wasn't a quitter; somehow she knew that. She might be confused, scared and needy right now, yet deep inside at her core burned the flame she'd recognized in the mirror. Now she knew she didn't like leg of lamb, but did like chocolate mousse. What else might she learn about herself tonight?

She turned up every gaslight in the room and then sat cross-legged in front of the bookcase. Book by book she went through the shelves. Tucked between a much-used copy of *Little Women* and what appeared to be a college psychology book, she found a leather-bound appointment calendar. Flipping through the pages, she saw that they were fairly blank for the last two months compared to the preceding months. August 9 was circled by a heart several times in red ink—in two weeks it would be her birthday.

She went back through the calendar, trying to recreate her life. Obviously she didn't have a job. Her days had been filled with trips to Jack's Gym, the beauty salon, tennis games and luncheon dates. Where were all the people who had filled her life? Again, gnawing doubts tore at her. Why had no one come to visit her in the hospital? It didn't make sense, especially after seeing this social whirl.

Carrying the calendar to the desk, she pulled out a pad and pencil and tried to duplicate her handwriting. Jack's Gym. Peter. Tennis with Randall, 2:00 p.m. Cut. Manicure. Pedicure. Massage. The Lodge. Mother Chambers's birthday and the big heart drawn beside it.

She couldn't make the handwriting fit. The longer she tried, the colder and more clumsy she became. Her wrist ached with the effort.

She drank more tea, trying to calm her doubts and fears. Randall was right. Her wrist was the problem. She'd just been through brain surgery—certainly there would be residual changes.

She paced the carpet from fireplace to window, trying to convince herself nothing was wrong. She threw her favorite oil into a steaming tub and soaked for thirty minutes, but the doubts refused to go away. She dressed for bed again, pulling a terry cloth robe over her nightgown.

She sat beside the fireplace, staring into the depths of the flame, willing her mind to open up and let her see into its deep recesses where her memory, her life, lay hidden. She dozed off and on, but never really slept. As dawn crept into her room, she still hadn't vanquished her fears.

Restlessly, she dressed in shorts and a cotton sweater before heading outdoors. Lady came bounding out of the woods. She called, but the dog ignored her, running back into the shadows beneath the trees. She continued on down to the dock, surprising Joe as he hosed down the pontoon boat, spraying off the bugs and leaves.

"Miss Amanda, you're up bright and early." Courteously he turned off the faucet and wiped his hands on his jeans, giving her his full attention. "What can I help you with?"

"I want you to take me to Dr. Taylor's house, please. It's across the lake."

"I know where Doctor Jonathan lives." His abrupt answer surprised her. So did the almost scared look he threw over her shoulder. "Do they know you're going?"

"Yes," she lied, hating to deceive him, but needing to get away. "Will you take me? Please."

"If it's all right with them, it's all right with me.

I'll just wipe the seat off for you first, Miss Amanda. Then we'll be on our way.''

Expecting someone to appear and try to stop her, she kept glancing back toward the house. She couldn't be so obvious as to rush Joe, but she was sure he sensed her anxiety.

He frowned, a spider's web of deep lines. She thought she was caught but he surprised her. He stared up into the sky. "There's a storm coming."

She couldn't see anything except a few pretty puffy white clouds. Holding her breath, she waited.

"But you know that. I can get you there and be back in plenty of time to beat it. Get in, Miss Amanda."

Eagerly she took his rough hand and jumped into the boat. The motor roared to life, and they glided out into the water. Midway across the lake, she finally relaxed enough to turn to him. "Do I seem different to you, Joe, since I came home?"

He gave her his gentle, sweet smile. "You're sure different than you've been lately, Miss Amanda."

His words fed the irrational idea taking root in her mind.

"You're more like you were when you first came here. Real innocent and sweet."

Something painful shifted inside her. When would she ever be able to understand again? Jonathan would help her. He had to. He'd always been her lifeline. The feelings she was experiencing now were making her feel sicker than she ever had in the hospital. Why did she feel weaker? Why was there more confusion?

Shouldn't she be getting her memories back, instead of feeling as if they were slipping farther and farther away?

The boat slowed, and before Joe could properly dock it, she jumped out onto Jonathan's pier. She ignored Joe's shout and raced for the house, but the door was locked and no one responded to her frantic knock.

Joe came up behind her. "Miss Amanda, how many times have I told you to wait before you jump out of a boat like that? Someday you're going to be sorry." He walked around the corner of the house. "Doctor Jonathan isn't home, but his car's here."

"Maybe he walked into town. I've got to find him. You go on back to the island, Joe. He'll bring me home later."

He hesitated, the spider web lines deepening as he thought it over. Finally he nodded and turned away.

Where could Jonathan have gone so early? She was determined to find him no matter what. She didn't have the faintest idea where to look, so she turned toward the town. A woman walking her dog smiled and waved. She responded, remembering what the detective had told her about that fateful night.

At the edge of town, she realized she'd been walking increasingly faster until she'd started jogging. She stopped to catch her breath. Her heart pounded against her ribs, and a matching pain beat behind her eyes. This was the most exercise she'd had since leaving the hospital. She felt a strange weakness in every cell of her body; undoubtedly her sleepless night hadn't helped.

A car pulled to a stop across the street. A man got out, wearing a badge pinned to his barrel chest. "Can I help you?" He had a broad face with a nose that looked as if it had been broken but never set properly. Suddenly he stopped to squint at her.

"Miss Braithwaite! I didn't recognize you at first."

"Why? Do I look different?" She could hear the panic in her voice. Obviously so could he. She saw him square his shoulders.

"Heard about your accident. You look real good. Can I help you with anything?"

"Yes, please. I want to find Dr. Taylor."

"Haven't seen him this weekend. You come with me and we'll find him for you."

He didn't touch her as he ushered her to his car, which smelled of pipe smoke. She decided she liked the slight cherry aroma. He didn't say anything as he drove across town to a small log building set off by itself. Once inside, she saw a sign on his cluttered desk which read: Sheriff Philip Eller.

He filled a paper cup with water from a cooler in the corner and handed it to her. "You just take it easy now, Miss Braithwaite. I'll make some phone calls for you."

Sipping the water, she stood at the window, staring out into the nearly empty street. Where could Jonathan be? He'd promised he'd come, and he always kept his promises.

A tall, thin man came through the door at the back

of the office. Before he closed it, she caught a glimpse
of jail bars.

"This is my deputy, Ernie Tyler."

He nodded and she smiled back automatically.

"Hold down the fort, Ernie. Me and Miss Braithwaite have to go to Dr. Taylor's."

"Jonathan's at home?" In her eagerness she spilled
water on her hands.

"We'll see. Let's head back over there."

She didn't see Jonathan when they pulled up his
driveway. "Where is he, Sheriff Eller?"

"Let's head down to the dock."

She ran ahead of him, anxious to see Jonathan. Out
on the lake, a power boat jetted through the water
toward her. She ran to the end of the dock, waving
so hard her arm hurt.

It dropped weakly when she recognized her aunt
and uncle. She turned on the sheriff, but he wouldn't
meet her accusing eyes. Instinct warned her arguing
would be useless. She had no choice but to wait until
Randall maneuvered the boat close enough to throw
a rope to the sheriff.

He held it as Margaret stretched out her hand. "It's
time to come home now, Amanda."

She was talking to her as if she were an errant
child. Resenting that, she ignored her aunt's hand and
jumped unaided into the boat.

"Thanks, Phil!" Margaret waved to him as she
pulled in the rope.

Randall twisted around to look at her. "Amanda,
why..."

She saw her aunt shake her head, silencing him. Never before this moment had she felt like a prisoner—not in the hospital when every aspect of her life had been strictly regimented, not on the island where everything had seemed strange. But now she was worried. Where was Jonathan? Why wouldn't they let her see him?

She felt as if the world were shrinking around her until she could hardly breathe.

The storm was coming. Gray clouds rolled across the sky, and Randall gunned the engine. This boat was much faster than the pontoon had been. In no time at all they were approaching the island.

There, on the dock, a man stood watching their approach.

"Jonathan!" She was so relieved, tears rolled down her cheeks. She stood and grabbed the side of the boat to steady herself.

"Where did he come from?" she heard Randall yell as he cut the engine.

She held out her arms, and Jonathan lifted her up onto the dock. Not caring who watched, she flung herself against his chest. When he closed his arms around her, she felt safe at last.

"Amanda, I'm here. It's all right now. Tell me what's wrong."

She buried her lips against his throat and whispered, "I'm not Amanda Braithwaite."

CHAPTER EIGHT

SHE CLUNG TO HIM and shut out everything else. Ignoring the sounds behind her—her aunt's sobs and her uncle's protests—she reveled in the safety of Jonathan's arms. Somehow she sensed when he sent them away.

"They're gone, Amanda. We can talk now." His voice sounded calm. Determined.

The wind shifted, sending a light spray of cold lake water against their ankles. The tension in her body seeped away.

"The storm's coming. Let's get off the lakefront."

Holding her tight against him, he led her to the covered glider at the edge of the garden. She faced the woods, deep and dark with the coming storm, and he sat across from her, facing the house. Their knees touched within the confines of the old-fashioned double swing.

"I know I must sound crazy, Jonathan."

"You *are* Amanda Braithwaite."

"I'm not sure...." she began, filled with a curious urgency to make him understand.

His voice overpowered her. "Yes, I understand." He gripped her hands in a velvet vise. "And I can make you understand. You are suffering from something called reduplicative paranesia. You think you've been mistaken for someone else. Dr. Newman says this is very common in patients suffering from your type of amnesia." He waited for the information to sink in. "You are not crazy. You are reacting very normally for someone who's been through what you've experienced."

She hadn't lost her ability to reason, just her memory. "What about the clothes that don't fit? The favorite foods I can't stomach? Even my handwriting is different."

"What about the fact the police found your driver's license in the evening bag you were carrying? The fact that you were wearing the Braithwaite family jewels. What about your Medic Alert bracelet and your blood type?"

She shook her head in denial.

"What about us? You remember that, don't you, Amanda?"

That brought her racing mind to a standstill. "I don't exactly remember us." She leaned forward and braced her hands against his thighs, which tightened instantaneously. "I want to be with you. Is that because I'm drawn to you or because I knew you before? I don't know." Practically climbing onto his lap, she brushed his mouth with her lips. "All I know is, I want to touch you, talk with you, know you. In every way. Was I this way before?"

He went utterly still. She drew back in the swing, as far away from him as she could get, feeling embarrassed for the first time. "I've done and said the wrong thing again, haven't I?"

"No. You're being honest." He sounded cool, but she could tell he wasn't. "We need to talk about our relationship. Just not right now. Think. Don't you have a sense of family now that you're home?"

She wrapped her arms across her breasts for protection, feeling cold and rejected. "I don't know what to think. I suppose I have a vague sense of Randall trying to take my father's place and lavishing me with affection." She swallowed, trying to soothe her suddenly dry throat. "I'm just not very comfortable with it."

"You're not comfortable with yourself yet."

"I never have been." The instant the words came out, she went hot and cold simultaneously. From somewhere deep inside her, and for the first time, a truth had surfaced. She wasn't comfortable with herself. With what had happened to her in the past, with what was happening to her now.

A physical pain started low in her abdomen and made its way to her temples. Soon she knew the buildup would be a raging storm in her head. Jonathan didn't want to deal with their relationship, yet it had become the most important part of her life. She didn't want to deal with her identity when it seemed he was so certain of the truth.

"I'm so tired my head hurts."

"The barometric pressure is a killer during these storms. Actually the best way for you to heal, physically and mentally, is to rest as much as possible."

He pulled her to her feet. Taking her cold hand in his large, warm one, he held on to her all the way across the lawn. She gave a shaky laugh at his expression of disbelief when they entered the house.

"It's exactly the same as when I was a kid! I haven't been here in years."

"I'm actually getting used to it."

They mounted the steps together. The gas lamps had been lit, presumably by Joe, against the darkening sky.

"Makes you feel like you're in a medieval drama."

"Your room, milady?" He pushed open the heavy carved door.

Someone had turned down her bed, and a fire blazed in the grate against the chilly day. It was as if someone knew exactly what she needed. But instead of making her feel cherished, she felt smothered. How could everyone else think they knew what was best for her? Why wouldn't they let her make her own decisions?

Still, for the first time she was glad about the dim interior. The room was warm and intimate. Jonathan stood so close to her she could feel the heat emanating from his body, but even that wasn't close enough. She wanted him in a way that she knew instinctively women longed for their lovers—stretched out in bed beside her, holding her, caressing her, loving her.

An icy fear assailed her. Did he know her thoughts? Would they drive him away?

"Will you be here when I wake up?"

"You know I will be. Rest now."

His familiar refrain made her feel safe. *He* made her feel safe. If only he could understand how her need had turned to desire. That she saw him as a man, not her doctor or her savior. She needed time to decide what to do next.

He stood in the doorway until she closed her eyes. Only then did she hear the door shut. But he didn't come to her. He hadn't been able to read her thoughts after all.

HE STOOD OUTSIDE her doorway fighting a battle with himself. There were those who would argue he was taking advantage of her if he gave in to his impulses. But he knew the truth. Somehow she'd found her way back into his heart. She wasn't just his patient or an old lover anymore. It was as if she were an entirely new person—a new Amanda, with a new face, and not just the physical one—he could no more leave her now than he could stop thinking about her.

"Thank heavens you got her calmed down!"

Margaret stepped out of the shadows, Randall silently following.

"I'm afraid she will have another seizure if she continues like this."

"She's resting. As long as she's taking the carbamazine, it will prevent further seizures."

"It might also hamper her recovery of memory. I know that can be a side effect."

He'd forgotten Margaret had been a nurse before she married Randall. "In this case the pros far outweigh the cons." He walked quickly away from

Amanda's door, ushering them ahead of him. "We should let her rest." He felt strangely angry with them. "What the hell has been going on since you brought her here, anyway? She seems more fragile now than she did at the hospital."

Randall squared his shoulders, as if he took Jonathan's words personally. "We have lavished her with our love and attention. Shared happy memories. Fed her all her favorite foods. However, she appears obsessed with you. How did that happen?" He lifted one eyebrow. "Surely that can't help her? Nor does it indicate very professional conduct on your part."

Jonathan caught the subtle threat but chose to ignore it.

Margaret jumped in. "Randall, this is the classic doctor-patient scenario. After all they're old friends, even if she *can't* remember. And Jonathan *did* save her life, so she thinks she can't live without him."

Was it an insult? Or was she just trying to let him know she'd seen through his pathetic attempt to hide from the truth? A part of him didn't want Amanda's attraction to be based on gratitude. God help him, Amanda was as much his obsession as he was hers.

"Mother requests your presence in the front parlor, Jonathan. It isn't necessary to guard Amanda's door in this house, I assure you." Randall's Old World manner had always charmed the women at the hospital, while masking his shrewd nature. For some reason, Jonathan resented it now.

"What's the matter with the two of you?" Margaret pushed between them. "Isn't there enough tension in this house already? Mother Chambers is waiting."

Penelope waited in the dim, overly warm parlor as if she were a reigning monarch. Joe dutifully hovered behind her throne, waiting for commands.

Jonathan shook himself mentally. This house was having a crazy effect on him. Maybe that was what was wrong with Amanda. She couldn't know this was the norm here. Even though he knew Penelope Chambers was an eccentric old woman, even though he knew the house hadn't changed in a hundred years, even though he knew Joe as the kindly, if somewhat confused, caretaker, he was having trouble keeping his mental balance. No wonder it was difficult for Amanda.

But they were her family. They loved her. They were trying to do their very best in a difficult situation. Misplaced anger aimed at them wasn't going to solve the mess he'd gotten himself into.

"Sit down, Jonathan." Penelope waved to the couch nearest her chair. "I need you to explain what is troubling Amanda so."

To his surprise he found the deep velvet cushions comfortable. Sighing, he leaned back. "She is suffering from what we call reduplicative paranesia. That means sometimes patients with traumatic head injuries believe they have been mistaken for someone else. They believe that either the accident happened to someone else, or, in Amanda's case, with her rare type of personal amnesia, that they are someone else.

Dr. Newman feels this is normal and that if we all stay patient, it will go away.''

"I see. Have you come to help her understand and accept her true identity, Jonathan?" Penelope pinned him with her eyes. "Or have you come to resurrect your former relationship with her?"

Her soft words hovered in the suddenly suffocating air. Instead of the cup of tea Margaret offered him, he wanted something potent, with ice.

He took a gulp of the scalding liquid and let it burn all the way down. "I've come to help her accept her identity. The other situation *was* between Amanda and me. No one else. Not even you, Mrs. Chambers.''

"So be it." The muscles in her thin arms tightened as she leaned on the cane to rise, slowly, majestically. Manners brought him to his feet. "Then you should begin at once, my boy. As you can hear from the thunder, there is a storm raging over the lake. Therefore Joe has prepared a spare bedroom for you. The one next to Amanda's.''

He intercepted the shocked expressions on Margaret's and Randall's faces before they could be disguised. He realized their reaction was exactly what Penelope had expected. What was the old lady up to?

"Amanda must find her way back to us. If we can't assist her, then nothing must stand in the way of someone who can." Her next words were all the explanation he needed. "Jonathan, I expect you to do whatever is necessary to restore Amanda to me—'' she banged her cane on the floor, the cat's eyes winking at him "—before it is too late.''

"I'm sure Jonathan will do everything possible within the boundaries of his professional ethics, Mother."

The look Penelope shot her son spoke volumes. For the first time, Jonathan realized that while she might choose to live in another century, supported by her family's indulgence, she had no illusions about the realities of the present.

"I have always been fully aware of Amanda's...activities. So consequently I understand precisely what might transpire now. Randall, you may escort me to my room. I wish to nap. Dinner is served promptly at six p.m. Do not be late," she said to Jonathan over her shoulder.

"To think I've been protecting the old lady from electricity in the study and she's known all along about sex in the boathouse."

"I'm not going to discuss this with you, Margaret," Jonathan interrupted her. He knew there was anger in his voice, as well as his posture.

She appeared contrite, even a little embarrassed. "I apologize, Jonathan. My only excuse is shock. Genuine shock. You must feel it, too. She just gave you permission to seduce Amanda if you think it will restore her memory."

Not bothering to hide his disgust, he headed for the door. "I'm going to my room."

Behind him, she murmured, "You know where it is."

He stood at the window in the bedroom assigned to him, looking over the lake, feeling every bit as tempestuous as the storm. After spending each summer of his life here, he had a healthy respect for thunderstorms.

A bolt of lightning streaked through the sky and plunged into the lake, the thunder blasting across the waves and reverberating off the house. Suddenly he recalled a freak lightning storm while Amanda and he had been waterskiing. She'd been terrified, on the verge of hysteria, as he raced the boat toward the shore. At the time, he'd been delighted to ease her fears. Later he'd thought it had all been an act.

Now he wasn't so sure. Maybe she was really frightened of storms. Maybe she was in her room needing him.

He crossed the hall and pushed open her door.

She was standing, her back to him. Suddenly she pulled her cotton sweater over her head and turned toward the bathroom. Her naked breasts rose free and full above her narrow rib cage. A dangerous shaft of passion ripped through him. He should turn and go. He stayed.

LIGHTNING FLASHED outside the lace curtains, and she turned toward the bath, pulling her sweater over her head. Sleep still hung like heavy tendrils in her brain. It took her a moment to register that Jonathan was standing in the doorway. She should be embarrassed. Instead her breasts tingled and her nipples grew hard, the sensation rippling down her body. As if in slow motion, she hugged the sweater to cover her nudity.

"I'm sorry."

They both spoke at once. Then they both laughed nervously.

"I wanted to check on you because of the storm. I'm right next door, you know." He gestured over his shoulder.

"Are you spending the night?" She liked the thought of him being so close.

"Yeah. Penelope reminded me that dinner is served at six." His dimples dented his cheeks. "What happens if we're late?"

Her nervous laugh died as his eyes traveled down her body. Suddenly she stiffened and turned away. He was too close and she was half naked. Her eyes stopped at the disheveled bed. She spun, a half-formed memory teasing her.

"I'll meet you in the hall in thirty minutes," he said lightly.

The memory blinked off. Her body relaxed. This was Jonathan. She could trust him. He backed out, closing the door.

She shuddered in delayed reaction. He might not want to talk about their relationship, but she needed to know all about it so she could fully understand her feelings for him. While she dressed she considered what the best approach might be.

She groped around in the closet, while she searched for memories in her mind. Any clue, anything that might lead her to him. She found a simple dress that fit her better than most. Fluffing her hair, which was filling out nicely, she considered her face in the mirror. The swelling was down—most of the black and blue just a memory now. Her skin, at least, was clear and smooth. She lavished mascara on her thick eyelashes—one bit of makeup she could use.

True to his word, Jonathan was waiting in the hallway. She knew instantly from his expression that he'd seen her in this white cotton sheath before.

"I've worn this before?" Her eager question made his expression go blank.

"Do you remember wearing it?"

She shook her head and his eyes softened into a dozen different colors. "It was your favorite dress one summer."

Margaret looked up as they entered the dining room. "Darling, that dress is at least ten years old, yet it still looks wonderful on you!"

A frame of reference at last. Jonathan recognized this dress and it was ten years old. So they must have spent a lot of time together them. She had been nineteen. Another piece of the puzzle to fit into place.

Outside, she could hear the thunder crash and the answering roar of the lake pummeling the island. But she felt safe inside, even though the room was heavy with silence. She and Jonathan seated themselves side by side at the table. They seemed to be waiting—for what?

From the kitchen came a faint clatter of dishes. Without warning, Margaret began to chatter about the weather and how she hoped Jonathan didn't mind being marooned with them. Randall appeared at the door, leading his mother in by the hand.

She looked over the room, a satisfied smile playing

around her mouth. Randall seated her at the head of the table and she lifted a small crystal bell.

Next to Mother Chambers, Jonathan held himself so tightly she could see the tension cord his neck. To comfort him, she reached under the table and gently pressed his knee.

She wasn't prepared for his hand to capture hers and hold it there. She could feel the heat rise through his slacks. Her own temperature rose in response. She looked at his face, a question in her eyes. There was a flash of desire, quickly suppressed. For a moment she held her breath. Was she imagining things?

Then his hand released hers, his cool fingers lingering to stroke her hand. An instinct was born in the depths of her soul. An intuition that felt right, that told her all of her future depended on him. With him beside her, the dark cloud would lift.

She tasted the soup course, not taking part in the conversation around her. The little bell tinkled and a fish course appeared. Suddenly she knew she couldn't endure another night of tasteless food and meaningless conversation.

"I'm tired. Jonathan, will you walk me to my room?" She jumped up before Mother Chambers could protest or Randall could turn one of those stricken looks on her. She didn't want to feel guilty. She didn't want to feel beholden. She wanted to be alone with Jonathan. Was that so wrong?

She felt so tight with emotions she was just beginning to identify, she was afraid to touch him. Until they reached her bedroom door. Then she couldn't resist sliding her fingers inside his shirt. She could feel the texture of his skin, the crispness of his hair as his heart beat strong and sure.

"We need to talk about us, Jonathan."

He jerked away. Even while his eyes risked, his hands gently held her at a distance. "Us? There is no us, Amanda. You need more time to recover. You're still confused."

She could hear the harsh edge in his voice, and while she understood, she wasn't giving up this time. She laughed low in her throat.

"No."

He stared at her as if she'd surprised him.

"You came here for a post-op. How am I doing, Dr. Taylor?" Tilting up her face, she closed her eyes expectantly.

He explored her eyelids, her cheekbones, her mouth, with his gentle fingers. Their light probe along the fading red scars at her hairline caused her to tremble.

She opened her eyes, watchfully. "What's the verdict? Are you still the best?"

"The best," he echoed.

"Then I guess I don't need a doctor anymore. Aunt Margaret says it's not allowed—a patient can't be involved with her doctor so you're fired." She spun around, raising her arms over her head. When she stopped, she hesitated long enough to make him lean toward her slightly. "Now we're just Jonathan and Amanda again."

His eyes blazed at her, and his smile was real, full

of life. "Okay, I'm fired. But I'm still not going to get into this tonight."

"So, when?" She swallowed, trying to cool her hot throat.

"Tomorrow," he said softly as he rubbed his thumb along her jaw. She could feel the difference in his touch. Slower. Deeper. She could see a new lightness in his eyes.

"Tomorrow I'm taking you on a picnic." He dropped his hands and moved away from her. "I'll see you in the morning."

For the first time in this house, she felt safe, felt right. She knew it was because Jonathan was close by. She slept through the night, a deep and dreamless sleep.

In the morning she bounded up full of energy. Today Jonathan would help her fit the puzzle together. She hummed through her shower, selecting a coordinated shorts outfit and floppy sandals. She even remembered to bring a big straw hat.

The hallway was empty. But of course he'd have no idea when she would be ready. She knocked on his door. There was no answer.

She ran down the staircase to look for him in the dining room, where Randall and Margaret were just finishing their coffee.

"Jonathan is in the kitchen with Joe." Randall rose and walked toward her.

She fought her need to see Jonathan to do what she knew was expected. She waited for Randall to kiss her cheek.

"I understand that Jonathan is taking you on a picnic to some of your favorite haunts." The sharp contrast between his smile and his tortured eyes confused her.

She didn't want to hurt anyone. "I'm sorry, Uncle Randall," she whispered, not fully understanding her feelings, and returned his light hug.

"I know." His breath smelled like coffee as he pressed a fleeting kiss at the edge of her mouth. "Please be careful."

"Yes, by all means be careful!" Her aunt pushed away from the table. "They're predicting more thunderstorms."

"Don't worry. I'll take good care of her." The voice came from the door behind her. Although she knew it was Jonathan, his voice was somehow different—younger, more carefree.

Twirling around, she found Jonathan carrying a picnic basket. Behind him, Joe held out a folded blanket to her. "Here you are, Miss Amanda. Enjoy your day."

"We will."

Jonathan took her hand. She felt as if the cares of the world—her world—tumbled off her shoulders. Outside, the air felt so soft and fresh, she laughed. Like kids, they ran across the lawn, laughing at nothing and everything.

Jonathan led her down a narrow path she hadn't noticed before. "C'mon. We're going to explore."

It felt cooler because the sunlight was filtered through thick overhead branches. She felt gloriously alive. He turned to warn her of low-hanging snares and took her hand to help her over obstacles in the path. Finally the woods opened up to a lawn leading down to the lake.

There was a small cottage made of weathered gray clapboard with shiny black shutters hung at two narrow windows. Beyond, a low boathouse perched on the rocky shore. To one side, a short covered pier had a single lounge chair on it. A sleek black boat was tied to its posts.

"This is Joe's place. When I used to come to the island, I always tied up here. Do you remember?"

Some quality in his voice made her search his face. She remembered nothing but understood that this place was important to him.

"Did we come here often?" She answered his question with one of her own.

"Sometimes during the day, when Joe was up at the house, we'd swim off this pier. It's so much more private." He took a ragged breath. "It doesn't bring anything back, does it?"

Disappointment glittered in his eyes, even though he tried to hide it. With Jonathan, she couldn't be anything except utterly truthful.

"No, I don't remember. But can we swim, just like before?"

His bittersweet expression tugged at her heart. "Yeah, maybe we can. C'mon. I'll show you where you like to picnic."

To her surprise, he led her deeper into the woods instead of along the shoreline as she'd expected. Suddenly she heard Lady barking, and an instant later the retriever darted out of the trees ahead of them.

"Hi, girl." To her delight, Lady trotted beside her, allowing her to stroke her silky head.

The minute Jonathan drew her into a clearing, something deep inside answered an unformed question. It was beautiful here. Beautiful and safe. The trees formed a cocoon of green; the short grass was scattered with tiny blue flowers; there was no sound, no intrusion. The mingled scent of flowers and pine was somehow exotic and secret.

They could be the only two people in the world.

Lady deserted her, dashing toward a mound of grass. Amanda was surprised to see that the mound had a cedar door on one side. "What's that?"

"The old icehouse. Someone told me it's still in use. Penelope has a ton of ice delivered to the island every summer."

She laughed at the tone in his voice. "She does. I saw the bill and couldn't understand why she needed it."

He spread the blanket on the sweet-smelling grass. "You must be hungry. Let's see what Joe put in here for us."

She sank down, knowing he wasn't ready to talk yet. His expression was wary as he took packages of food out of the basket. Now that they were together, alone, she could wait.

"God, I can't believe he remembered," she heard him mutter. He glanced up at her. "Joe packed everything we used to ask him for."

A sudden chill made shivers run along her skin. Once before Joe supposedly had prepared her favorite dinner and she'd hated most of it. Would she like Brie spread on crusty French bread? Seedless green grapes and strawberries? Chocolate chip cookies still warm from the oven?

"Are you all right, Amanda?"

The question startled her. "Yes, just hungry," she answered as naturally as possible.

Tentatively, she took her first bite. Then she devoured everything in sight, including Jonathan's share of cookies.

"I love everything!" Torn between relief and confusion, she sat back on her heels. Jonathan handed her a glass of champagne.

"Slow down a bit," he ordered, and knelt in front of her. "Does that make you happy or sad? I can't tell."

"*You* make me happy." She couldn't stop until she knew. "Did you always?"

She could tell by the stiffness of his shoulders that he didn't want to tell her. But that was why they had come here.

He reached out a hand, slipping it under the hair curling at her neck, and his smile was gentle. "Ten years ago we had a relationship. A physical relationship."

Her heart crashed against her ribs. She couldn't *remember* it, but she felt it, believed in it, and him, completely.

"Were we in love with each other?"

He dropped his hand and sank back on his heels. "I don't think I can answer that," he said at last.

She stared, trying to see beyond the glitter in his eyes and his shadowed expression. "What happened to end it?"

"I was an arrogant young fool and you were even younger. I found you in bed with someone else." He spoke the words almost casually, yet each one pierced her heart.

She would *never* betray him so cruelly. "I don't believe that."

Suddenly he looked years younger, vulnerable and hurt. "Neither could I."

She'd hurt him. He'd given her everything: his love and trust then; her life now. Somehow she had to make it up to him. She reached out to smooth the hair away from his forehead. He leaned into her touch, almost as if he couldn't help himself. That small movement sealed her decision.

She pressed her mouth against his. He tasted of champagne and chocolate. It was good.

Passion rose inside her, just beneath her hot skin, as his mouth opened for her, to her. He stroked her lips with his tongue, eliciting a hushed moan from her throat. She threaded her fingers through his hair, holding him, seducing him with her mouth, being seduced by his.

This was beyond memory; behind, before, beneath, above anything she'd sought through the dark corridors of her mind. Life itself blazed like fire inside her. Her body had a will of its own, leading her to press against him until she could feel her breasts swell beneath her thin knit top and tremors sweep through her.

She felt his response build. She knew he was fighting it, but knew the battle was hers when he put his mouth to the hollow between her breasts.

"Are you sure you want this, Amanda?"

"Yes." She urged him down onto the blanket. A deep shudder shook her body as his hands slid under her shirt to stroke her aching breasts. She tugged at his lower lip with her teeth and slid her tongue inside his mouth. Her hands went around his back, coaxing him closer. As much as she wanted to, she couldn't capture any memory of being with him like this, but it ceased to be important. She only knew she wanted to feel his hot skin next to hers.

Eagerly she pushed her hands under his T-shirt, down his hard stomach. She slid two fingers beneath the zipper of his jeans and felt him harden. She parted her thighs, allowing him free access. Trapped beneath his weight, she felt new again.

One hand stroked her breast, while the other trailed down her quivering stomach. A deep, sensual yearning grew within her. She had no fears, no doubts. She was willingly drowning in these new sensations, falling into him.

And then it came. From deep inside her—not from the center of her sensations, not from her muddled brain, but from some yet-unidentified source—the one question that wouldn't let her be free. She pressed her lips to his ear.

"Are you still certain I'm Amanda?"

Jonathan went completely still. Icy cold replaced the heat of passion. She found she couldn't look at him.

"Yeah, now I'm positive. You are Amanda. You always were a tease."

She couldn't move, didn't, even when he lifted himself off her to sweep her body with his dark eyes. "I guess there are some things a guy never forgets. So long, Amanda."

He walked away, casually straightening his clothes, as if what had just happened between them didn't matter at all. He was actually going. This time, forever.

Mesmerized by the enormity of her mistake, she felt paralyzed. The exotic scent of this place and their shared arousal taunted her.

Lady whined, then licked her cheek. Finally she was forced to act.

"Jonathan!"

She screamed his name, pulling her clothes together even as she ran through the woods after him. By the time she reached the dock, he was gone, his boat already out in the lake, the motor gunned to full throttle.

She raced to the edge of the pier. "Jonathan, wait!" The wind caught her words, flinging them away.

She knew she'd lost him. Large, hiccuping sobs convulsed her as tears poured down her cheeks. Somehow she had to stop him. Had to explain. If there had been another boat, she would have gone after him even though she wasn't sure how to drive one.

There *was* another boat! The powerboat Margaret and Randall had used to fetch her from town. It had to be as fast as Jonathan's. Before she could decide how to reach it, the sky opened up.

Sheets of rain pelted against her body. She ran up the pier, past the boathouse. A bolt of lightning struck a treetop at the edge of the woods. She could smell the heat, feel the power. She fought a rising panic.

Instinct drove her toward Joe's cottage.

The porch floor planks creaked as she ran under the sheltering roof. She banged on the door as the wind shifted, sending a torrent of rain against her back. Lightning flashed and thunder crashed. She began to shake. Vague, dark memories of storms assaulted her mind. Frightened, she pushed at the door frantically and sobbed with relief when it creaked open.

Inside it was snug and dry and warm. The living room held a green-and-red-plaid sofa and matching chair on one side and a round dining table with two chairs on the other. Bouquets of flowers covered every surface, their scent swelling in the heavy damp air.

"Joe, are you home?" A loud banging, from behind a closed door, answered her.

"Joe?" she called as she cautiously crossed the room and opened that door.

It was a bedroom. Empty. The rain was blowing in

from an open window that banged against the wall. She rushed forward to shut and latch it.

Rainwater dripped from her saturated clothes and soggy sandals as she turned around.

She forgot to breathe as she realized what she'd seen hadn't been a trick of light and shadows. She stared at picture after picture of herself, nailed onto Joe's bedroom wall in a monstrous collage.

A floorboard creaked and she looked away from her own face to the open door.

"What are you doing in my bedroom, Miss Amanda?" Joe asked in his quiet singsong voice.

CHAPTER NINE

SHE FROZE FOR A MOMENT then started backing up slowly.

"What are you doing here, Miss Amanda?" He stepped over the threshold and shut the door behind him.

She heard a bolt snap, and a small tremor started in the pit of her stomach. Instinctively she kept her voice soft, calm and low. "I was looking for you, Joe. I'm afraid of the storm."

His eyes turned opaque, and he nodded as if he believed her. She took a shallow breath of relief. Inching closer to the wall, she commented, "These pictures are wonderful."

"Remember this one, Miss Amanda? I took it the day you came here."

In an enlarged picture in the center of the wall a blond child with chubby cheeks and big, sad eyes stood clutching a doll to her chest. Amanda squinted, desperately searching for a memory.

Joe brushed past her to point to the upper left. "And this one when Mr. Chambers was teaching you to play tennis."

This time the little girl was smiling. She wore all

white, with Randall and Margaret similarly attired, all holding tennis rackets. They appeared happy. Did she play tennis? She searched her mind and suddenly came up with the scoring system: love—15—30—40—game. But that didn't prove anything.

After a moment she realized that, except for the first picture, Joe had arranged his wall in chronological order. As the pictures progressed, she could see herself get older and harder.

"How about this one, Miss Amanda? I took it the summer Dr. Jonathan spent so much time on the island with you."

In that picture she was wearing the white dress she'd chosen to wear last night. The girl she had been was beautiful: hair flowing about a classic face, voluptuous figure, long, tanned limbs. But it was the eyes that caught her attention. Eyes full of wild rebellion. Eyes that demanded and commanded. Had she ever really been that out of control?

Remembering how she would have willingly abandoned herself to Jonathan, she could recognize a glimpse of this other Amanda. She searched the wall. There were so many similarities. Why couldn't she accept herself? Accept this as her world?

Because something, somehow, didn't feel right.

"I'm glad you like my pictures, Miss Amanda."

Joe's sweet smile lulled her. She relaxed a little. "Yes," she said, sighing as she followed the direction of his callused finger pointing from one picture to the next. At the bottom right-hand corner of the wall, he stopped at a crumpled photograph that had been smoothed and tacked up with four pins.

At first it seemed to be a recent picture of her, but it was somehow different from the rest. More posed. Different grain. Something about it made her reach out to touch it.

"No." He slapped her hand away. "Don't touch."

Joe, harmless, helpful, smiling Joe. He wouldn't hurt her. He treasured her, if she could believe the evidence before her. Or was it some sick obsession?

She made herself smile at him. Made herself stand still when her instinct told her to run.

"It's…it's so pretty, Joe. But why is it creased?"

"Because they threw it away. I took it from the trash." His gray ponytail swung over his shoulder as he turned to her with clenched fists. "Don't tell them, Miss Amanda, or you'll make trouble for me."

As hard as she tried, she couldn't prevent the flinch. It seemed to unleash something in him. He stepped toward her. She backed away. He pursued her until she was trapped against the door, the knob biting into her back.

He leaned so close she could smell the rain musty on his skin and clothes. "You better not tell them, Miss Amanda."

"I won't, Joe." Horrified at the fear she heard in her voice, she cleared her throat. "I promise."

"That's all right, then." He smiled again, as if all was forgiven and forgotten. "We gotta go now. They'll be looking for you."

He reached toward her and she scrambled away

from the door, but he only turned the lock. "I gotta go up to the big house and check on things. The boats are secure."

She followed him into the living room. This time she paused to look for clues, as much to find out who he was as anything that might have something to do with herself. By the front door there was a row of hooks holding keys. Two had red cork bobbers—boat keys. She gripped her hands together, trying not to give her thoughts away.

"We better go, Miss Amanda." Joe pushed the front door open, obviously expecting her to leave.

She cringed from the rain still pounding down.

"You scared?"

Holding onto her self-control, she nodded.

"You always been afraid of storms since you ran away." He peered at her. "Once, when you were thirteen, you took the boat without permission and got caught out in the middle of the lake by a whopper of a storm. You don't remember that, Miss Amanda?"

No memories came, but the fear of storms beat inside her like thunder. "You go on ahead, Joe. I'll stay here on the porch until the rain stops."

"No. They're waiting for you. I'll just go up to the house and bring you back an umbrella."

He sprinted out into the downpour, disappearing up the path. She knew she didn't have much time. Her desperate need to know the truth, to understand who she was, gave her a raw kind of courage.

She slammed her hip into the door. When it opened, she raced to his bedroom, unpinned the creased photo from the wall and tucked it into her shorts. Grabbing the two sets of keys, she ran all the way to the pier.

She wasted precious moments looking over her shoulder as she clawed at the canvas boat cover. Finally she got it pulled back enough to squeeze down into the driver's seat.

The first key didn't fit. She threw it behind her under the canvas. With the second, the engine roared to life. She jumped back out and loosed all the lines. It took her too long to figure out how to reverse out of the boat slip. Every second, the blood beat harder and harder in her head.

At last she made it. In her haste, the front of the boat clipped the end piling, and a huge splinter of wood flew past her cheek.

With a sob of relief she shifted gears, and the boat shot into the waves as she headed across the lake. The rain blended everything into shades of gray. For a moment she wondered if she'd find the shore or plow in endless circles until she ran out of gas or the rain stopped. She gripped the wheel, holding the boat on what she hoped was a straight course.

She was alone on the lake. No one else would be desperate enough to go out with lightning flashing all around them. She pulled the canvas over her head, trying to keep the rain off, but it was hard to steer with one hand, fighting the wind and waves.

The mist shifted and she saw lights ahead. Thank God! Tears of relief streamed down her cheeks, mixing with the rain. Then reaction set in. She began to tremble until huge shudders racked her body. She had to keep control until she could dock. She had to finish this.

No matter what the cost, she would reach Jonathan and get help.

Light streamed from his windows, a haven beckoning to her. She took a breath and steadied herself. Then she saw his black boat in the pier slip. What should she do? She didn't know how to dock this thing, especially in this weather. She sobbed, slumping over the wheel in defeat.

The horn blared, startling her.

Without thinking, she pressed it again. And again. She didn't know what else to do.

THE STORM ROARED outside, matching the anger raging inside him. How dare she play her little tricks on him again?

He didn't know how long he'd been sitting there when he heard the faint horn. Couldn't be anyone out on the water. No one would be so foolish in this weather. Then it came again. And again.

He opened the front door, and there, bobbing just a few feet from his pier, was a powerboat. Randall's boat.

Without thinking, he raced to the end of the dock and plunged into the water.

"Are you trying to get yourself killed?" He hauled himself over the side and pushed her out of the driver's seat. Holding his anger in, he nosed the boat to the pier and tied it to one side.

They were both soaked through, but her lips were tinged a faint blue. With her hair plastered against her skull, he could see the area Carl had shaved for surgery. Her eyes were huge with fright.

What could have made her pull such a damn dangerous stunt? He remembered how frightened she'd always been of storms, especially lake storms, when the waves tossed and the lightning streaked to the waterline. The anger leeched out of him, leaving him concerned for her health. She looked like a half-drowned kitten, a woman in need of his strength and warmth.

He tried to retrieve his sense of outrage. He'd need every defense to keep from going overboard again.

Unbidden, the remembered taste of her filled him with desire. "C'mon. I've got to get you out of this storm." He hauled her out of the boat, not bothering to secure the canvas cover. Catching her up in his arms, he carried her into his house.

She wound her arms around his neck and buried her face in his chest like a trusting child. But all he could feel was woman. His body went hot everywhere it pressed against hers.

Even in the warm living room, where flames roared in the fireplace, she continued to shudder. Slowly, carefully, he lowered her to the carpet. She staggered, her knees buckling. She clutched at him.

He couldn't let her go. "Amanda, what..."

"Don't call me that." She pushed out of his arms, her eyes blazing out of a pale face. Fumbling under her top, she pulled something from the waistband of her shorts. "Look at this."

He glanced down at the crumpled photo. "Beautiful girl. Who is she?"

She looked ready to shatter. "I...I think it's the face I saw in the mirror."

For the first time in his career, he wanted help. Pat, or someone more qualified to deal with this, standing at his shoulder, telling him what to do. He stared down at the picture—a smiling woman with a straight fall of blond hair.

"Where did you get this?"

"Joe." Her eyes were swimming with tears. "It was on the wall with all the other pictures in his bedroom." Her voice sank to a hoarse whisper. "He has dozens and dozens of pictures of me. Of Amanda. Like some kind of shrine."

He had to be very careful; she seemed at the breaking point. "Joe is easily confused, but he would never hurt anyone, much less you. He's adored you since you first came to live on the island."

He turned the photo round and round. Yes. In a way this picture looked like Amanda. But anyone who knew her well would realize this wasn't her. He turned it over. The printing on the back made him smile.

"Do you know Tori Owens, five foot seven inches, a hundred and fifteen pounds, size six?" He offered the picture back to her. "You didn't see this face. Some trick of the lousy light in that house threw shadows on your face, so it might have resembled hers. You have similar bone structure.''

The dazed look in her eyes hit him like a blow. ''It's a model's composite,'' he said gently. ''I don't know where Joe got it. But trust me, you've never been near a modeling agency.''

''Joe said he found it in the trash.'' She looked ready to drop. ''He said *they* threw it away.''

The way she said *they* brought him up short. This whole thing was going in the wrong direction. Something had gone very wrong at The Lodge. She didn't look well and she was getting more and more confused.

Decision making, especially in a crisis, was his specialty. ''I'm taking you back to the rehab center. Now.''

''Yes. I want to get away from here.'' He hardly recognized her voice. He couldn't figure out the shuttered look on her face. There was nothing to say but plenty to do. He opened the bathroom door and handed her his own navy terry cloth robe. ''Leave your clothes outside the door. I'll put them in the dryer while you take a hot shower.''

While he waited, he picked up the phone. The storm had taken out the lines. No great surprise there. He'd have to figure out another way to let Randall and Margaret know that she was safe.

He heard the door creak open and turned just in time to see her hand snake out to drop her shorts and shirt. He threw them in the dryer before he fixed steaming mugs of tea, hers with double sugar.

By the time he came out of the kitchen, she was sitting on the couch, enveloped in his robe, staring at the fire. She seemed miles away as she absently took the cup and warmed her palms around it.

Leaving her, he went to his bedroom, stripped off his own wet clothes and tossed some things into his leather duffel. He'd failed her somehow. It was his job to keep her safe. Not once in his professional life had a patient affected him so profoundly. Not once had he failed any of them. Why now? Why wasn't he able to help her the way he wanted to? Now, when it had never been more important?

By the time he was dressed she had found the dryer and put her clothes back on. Her hair was still wet, but she'd fluffed it out. She looked more like herself, yet seemed resigned—to what he couldn't tell.

He tried a new tack. "How about a truce?" he asked, trying to get some sort of response from her. "We'll just forget what happened on the island today. We'll go back to where we were at the rehab center and start again."

"I've already forgotten enough. No more. I'm only going forward." Her icy calm rubbed his already raw nerves. This was yet another side to Amanda. Damn it, all of her personalities were going to drive him a little crazy.

They drove into town, but he was reluctant to leave her alone in the car. He laid on the horn outside the sheriff's office until a deputy sprinted out in the rain.

"Have Phil notify Mr. and Mrs. Chambers that I'm

taking Amanda Braithwaite back to the hospital. Oh, and they can find their boat at my dock.''

Ernie squinted into the car before he nodded and turned away. Jonathan gunned the engine, making the car fishtail a bit as he started up.

As he drove south toward the city, she remained quiet. He kept glancing at her profile. There were no tears, no telltale signs that she was upset, but her hands remained clasped in her lap—almost as if she were praying.

The closer they got to the rehab center the more he fought with himself. A crazy part of him wanted to keep her with him, wanted to take away all her pain, wanted to taste her mouth and feel her come alive beneath him. What the hell was wrong with him? He had to do what was best for her—he had to get away from her.

It wasn't possible.

''I'm not going to the rehab center, Jonathan.'' As if she'd read his thoughts, she finally turned to him. ''Take me home with you. I need to talk to you.''

When he hesitated for a second, she shrugged. ''Then take me to a hotel. With you or without you, I'm going to find out the truth.''

There was no decision to make. He'd already made it. ''I'll take you home with me.''

JONATHAN'S CONDO overlooked Lake Michigan. It seemed stark, almost empty compared to The Lodge. She liked the natural wood floors, the smell of the leather furniture and, most of all, the sense of open space.

While he checked with his answering service, she stared out the plate-glass window at the waves crashing against the shoreline twelve stories below. It had taken her almost the entire trip here, but at last she had a plan. No more would she allow other people to direct her life. She would focus. If her mind wouldn't let her remember her past, she would force it to help her carve out a future. She might never again be the Amanda she had been—if that *was* who she had been. She might never learn the whole truth. But what she could learn, she would. What she could accept of her past, she would. Then and only then could she plan the future.

She felt Jonathan come up behind her and turned slowly. His hair had fallen over his forehead, and he looked young, vulnerable, as he had earlier this afternoon. It seemed a thousand years ago. He attracted her in an elemental way that was almost too powerful to understand. If she didn't do what had to be done right now, she might lose her nerve.

"I don't want to go back to the rehab center. I don't want to go back to The Lodge. I...I don't feel well there." She shook her head when she couldn't find the right words. "I can't explain why. Maybe because I don't feel comfortable with my family. I only feel right with you."

With a jolt of surprise, she realized he wasn't as calm as he appeared. His legs were braced apart, his fingers were jammed into his jeans pockets and his jaw was clenched as if he faced a great foe. Her survival instinct was strong, she knew that from the description of how she'd fought off her attacker. But bound up with that instinct was a new perception—a knowledge of who she was right now and what she needed to survive.

"You make me feel safe. But it's more than that, and we both know it. I can't live with my doubts anymore. I'm going to find the answers I need." She put her arms around him, leaning her head on his chest. The accelerated beat of his heart echoed beneath her ear. "Will you help me?"

Lightly, yet firmly, his arms closed around her. "We're both so tired tonight, neither of us can think straight. You need to rest." His chest heaved with an ironic laugh. "Now that sounds familiar, doesn't it?"

She recognized he was trying to distract her, and on one level she accepted the sanity of it. So she allowed him to loan her a Bulls T-shirt to sleep in and to put her in his own bed. But that didn't change her need or her desire. She closed her eyes, willing oblivion to claim her quickly. Tonight there was no reason to lie staring at the ceiling, trying to find answers. Tomorrow either he would help her or she'd go it alone.

Her body involuntarily twitched, but she forced it to relax. She must fight her unreasonable fear of being alone, a fear that seemed to grow with each passing day. No matter what she found or who she was, she would have to be strong enough to start anew—and to keep Jonathan by her side.

It was his voice that brought her awake from a peaceful sleep, as it had when he called her back from the threshold of eternity. Now, as then, she opened her eyes to find him leaning over her, silhouetted in bright light, although this time the brightness was the sun blazing through the window.

"There's an emergency at the hospital. A five-car accident on the Edens expressway. I don't want to leave you, but I'm needed."

She managed a faint smile. "Go. I understand." She watched the tension drain out of his body.

"I'll be back by early afternoon. If you get hungry, I've left money and a spare key for you. My fridge is bare but there's a good restaurant right around the corner." He hesitated. "The door will lock behind me. You're safe here."

Even after he finished speaking, he didn't move away from the bed. She searched his face and read a question there.

"I promise I'll be here when you get back."

He turned and she held her breath until the door shut. Then she rolled over and slept for another two hours, exhausted from her ordeal the day before.

Once fully awake, she took a long leisurely shower, then dressed in the clothes she'd had on the day before. They were wrinkled but she had no choice. She didn't feel she could go poking about in his things for another T-shirt, but she was eager to explore his kitchen when her stomach started to growl. He had been utterly truthful about the state of his refrigerator. There was only a bottle of red and a bottle of white, and she wasn't up to wine in the morning. Not even a frozen orange juice in the freezer. So she took the thirty dollars he'd left on the table, along with the key, and headed out.

She was alone on the elevator until the eighth floor. When the doors opened, a man in shorts got on with a small towel draped around his sweaty neck. Before the doors swished shut again she saw the sign for the health club.

Health club! She could hardly control the little shiver of excitement that ran up her spine. She'd almost forgotten the appointment book with Jack's Gym scheduled practically every other day. And beside the gym listing, a name. Peter.

In the lobby she headed directly to the pay phones, discreetly hidden by a potted palm. The phone book had two locations for Jack's Gym. The doorman pointed her to the closest one, only six blocks away.

She wouldn't look at all out of place in shorts at a gym. She pocketed the key and the cash, forgetting her stomach, and set out at a brisk pace. The sun reflected off the sidewalk, and she grew hotter and hotter. She had to slow down, but she couldn't stop. For some reason, seeing Peter had become of paramount importance.

Peter wasn't there. He didn't work at that site. The young man who welcomed her was tanned and muscled, reminding her of Tori Owens's picture.

"You have to go crosstown to the other gym. Want me to call you a cab?" he asked, white teeth flashing.

Considering she was spending Jonathan's money, she shook her head. "I'll walk."

The muscular young man had a hearty laugh. "No way. It's too far in this heat. You'd melt. The bus stops two blocks west of here."

She caught it and had to get a transfer before finally reaching an impressive complex of shops and condos.

Jack's Gym II occupied one whole side of the main floor. The noise of the machines and the crowded floor disconcerted her for a moment. She wandered around the empty reception area, trying to decide how to find Peter.

"Can I help you?"

She whirled around. A tanned, attractive body-builder tried to hide a gasp. "My God, Amanda!"

"Peter?" Her question seemed to startle him.

His expression shifted. "God, I forgot. The police told us about your mugging and the amnesia stuff when they questioned us. How are you feeling? You look...great."

Detective Savage had been here. Maybe, finally, she was getting somewhere. "How well do you know me, Peter?"

Suddenly he looked as if he wanted to take off, but she'd come too far to let that happen. "Could we go somewhere private to talk?"

His eyes lit up and he nodded. "Sure, hon. Come into my office."

The cluttered office was smaller than her closet. Too small, she realized, once he shut the door.

"I've missed you."

There was a tone in his voice she didn't quite understand. She wasn't sure she was going to like what she found out here, but she held her ground. She looked him straight in the eyes. "I know from my appointment calendar that we...got together often. When was the last time you saw me?"

"A couple of weeks before you got mugged."

"If the police told you about what happened to me, why didn't you visit me in the hospital?"

He shrugged his massive shoulders. "Hon, you made it real clear it was all over between us."

The implication made her stomach churn, but she persevered. No matter what, she had to know the truth.

"How did I do that?"

A deep flush spread up his tanned cheeks. His whole body stiffened as he looked everywhere in the office except at her.

"What happened between us to end it, Peter? I need to know."

At last her urgency seemed to get through to him. He stared down at her from close range. "You never were subtle, honey. So why should I be? I got home early one day and you had another guy in my bed."

CHAPTER TEN

THE SILENCE IN his condo should have alerted Jonathan. He called her name repeatedly, unable to believe she was gone. He searched the empty apartment, disbelief, anger and fear all merging to the realization that he'd failed.

Amanda was gone despite his wish to keep her safe, despite her promise to stay. He'd repressed everything while performing surgery, as always concentrating on the task at hand. For once, his iron control, his supreme confidence deserted him.

She was out *there*. Alone. And he had no idea where she might have gone, who she was seeing.

Even though the money and the key were gone, it was way past lunchtime. She should have been back long ago if she'd just gone out for food.

Pat Newman stood behind him, silently waiting and watching from the foyer. Watching him lose it, he realized.

"I left her thirty dollars." He tried to explain. "Just in case. She was supposed to go to lunch and come right back. She's so confused, she could be anywhere. I shouldn't have left her alone."

"You had a job to do." Pat jabbed at his glasses,

pushing them up on his forehead. "Stop acting like her lover instead of her doctor."

Even though Pat's words stripped his soul bare, he tried to bluff, "Don't psychoanalyze me. I brought her here and I'm responsible for her, that's all."

Pat's laugh sounded cynical. "Yeah, right. If she promised, she'll be back. Amanda keeps her word. That's one fact I can tell you from my evaluation of her."

"Meantime, anything could be happening to her." Without warning, Jonathan remembered how she'd cried in the hospital, how he'd held her. He could taste her kiss, feel her arms around him. She had shown him over and over how she needed him, but he had to keep his professional distance—always so correct! The great doctor, hiding behind his rules and regulations; never wanting to be hurt by her again. "She's alone out there. She's afraid to be alone, you know."

"Jonathan, we need to talk about this."

He met his friend's eyes briefly before jerking his head away. He realized that even that brief contact revealed more than he wanted Pat to know. "I understand what's happening."

"Do you? Do you really?" Impatiently, Pat walked around him. "So what are you going to do about it?"

Whatever answer he might have given was cut off by the sound of a key in the door. Before Pat could react, Jonathan wrenched the door open to reveal Amanda standing on the threshold, very pale, very confused.

Jonathan pulled her into his arms, holding her against his body, not caring that Pat was a witness. She went completely stiff. Not like his Amanda at all.

"What happened? Are you all right?" He held her away to study her reaction. She seemed all right—no cuts or bruises. Her clothes weren't mussed. But she had a faraway look in her eyes, as if something had taken her to a place so dreadful, shown her sights so heinous, she just wasn't able to deal with it.

Moving past him, she ignored his questions. "Hello, Dr. Newman."

"Hello, Amanda. I came to talk to you about returning to rehab."

"The hospital?" She threw Jonathan a look of reproach. "I'm sure Jonathan told you how I feel. No disrespect to you, Dr. Newman, but I won't find the answers I need there."

Her color seemed to be returning. Whatever had happened to traumatize her was beginning to fade. Jonathan stood back, content to let Pat handle her state of mind in his gentle way. There would be time enough to confront whatever demons she'd encountered when they were alone.

"I disagree, Amanda." Pat said. "However, the choice is yours. If you should ever wish to return, I'll be available."

"Thank you. Goodbye." It was a dismissal, plain and simple.

Cool and composed, smiling graciously, Amanda ushered Pat out the door. But despite his shock, Jonathan knew she wasn't in control at all.

She turned from the door. "I told you I wouldn't go back there." She shook her head, as if ending the subject once and for all. "I'm sorry if my being gone upset you. I didn't plan to be away so long. I went to Jack's Gym."

A gym? What the hell did a gym have to do with anything?

"Why?"

"Because I...Amanda went there three times a week to see Peter. Her very *personal* trainer." Tears welled up in her eyes. "Now I understand why you don't want me. I'm not a very likable person, am I? Maybe that's why I don't *feel* like Amanda Braithwaite." She crossed the room to the large window, avoiding him completely, as if she were talking to herself now. "I don't like her much, or understand her. Except in her affection for Mother Chambers. Otherwise she's pretty...horrible."

The way she referred to herself in the third person, in a too calm voice, frightened him. He moved toward her slowly, afraid of how she might react. He kept his voice gentle, even though what he wanted to do was grab her and shake some sense into her.

"A good doctor would insist you return to rehab. I've decided I'm not a very good doctor. You were right. What's between us is more than a doctor-patient relationship. It may not be fair and it may not be good. It may lead us astray. But we have to let it lead us somewhere, because, whatever it is, it's driving us both crazy."

He stopped a foot from her, still careful not to

touch her. "But before we can deal with us, you have to deal with you. You have to accept once and for all who you are."

She shook her head in denial.

"If there are things about your old self you don't like, you can change them."

Her breath caught on a sob. "Do you really believe that?"

"Yeah, I do." It took every fiber of his control not to reach out and comfort her. She wasn't ready for that yet. "I'm going to help you find the truth, Amanda, because only then can you get your life back. What you do with it from then on is up to you. I already know the truth. You are Amanda Braithwaite, and our search will prove it."

SHE COULDN'T FALL ASLEEP. Despite Jonathan's words, his assurance that she could build a new life, she couldn't get the dark picture Peter had painted out of her mind. And now her greatest fear rose up to confront her. Maybe she felt so disconnected because she wasn't a person worthy of friendship. Maybe Amanda was so awful that she'd driven everyone away. She'd disgusted Peter, even though they'd had an intimate relationship. She'd pushed Jonathan away ten years ago, when she'd only been a young woman. Her family seemed to love her, but they had to—wasn't that what family was all about? And Joe, well that was just too weird. The puzzle of Amanda, just beginning to take shape, wasn't a pretty picture at all.

And then a new thought struck her. Maybe Detective Savage had it all wrong. The truth about Amanda was proving to be ugly. Maybe someone had a reason to want her dead.

Suddenly she couldn't bear being alone in Jonathan's bedroom. It was too dark, too quiet. Barefoot, she padded into the living room, dragging a blanket behind her.

Jonathan was sprawled across the couch, a white sheet wound around his waist and thighs, as if he'd been tossing and turning. His hair was mussed and he had a day's growth of beard, but he looked wonderful to her.

Wrapping the blanket around her shoulders, she curled up in the leather chair across from him. Fascinated, she watched the even rise and fall of his bare chest as he slept.

She had tasted him and touched him. And in her dreams she had felt him shudder when they lost themselves in each other. Her dreams had been miraculous, full of love and rightness. She refused to believe she'd felt that way about Peter or the faceless man who had been her way out of that relationship. Supposedly she'd used the same trick on Jonathan ten years earlier. The pattern seemed unmistakable, and it sickened her. What kind of woman was she?

Jonathan believed he knew the truth. Part of her prayed he was wrong. She didn't want to be that Amanda—a betrayer of hearts.

When she woke, the shower was running. Jonathan had left the sheet twisted in a heap at one end of the couch. How long had he been awake, watching her sleep? she wondered. Or didn't he care at all?

Then she saw the picture of Tori Owens. It was propped up on the glass-and-iron coffee table along with an enormous phone book open to the yellow pages. Next to it, a legal pad listed twelve modeling agencies' addresses.

Excitement surged through her. He'd meant what he said. At last, she was going to make some progress.

The doorbell startled her. He'd never hear it in the shower. Dropping the blanket, she scrambled out of the deep chair. The bell rang and rang, as if there were some dire emergency.

Randall stood in the doorway, his finger still pressed to the button. When he saw her, his face drained of all color, leaving him looking old and haggard. Only then did she realize what she must look like with her hair sleep-mussed and wearing only Jonathan's oversize T-shirt.

"Was that the doorbell?"

She spun around at the sound of Jonathan's voice. Barefoot, his jeans zipped but not snapped, he walked across the living room as he rubbed at his damp chest with a towel.

Disbelief and rage blazed from Randall's eyes. Suddenly afraid, she backed up. Jonathan, smelling of shampoo and soap, caught her, and put up his hand. "This isn't what it looks like, Randall."

Ignoring him, her uncle turned on her. "Do not do this, Amanda. I want you to return to The Lodge with me, now."

It took all her newfound strength to hold back her tears. How could she go on hurting these people— her family—until she found the truth? A sob rose in the back of her throat so hot and thick she couldn't speak. She shook her head in denial.

Something dark and terrifying flashed across his face. *He hates me!* she thought. Panic made her step back into Jonathan's embrace.

"Randall, you're being ridiculous. I…"

Her uncle cut him off. "Your behavior is not only despicable, it is unethical." He spat the words out. "It remains to be seen how I will handle this with the hospital board."

At his threat, Jonathan stiffened behind her. "All I'm thinking about is Amanda's welfare. I'd think you would feel the same way."

"How dare you!" Gathering his dignity, Randall flung back his head. "Nothing but concern is motivating me. After all, I'm family. I doubt your actions spring from any familial feeling." He reached behind him to grab a suitcase and shove it over the threshold. "Even though you have broken your grandmother's heart, she insisted we pack this for you."

He spun on his heels and walked away from them, his back and shoulders rigid.

"He hates me." The whisper tore from her tight, hot throat.

"No, he loves you." Jonathan shut the door. "They all do. Your family spoiled you rotten from the day you came to live with them. He just doesn't like not being in charge. But that's your job now. It's your life.''

The tenderness in his eyes was unexpected. It made her feel vulnerable, not in control at all. Suddenly she was painfully aware that she wore only a thin T-shirt and he was bare-chested. Surely she had seen him that way plenty of times, but here, in the intimacy of his apartment, the implication was overwhelming. She wanted him—in a relentless, fascinating and breathtaking way.

''Good morning,'' he said softly, diffusing her thoughts.

She barely managed a smile. ''I see you're already ahead of me. I'll shower and change as quickly as possible.'' She picked up the suitcase, trying not to think of Mother Chambers's thoughtfulness. Of all the new people in her life, she was the one who shouldn't be hurt.

The white dress was on top. Since it fit her better than anything else, she wore it. Jonathan was on the phone when she went back into the living room.

''No Tori Owens? Well, thank you, anyway.'' He hung up and scratched through one of the listings. ''So far, none of these modeling agencies has panned out.''

She could hear the frustration in his voice. ''Why don't we look her up in the phone book?''

Amusement lighted his eyes. ''Do you know how many people live in the city? Not including the 'burbs?''

''Why not take a look? Maybe we'll get lucky.''

Shaking his head, he sprang up off the couch. "Be my guest. I'll go get some breakfast."

Their eyes met briefly as he opened the door. He must have been satisfied by the look on her face, because he nodded almost imperceptibly before leaving.

She knew she'd frightened him by disappearing the day before. She vowed to do her best not to repeat that mistake. She opened the phone book and found that the list of Owenses went on for three pages. Scanning the names, she found a T. Owens and dialed. She got an answering machine—with a man's voice. One by one the list dwindled: a Taylor, Terrance and Thomas were quickly eliminated. There was no listing for Tori Owens.

"Any luck?"

She looked around as he entered with a white paper bag.

"Not so far. What did you bring us?" she asked curiously, real hunger gnawing at her stomach for the first time she could remember.

"Bananas, warm bagels and cream cheese. Tea with double sugar." He laid plastic containers on the coffee table and pulled out napkins and utensils. "Hope you like something."

The tea tasted wonderful and warmed her through and through. After a banana and three half bagels smothered with low-fat cream cheese she finally stopped eating. She laughed. "This stuff must be brain food. Why didn't I think of this earlier? *Victoria Owens.* Tori is probably a nickname."

"Or a professional name. Her real name might be Mary Smith. There are only ten thousand of those."

She looked at him, trying to decipher his mood. Suddenly dimples creased his face. "I'm just kidding. Let's take a look." He pulled the heavy book onto his lap and ran his finger down the page.

There were three listings for Victoria Owens. Jonathan went into the other room and got a spare phone so he could listen in.

The first was an elderly woman who didn't have a clue what they were talking about, however she wanted to talk. After Amanda listened politely for five minutes, Jonathan signaled her to cut it off.

A machine picked up on the second listing.

The tea she'd just sipped caught in her throat as she forgot to swallow. She hung up and looked at Jonathan, waiting for a reaction. There was none.

Trembling, she dialed the number again and listened to make sure she hadn't imagined it. Her pulse pounded so hard she thought she might explode.

"Hi, this is Tori. Sorry I can't come to the phone. Please leave your name and number and I'll get back to you as soon as possible. Bye."

Couldn't Jonathan hear what she heard?

She dialed again. "This time, listen."

His expression darkened. "Where does this Victoria Owens live?" he asked as he slowly put the phone down on the coffee table.

She could feel her body tensing with anticipation. "You heard it, too, didn't you? She sounds like me."

"Maybe a little." He caught her hand, absently

stroking it. "I know *you* think she sounds like you. Let's go meet her face-to-face so you can forget about this."

Jonathan's Jaguar looked out of place on the street where Tori Owens lived. Amanda glanced around at the nondescript apartment buildings pressed together, the cars crowding the dirty curbs. This was a far cry from The Lodge or Jonathan's condo. She opened her mouth to ask what part of town this was, but stopped when she saw Jonathan eyeing a group of young boys loitering near a fire hydrant. He made a big deal of using his remote lock. It beeped loud enough for the kids to notice.

"My guess is they're going to break open the hydrant to cool off in this heat." She tried to deflect Jonathan from assuming the kids were out to get his car. The neighborhood might not be upscale, but she instinctively felt that the kids were okay.

She didn't recognize the building half a block away. It was yellow brick, and some leggy geraniums in pots attempted to soften the concrete entrance. The heat was overpowering. In the dark, musty foyer, she had to strain to read the names on the mailboxes.

"Five A." Jonathan pressed a black button and turned toward the inner door. They waited impatiently. When there was no answer, he jabbed at the button again.

"Damn! She's not home."

"Maybe she's just not answering. Let's go knock on her door."

"We can't get in unless she buzzes us through."

"All right. Then buzz someone else until we get an answer."

"Good idea." He pressed one button after another. Finally an answering buzz let them in. "Let's go, and hope someone doesn't come after us with a gun."

They made it up five flights without being challenged, but they were both breathless by the time they got to the top. Her dress clung to her back and stomach in damp patches. She felt exhausted, suffocatingly hot, and her nerves were stretched on some sort of emotional rubber band. It was hard to maintain the control she'd assumed when she decided to begin this search. It could be ended abruptly if the woman in the picture she kept so carefully folded in her purse opened to Jonathan's thunderous knocking.

Tori Owens's door stayed shut. But after a few moments a door across the hall opened the width of a safety chain.

"If you don't stop that noise, I'm calling the super!" an elderly feminine voice challenged them.

"Go right ahead!" she replied loudly.

Jonathan looked shocked by her outburst. He stopped knocking.

She shrugged. "Maybe he'll let us in."

An overweight, unshaven man stomped up the stairs. Their prospects didn't look too promising.

"What d'ya want?" The man's jeans rode low under a massive protruding stomach. "Hey, Tori! About time you showed up. Your junk was hittin' the street next week."

His voice boomed along the narrow hall. Jonathan

frowned at her and started to say something, but she shushed him.

When the super got closer, he squinted, lines creasing his forehead like ruts in a road. "Thought you was Tori," he said flatly. "See that you ain't. What's your problem? The neighbors are bitchin' 'bout the noise."

"We want to get into Tori Owens's apartment." Jonathan held out two fifty dollar bills.

Fortunately she had her back to the wall or she might have collapsed from shock. The man snatched the cash, cramming it into his pocket.

"Five minutes. No more," he growled. "Don't try to steal nothing. I'll be standin' right here."

While he searched for the right key, she pushed Jonathan down the hall and whispered, "I can't believe you just gave him a hundred dollars."

"It's worth more if we get some answers." There was a look in his eyes that suddenly made her very afraid.

"What do you think we'll find?"

"I don't know, but there's something very strange about all of this."

The super pushed open the door, kicking aside a pile of magazines and mail. "She ain't been here for weeks. My guess is she's skipped town."

He flipped on an overhead light, which revealed a light layer of dust on the floor. "I been emptyin' her mailbox, but only lookin' for a rent check."

She could feel tension growing in Jonathan as they moved into the small two-room apartment. A heart-

shaped lace pillow at one end of the shabby couch
was the single homey object in the dingy room. Drab
gray carpet, beige walls and a couch and chair so
faded their pattern was indistinguishable gave the
place a sad feeling. On the opposite wall, the kitchen
comprised a small refrigerator and a hotplate.

Tears burned behind her eyes. Whoever lived here
was alone in the world. She could see it; she could
feel it. There wasn't one photo on the scarred wooden
end table or the tiny desk under the window.

Jonathan made his way over to it and began to go
through the drawers.

"Don't you be tryin' anything funny." The super
appeared to be having a belated attack of conscience.

She managed to smile at him over her shoulder.
"We won't. I promise."

Jonathan went very still, staring at a receipt of
some kind.

She was almost afraid to ask. "What did you
find?"

He looked at her as if he wanted to observe her
reaction. She had nothing to hide, but it was scary
nonetheless.

"What is it, Jonathan?"

"It's a receipt from the Well Women's Clinic run
by Memorial Hospital. The Braithwaite family
founded the clinic years ago, before your parents died,
to aid low-income women. Both Margaret and Randall are actively involved in its program. And Tori
Owens had a routine physical exam there three weeks
before you were attacked."

CHAPTER ELEVEN

SHE UNDERSTOOD what he *wasn't* saying immediately, and a shiver raced up her spine. "It's a connection between Tori Owens and Amanda's family. But we knew that already, or why would her picture have been at The Lodge for Joe to find?"

"That's the question." His eyes searched her face. "How does this place make you feel?"

"Lonely." She gazed around the room. "Sort of sad."

"Maybe you've been here before. Maybe Tori Owens is a friend of yours."

"I don't think the person who lives here has many friends." A growing anxiety drove her across the room to the bedroom doorway.

"Where ya goin'?" The super's voice stopped her.

"Into the bedroom." She realized this room was smaller than her closet at The Lodge.

"I'm right behind ya. Ya got two more minutes." He took a belligerent stance at the bedroom door as Jonathan slipped past him.

The light on the answering machine was blinking. She couldn't resist touching the Play button. Six messages. The machine had a day and time marker—and the first message was from the afternoon of the day she'd been mugged.

"This is the agency calling. Sorry to leave this so late, but we just firmed up a print shoot for you for 6:45 tonight. Wait under the marquee at the Majestic Hotel in Evanston for the photographer. If he doesn't show by 7:00 p.m. go across the park to Evanston Beach. Someone will meet you there. Wear an evening dress and plain pumps. No jewelry. Call tomorrow and let us know how it went."

The words struck her like a physical blow. She sagged down onto the bed.

Another connection. There were too many connections. They got all tangled up in her mind with the other loose pieces of her life, critically altering the puzzle.

"The other messages are demands for rent," Jonathan said flatly. "I wonder why the agency didn't call her back after all this time."

His eyes burned through her. She hadn't even heard the other messages. The first kept echoing through her head. "What does this mean?"

It was a simple question, but she knew there would be no simple answer. She did her best to stay calm, to still the swirling blackness in her mind. Jonathan just stared at her.

"Time's up. Outta here! The both of ya!"

Jonathan's hand moved so quickly, she barely realized he was flipping the microcassette out of the machine. She jumped up to distract the super and rushed toward the bathroom. There was nothing unusual to see. A large bottle of cheap bubble bath, a blow-dryer beneath a rusty sink, and on the back of the toilet a brush and comb. Without a conscious reason, she slipped the hairbrush into her purse. She could hear the super complaining in the other room.

She stepped back into the bedroom and lifted her eyes to Jonathan's face. She could tell he was upset, but he shrugged it off. "Let's go."

She slipped past the super, who was still standing in the doorway, suspiciously watching their every move. He gave them one last sour look and slammed the door. "Don't come back. I don't want no trouble here."

The door across the hall closed quietly. Jonathan practically pushed her down the steps in front of him. She was anxious to get away from that room, that depressing, shabby room. What kind of person lived there? Where was she? Amanda dreaded the answer.

Outside, the sun still shone, and shrieks and giggles proclaimed the hydrant had been breached. Water spewed out onto the street. They skirted the kids and the puddles and ran the rest of the way to the car.

Jonathan pushed the beeper, but the heat pouring out of the car made her look longingly toward the kids. She waited to get in until he started the car and the air conditioner kicked in.

"Where to now?" She was almost panting from fatigue.

"Detective Savage. Tori Owens was supposed to be in the park on the same night someone tried to kill you. I think the police might be interested in that little fact.''

Little fact, indeed. There was no question in her mind that what they had found this afternoon would change the course of her life forever.

HE WATCHED PANIC grow in her blue eyes. If he had the power, he would take it away. He wanted to wrap her in his arms and tell her everything would be all right. But he couldn't do that, because he didn't know it would.

How could this be? How could this growing pile of evidence be the truth?

He drove to the Evanston Police Department at breakneck speed, almost hoping a cop would dare to pull him over. His anger grew as the blocks sped past. They had told him it was Amanda. There'd been plenty of proof. This all *had* to be some nightmare coincidence.

He practically dragged her into the station, demanding to see Detective Savage.

In contrast to his sloppy dress, Detective Savage's office looked as sterile and neat as an operating room before surgery. The man was totally professional. Just his attitude relaxed Jonathan somewhat. Amanda sat in a chair in front of the desk, but he was restless and chose to stand.

The detective eyed them with barely concealed suspicion. ''Well, this is a surprise. How are you feelin', Miss Braithwaite?''

''No small talk. We came here for a reason.'' Jonathan was impatient to get to the truth now that it stared him in the face. "Here. I want you to do a voice print on the message on this tape."

He pulled the microcassette from his pocket and threw it onto the desk. The detective looked at it, then at him, waiting for an explanation.

"Wait." Amanda's voice was soft and trembling. "I have something, too." She pulled a hairbrush from her purse and handed it to the detective.

It was full of light blond hair. Long silky strands. Not like her unruly mop at all. But then, they'd shaved part of her head and cut the rest after her surgery.

"I know you can do DNA testing on the hair from this brush. I want you to compare it to mine." She looked at Jonathan as if expecting him to protest.

Instead, he pulled out a pocket knife and carefully cut a small section of her hair from the back where it wouldn't show. The detective held out a fresh sheet of paper to receive it.

But she wasn't finished. She tangled her fingers in her hair and pulled out a few strands without even flinching. "It works better with the follicle, right?"

She seemed so calm, while he was a raging torrent of emotions.

"What's goin' on here, Dr. Taylor?" Savage had never looked more like a policeman, suddenly all efficient authority. Gone were the gentle questions. This man wanted answers.

"I found this picture on the island and it seemed familiar to me," she answered in a shaky voice that made Jonathan want to comfort her. "We went to Tori Owens's apartment and took the tape and brush."

He saw how her hand trembled as she pushed the creased photograph across the desk. But she seemed composed, and he was amazed at how well she was dealing with this incredible turn of events. Better than he. But then, she'd suspected something for a long time. And he, in his arrogance, had discounted everything she said. Even the evidence of his own heart.

The detective studied the picture. "There's definitely a resemblance here. Is this girl related to you, Miss Braithwaite?"

She turned her head to look at him with trusting eyes. "I don't think so. Jonathan would know."

"No. Not related. They are simply both beautiful women with almost identical bone structure."

Her skin flushed a bright pink. Jonathan rammed his hands into his jeans pockets, making it impossible to reach out to her. He fought to control the feelings rioting through his blood, reminding himself of the night of the attack when he'd had to distance himself to stay objective. It was a whole lot harder when the woman he had sworn to help and protect was in ultimate jeopardy. His gut burned, his palms were sweaty. But she stayed perfectly calm.

"What does Miss Owens have to say about all this?"

"She wasn't home. It looked as if she hadn't been there in weeks." She answered firmly, apparently unafraid of the consequences.

He should be so brave. He met the detective's eyes without blinking. They understood each other. Understood the danger here. Understood that she didn't need to be frightened now. That could wait until they were sure. He wasn't going to do or say anything until he was absolutely certain of the truth.

"Do you think Miss Braithwaite might have been stayin' with Miss Owens during that six weeks she was unaccounted for?"

"We found a message from a modeling agency on that tape that places Tori in the park the night in question. We think it might have been Tori Owens who was attacked that night, not Amanda Braithwaite."

Jonathan stared at her perfect profile, the one he had re-created, as she spoke. It was as if she'd read his darkest fears and had the courage to articulate them. At the same time, he could feel Detective Savage's eyes stab into him.

No! He didn't believe this. He couldn't. A part of him just shut it out, rejecting everything she said. *He had made her Amanda.* But she'd had Amanda's identification, jewelry, blood type. Of course she was Amanda!

He'd fallen in love with her all over again when he'd believed he could never feel this way about her after her betrayal. Now, all he could think about was her need, her pain. Her. Loving her. She touched his soul, his body, because...

Because she was different! Only the beautiful face remained the same. He tried to reject the idea, wanted to tear it out of his mind and soul.

"Is that what you think occurred, Dr. Taylor?" The detective repeated his question. She was looking at him, too, waiting for his response.

This time there could be no mistakes. "A good doctor rules out all other possibilities before he makes a diagnosis. I'm disturbed by the coincidences, but not convinced. That's why I want you to do the voice analysis and DNA." The hoarseness underlying his words surprised him.

He must have surprised her, too, because her eyes widened, making her look vulnerable and fearful. Unable to prevent himself, he went down on one knee, sliding his arm around her shoulders. Without hesitation she leaned into him.

The detective coughed abruptly before stating, "DNA testing takes weeks, Dr. Taylor. We might be able to eliminate this possibility right away. I didn't see a need before, but now I think it's time for Miss Braithwaite to meet Lois Langley, the lady whose dog she rescued. She'll recognize which of these young women was in the park."

DETECTIVE SAVAGE DROVE. She and Jonathan sat in the back seat, and it took every resource within her to bolster her strength. She didn't want him to see how close she was to the edge of hysterics.

She'd lived with the fear and confusion of an identity crisis, but now rage burned into all the other emotions. Hers had been no random mugging in the park. Someone had purposely lured Tori Owens to the park that night. She tried to remember the voice that had left the message on the phone. It had sounded sexless and hollow somehow. She was certain when the police checked, the agency would say no such call had been made.

Who could it be? Had he lured Amanda Braithwaite there, as well? Both women had disappeared about the same time. Which one was she?

Pain throbbed through her chest. The bleak look in Jonathan's eyes didn't help. He was obviously as confused as she, but suddenly he leaned toward her and smiled. Tears burned behind her eyelids.

"Are you all right with all of this?"

She could only nod and pray. Except she didn't know what to pray for. In her heart of hearts she knew she didn't want to be Tori Owens, that lonely lost soul, or Amanda Braithwaite, who despite her riches was as lost and alone.

Detective Savage pulled up in front of a white bungalow on a pretty treelined street. It seemed a million miles away from the place Tori Owens lived. He led the way to the front door. She went willingly, anxious to hear what the lady had to say. Jonathan stayed close, yet seemed separated from her by a yawning gulf.

A woman with short curly gray hair opened the door, and a small white poodle escaped. "Ralphie." The woman's querulous voice brought him to a standstill. He sniffed at Amanda, then began jumping up and down frenetically.

"See. He recognizes you. Come in, won't you." Mrs. Langley urged them into a house redolent with the aroma of fresh-baked cookies. It was a cozy room, with opera playing from a stereo at one end. She switched it off, apologizing. "My one indulgence. My son knows how I love music, so he bought me that expensive system." She sighed and invited them to sit on three chairs circling a fireplace whose grate was filled with potted plants.

The poodle followed Amanda and lay at her feet. "Hi there, guy." She patted his head, concentrating on his affectionate response, afraid to look up, afraid to hear what the woman had to say.

Her future rested in this woman's hands. A part of her didn't want to know, while another craved the truth like a child hungers for love. Where had that thought come from? Something about that shabby apartment had broken loose bits of memory she couldn't quite place yet.

"Mrs. Langley, thank you for seein' us. We just want to confirm that Miss Braithwaite is the young woman you encountered in the park the night of the attack."

She could feel them all turn to her. Keeping her hand on Ralphie's soft head, she looked up. Beside her, Jonathan's tension had grown unbearable.

Mrs. Langley's eyes were soft. "Must be. Ralphie remembers you. And the voice is the same." She shook her head, looking embarrassed. "You look similar, but I know how badly you were injured. Your doctor did a remarkable job, dear," she added quickly. "It was dark in the park, and my eyes aren't what they used to be. I remember your hair was much longer," she rambled on.

Ralphie whined, deserting her to go to his mistress, as if sensing her distress. Absently, she picked him up and put him in her lap. "I'm almost positive. Yes…yes, I'm almost positive you're that same sweet, dear girl who rescued my Ralphie." Her hands fluttered to her throat. "Did I ever thank you for that, dear?"

"I'm sorry, I don't remember, Mrs. Langley." Somehow she forced herself to go on. "How did I look that night?"

"Lonely." Mrs. Langley seemed embarrassed, her hands fluttering helplessly. "At least that's the impression I got. I mean, why would a beautiful girl like you be in the park by herself on a lovely summer night?"

That was a question no one could answer, least of all her. Her nerves had stretched to their limit, so she stood and turned slowly. "Mrs. Langley, look at me. Are you sure I'm the woman who helped you?"

"Of course." She put the dog down. "Ralphie knows you. And you look almost exactly the same." Squinting across at Amanda she continued, "The differences are so slight… No, no, I'm sure."

"Could this have been the young woman, instead?" Detective Savage showed her Tori's picture.

Amanda stood perfectly still, waiting for the reaction that would send her life hurling in another direction. Jonathan rose beside her, but didn't reach out to her.

Mrs. Langley looked at the picture, then up at her. "My, my! Why, you could be sisters. Really you could." She squinted again, staring down at the creased photograph. "I've ordered new glasses, you know. It's so hard, isn't it? What with night falling in the park and your hair being so different and all. Ralphie and I are certain it was this nice Miss Braithwaite."

"Thank you, Mrs. Langley. You've been very helpful." Detective Savage took pity on all of them and stood to go.

"I'm glad I could help. Now, you'll want to stay and have something to eat, won't you, dear?" Holding the poodle tightly to her side, the elderly lady sighed in contentment. "Ralphie and I are so happy you've recovered from that horrible ordeal and we want to thank you for saving him that night."

She felt numb all over. The last thing she wanted to do was disappoint this nice woman, but she didn't think she could stay here another minute. She looked at Jonathan, begging him to intervene.

"Thank you, Mrs. Langley. That's very generous of you. I'm sorry, but I have to get back to the hospital. We need to go now."

Detective Savage got the message, took the picture carefully out of Mrs. Langley's hand and moved toward the door. If Jonathan hadn't had a hold on her arm and urged her out, she wasn't sure she could have moved.

What good had it done, after all? Nothing had really been settled. She tried to hide her disappointment as she slid into the back of the police car.

Detective Savage turned from the front seat. "I don't feel comfortable with Mrs. Langley's identification. I'm proceedin' with the tests. I'll also get a warrant to search Tori Owens's apartment. We need to find that modeling agency."

"I agree." Jonathan's arm felt like an iron band around her shoulders, but for the first time she got no comfort from it. "Why don't you run a check to see if anyone's reported Tori Owens missing?"

Detective Savage turned around and started the car. "I checked that before we left the station. There hasn't been any report."

Emotionally drained, it was easy for Amanda to be quiet on the way back to the police station. She listened while they discussed the case and how to tell her family the police were reopening the investigation. She nodded when she knew she should, but more than that was beyond her ability at the moment. Detective Savage shook Jonathan's hand and briefly touched her shoulder before they left. Once she was in Jonathan's car, she put her head back and let the tears flow. He didn't say anything at all as they returned to his condo.

Once inside, she wandered to the window and stared out into the darkness. There were no lights tonight; clouds covered the stars and no boat had ventured out. There was no sign to guide her. No magic from heaven to make everything right. She felt disoriented, as if she was floating above her own body.

That, at least, was hers; but which was her face: the one in the picture or the one in the mirror?

Jonathan came up behind her and stood for a long time, staring out into the nothingness with her.

"I know this is a lot for you to take in," he said with a strangled voice that matched the bleakness of his eyes. "But we *will* discover the truth. I promise you."

All at once she could hardly see his face through her haze of tears. "In a way, it doesn't matter. Either I'm Tori Owens or Amanda Braithwaite. But both are unhappy women, aren't they? Amanda has no friends. And no one cares enough about Tori Owens to notice she's missing. Either way, whoever I turn out to be, I'm alone."

Jonathan took her into his arms. He caressed and patted her while she sobbed into his shoulder. She hadn't meant to cry. She didn't mean to cling to him as if she could never let go. She must stop, she told herself. But she needed just a minute more to feel safe, to push away the loneliness.

"Listen to me." His lips brushed her ear. "You are not alone. I'm here now. I'll always be here for you."

Some new quality in his voice made her gaze up at him. She hadn't realized she knew what vulnerability was until she recognized it in his eyes.

"Pat Newman asked me what I was going to do about us. Now I know the answer. I'm going to love you." He touched her mouth gently, then drew back and studied her face. "If you'll let me."

She tightened her arms around him in answer. Deliberately, she kept her eyes open until the last second, watching the passion intensify on his face. He took her mouth again. This time there was no tender question; this time there was need and desire.

A thousand emotions rushed through her, all flowing into him. Reaction rocked her as his lips feathered across her eyelids and his mouth took little bites of her throat, shooting pleasure pinpoints deep inside her.

"Jonathan...I don't want to be alone anymore." She barely breathed the words, overcome by sensations that kept building until she began to shudder. She arched back, craving more from his lips.

Then she was floating again, except this time in his arms. She could feel the power in him as he lifted her and carried her into his bedroom. He hesitated only to kick the door shut behind him before placing her on his bed.

Once she had asked him the question tormenting her soul and he'd turned away from her. But *she* couldn't turn from it, couldn't let it go. "Who are you making love to, Jonathan? Tori or Amanda?"

This time he stayed. His eyes searched her face, caressed her body. She could see how much he wanted her.

"I'm making love to you," he said simply. "Whatever comes tomorrow, we'll still be who we are right now. But we won't be alone anymore."

Now the floodgates opened. All her emotions poured out freely, joyously. There could be no more doubts. No more fears. She knew she'd never felt this burning need for anyone else. Tori and Amanda disappeared. The world dissolved except for the two of them. The feelings beating between them couldn't be denied.

She rose to her knees on the bed and with shaky fingers stripped the clothes from his body. He stood before her questioning gaze, all long, golden muscles. "I could never have forgotten this body," she whispered, aching to touch him but waiting.

Their eyes met and held while he reached behind her to pull down the zipper of her dress. She became lost in the heat and smell of him. Gently, he pulled her off the bed. The white dress pooled at her feet. Still they looked at each other as his fingers traced the bikini briefs she wore.

He groaned, and with that sound his patience ended. He cradled her against his body, murmuring his need as they slow-danced around the room. No music was needed. His steps were sure, their rhythm strong and measured. She grew light-headed as her body curved into his; they fit together as if they always had, always would.

He stopped abruptly and tumbled her onto the bed. She couldn't control her response when his mouth found her breasts, kissing and licking them until they ached.

She began to tremble deep at her core. She might have done this a hundred, a thousand times before, but she knew this was the first time that had meaning. Her legs moved restlessly between his strong thighs.

"I want to make this last forever." His words, the taut passion on his face, the way his hands stroked her, were like nothing she'd ever experienced before. It felt new to her even as she recognized it on some level beyond memory—an instinct born before time.

She didn't, couldn't, stop him when he trailed kisses down her stomach and onto her awakened thighs. She could feel his power grow. She had to touch him, to give him the pleasure he gave her as his lips nipped at her skin and his palms soothed her swollen breasts. She reached for him and he groaned, holding her hand there so she could feel his mounting tension.

"No. You're not ready yet," he murmured.

He slid his fingers up her silky inner thighs, separating them. Then he kissed her slowly, his tongue meeting hers. His sweet, coaxing kiss called up such desire it amazed her.

She couldn't wait anymore. She didn't want to. She threaded her fingers through his hair and wound herself around him, giving him her mouth in an open, melting kiss. He was taking her somewhere she knew she'd never been before. Nothing in the universe could have made her forget the torrents of emotion pooling deep inside her. She sobbed against his shoulder, not knowing how to tell him what she wanted.

"Now, touch me." She thought he said the words, but she couldn't be sure. Still, she held him between her hands, leading him where she needed him to go.

In accepting his mouth, his tongue, all of him surging into her, she lost herself. She ceased to exist as waves of white-hot pleasure ripped through her. He vanquished her emptiness forever with a powerful thrust that connected them, body and soul.

Within her, something broke apart, and she arched up higher to dissolve into his body. She drank from his mouth, tasting his pleasure, gasping when he gave her everything she wanted.

She lay beneath him, drained and trembling. Only one thought pounded through her mind: no matter who she was, she would never be alone again. Now, they belonged to each other.

CHAPTER TWELVE

Moonlight dappled the room with silver light that played across her cheek and hair. She slept curled trustingly against him, and he lay perfectly still, reluctant to disturb her as thoughts jumbled together in his head. Tension built in his body. He wanted her again. He wanted to stroke her silky thighs, taste her skin, lose himself and all his confusion inside her.

Carefully, so he wouldn't disturb her, he slid the sheet off her body. She sighed and stirred, tucking one of her hands under the pillow.

Her body felt new to him. But so did everything else. A new world of sensation and emotion was there beside him to explore. For he hadn't anticipated her response, so sweet and generous, so overwhelmingly passionate. He didn't remember her this way.

Doubt, ugly and unbelievable, crept into his head. He tried to rationalize it away. They'd both been young, arrogant and selfish. Thank God they'd both changed in the ten intervening years to become deeper, more complete human beings. More willing to give than to take. More able to understand and appreciate each other.

She rolled onto her back, searching for the covers.

The moonlight caressed the peaks and valleys of her breasts and stomach. His mark was everywhere on her creamy skin. He feared to touch her, because he knew once he started he wouldn't be able to stop.

Still trying not to wake her, he inched toward the edge of the bed. Instinctively she reached for him, her hand feathering across his thigh, searching for the warmth of him.

He held himself perfectly still, desire making it hard to think straight. She had to be exhausted, he told himself. He should do the right thing.

Murmuring in her sleep, she shifted, still searching. Her head found his stomach and pillowed there. Her gentle breath tickled the hair curling down between his thighs. His response was automatic.

He would explode if he didn't touch her.

He tilted her face upward and bent to meet her lips. Instantly her mouth responded eagerly. Excitement rippled through him, and he groaned deep in his throat.

"I'm awake," she whispered against his lips. Her smile took his breath away as she pressed her swollen breasts into his chest and rocked her hips against his. "I was dreaming about this."

He sucked gently on her lower lip. "This isn't a dream."

Laughing, she pulled away from him. The happiest sound he'd ever heard. "I know. I can't control my dreams, but I'm in charge here. Isn't that what you said?"

She placed her hands on either side of his head,

effectively pinning him in place. Her kisses were wet and deep. He couldn't get enough of her sweet mouth, couldn't remember when a woman had captivated him so completely. Burning for her, he pressed against her undulating body, savoring every silken inch.

"Let me share my dream with you." Her whisper sent shudders scudding through him.

Slowly, deliberately, she lifted herself and lowered onto his hardness. He watched her face as she settled herself, catching her breath in amazement. "Yes. This is what I want."

"Yes…" he agreed, cupping her hips to guide her.

In awe of her beauty, he watched every nuance of emotion filter through her eyes as they surged together in a perfect rhythm. She *was* perfection.

He writhed beneath her, caressing her, giving her what she so obviously wanted and needed, but he held himself in check, waiting. Waiting until at last he felt her body convulse around him. She flung back her head, her face more beautiful than he'd believed possible. Only then did he let himself go, pulsing into her until sweet oblivion took him, too.

He woke slowly. He didn't know the time, didn't care. She lay on her side, her legs tangled with his. He stroked the long, beautiful curve of her hip.

She turned to him and smiled, the sweet contentment of a satisfied woman. He wanted to tell her all he felt, needed to explain his discovery. With his thumb, he tilted her face toward him. "Last night you asked me a question."

She placed her fingers across his lips, stopping him. "It doesn't matter now. I thought my life began when you helped me breathe so long ago in the ER, but I was wrong. My life began last night."

He saw a new tenderness in her eyes. It was love, not gratitude or a patient's infatuation for her doctor. That realization shattered him, forever rearranging his life, too. Whatever had been between them in the past was gone; whatever the future held would not change this for them.

He turned his lips into her warm palm. "I lo…" The phone's shrill ring cut him off. In the heat of the moment he'd been ready to tell her. Now the world intruded. He didn't want that just yet.

"It might be the hospital, Dr. Taylor." She reached across him, her breasts teasing his chest, and handed him the phone.

"Jonathan, I wish to speak with my niece at once!" Margaret announced before he could even say hello. "Her grandmother has collapsed. Amanda is needed here, immediately."

"It's your aunt." He kept his voice mild. "Do you want to talk to her?"

He could feel her withdrawal, but she took the phone. He felt powerless to do anything as he looked down at her stricken face.

"We'll be there as soon as possible. Please tell her I'm on the way."

He wasn't sure what to expect. She placed the phone in the cradle, stretching across him to do so. For a moment she lay there perfectly content, then she looked at him. Fear, guilt and regret marred her perfect face. Her fragile state of mind tore at him— she had nothing to feel sorry for. Nothing that had happened was her fault—the attack, her memory loss, her hesitation about her family. Because of her, he felt things more powerfully than ever before, and he understood her hesitation.

"You want to go back to The Lodge." Maybe saying it for her would make it easier.

"I don't want to go, but Mother Chambers needs me. And then we can tell Margaret and Randall face-to-face about the police reopening the case. But we won't tell my grand..." She stopped and swallowed back a sigh. "Not her. She's not strong enough. And anyway, we don't know the whole truth yet."

Overcome by the need to protect her, he cupped her face. "Are you sure you want to do this? I could go alone and tell them and check on Mrs. Chambers for you."

"No. However this turns out, I owe them at least this much for their kindness."

He kissed her then. "Rest awhile longer. I'll shower and get us breakfast. Then we'll do this together."

SHE TRIED TO REST, but every time she closed her eyes, strange pictures formed in her head. Incomplete pictures. There were too many new facts to think about. Amanda and Tori were both the past. She could, she *would*, make her own future.

She heard the shower as Jonathan started humming off-key. She loved the sound of it. She loved him.

Let me count the ways.

Her heart pounded against her ribs, forcing her to sit up. That was a line from a famous poem about love. A poem she knew well. The heavy darkness in her head seemed somehow lighter. She could almost see herself in a classroom, hear the teacher reading aloud from a book of poetry.

Ever since she'd visited that shabby apartment, she'd felt the darkness in her mind paling to gray. But this was the first real sense of recognition she'd had. She wanted to tell Jonathan, to join him in the shower, to hold him and be held. Maybe it wasn't that awful apartment at all that had changed her. Maybe it was the freedom of making love with him. Hadn't he always been her lifeline, the only person who could calm the storms in her head?

The phone rang again. Jonathan would never hear it with the water running, so she answered. Detective Savage didn't seem at all surprised to hear her voice. "I thought you might be there, Miss Braithwaite."

Hearing herself called by that name made her feel funny. Suddenly she realized Jonathan hadn't called her Amanda since they'd been to Tori Owens's apartment.

"Thought you should know I spoke to the agency Miss Owens worked for. They have no record of callin' her that night and they haven't heard from her in several weeks. I'm havin' the tape analyzed by a sound lab. See what we come up with."

She closed her eyes, trying to push back the fear. "Could this type of a mistaken identity really happen, Detective Savage?"

"Well, Miss Braithwaite, I'm afraid so. When I was a new cop, I was first at the scene of a bad traffic accident. Two teenage girls, same age, same color hair and same build. Both were thrown from the car, so we didn't know who had been drivin'. One was killed instantly. Both had massive head and face injuries."

Like me. Anxiety consumed her. She wrapped the sheet around her trembling body.

"One family buried their daughter. But when the other girl came out of her coma, confused like you, some things she said got everyone thinkin'. They ran more tests and found they'd made a mistake. The family who thought they'd lost their daughter found she was still alive. Of course the other family realized they'd lost theirs."

She rubbed her hands over her arms, trying to ward off the chill spreading through her body. The silence stretched on.

Finally Savage cleared his throat. "Miss Braithwaite, you still there?"

From somewhere deep inside her came the courage to answer him; the same courage that had started her on this journey. "Yes. Do you think something like that has happened to me?"

"Miss Braithwaite, those girls didn't have any ID. You had your Medic Alert bracelet, family jewelry, driver's license. Why would Miss Owens have your stuff? We try to make sure of identity before we go notifyin' people their next of kin's been in an accident.''

"Could Amanda have given that stuff to her? You yourself asked if Amanda might have stayed with Tori all those weeks she was missing."

He laughed, but the sound wasn't reassuring. "You let me do the detective work, Miss Braithwaite. Remember, I told you once I was on the job for you. I still am. You relax and concentrate on gettin' better."

She took a deep breath, trying to regain her equilibrium. "Jonathan and I are going up to The Lodge to tell the Chambers what we've discovered. We'll call you from there to see if you've found out anything else."

"You do that. I have the number up there and I'll be stayin' in touch."

He hung up, but she didn't move, cradling the dead phone to her ear. Part of her wasn't surprised by what he'd told her. Why was that? Because of her fears? Or because on some level, not yet fully realized, she already knew. In some fundamental way, even though she felt her life had begun again with Jonathan, she realized she couldn't really give him everything he deserved until she reclaimed her past. Whatever the consequences might be.

She'd always known what she had to do. Last night, lost in Jonathan's arms, she'd forgotten everything but him. Now the questions resurfaced within her, demanding the truth. Last night had been wonderful, beyond expectation and never to be forgotten, but it wasn't reality.

Jonathan came out of the bathroom with a towel wrapped around his hips and found her sitting there. "Who is it?"

"It was Detective Savage." Slowly she replaced the receiver. "Tori Owens's modeling agency never called her that night."

He sat beside her on the bed. His gentle hands cupped her face and his mouth brushed across her eyelids. His arms went around her and held her as tears welled up in her eyes.

"You aren't alone in this."

In contrast to the gentleness of his hands and mouth, his face looked hard, determined. "You're never going to be alone again. Do you believe me?"

"Yes."

But deep inside, doubts remained. What if she wasn't who he thought she was? What if she turned out to be someone unworthy? Someone even she couldn't love? She forced a laugh and flung herself out of the bed. If she stayed, she'd wrap herself around his freshly showered body and never leave this room.

"I'll get dressed so we can be on our way."

HE WATCHED HER disappear, naked, into the bathroom. Something had happened while he showered. Something to make her pull away from him. He stood outside the door, listening to make sure she was all right.

When the shower came on, he called Detective Savage, determined to find out what had frightened her, but he was already gone.

He was frustrated, feeling as if his emotional life had been stunted until she entered his life those few short weeks ago. That one violent act perpetrated by a sick human being could transform him was amazing to him. He couldn't imagine going back to the man he had been, couldn't contemplate how empty his life would be without her. She had opened his eyes and his heart. He would do anything to make her feel whole again, just as she had transformed him.

This afternoon would only be a skirmish in the battle plan ahead. But he would make certain that the Chambers family would accept the truths they had to tell, and with a minimum of hurt to her.

She came out of the bath with a huge towel wrapped around her. He turned to give her some measure of privacy, as silly as that seemed after their intimacy. But her eyes demanded it—vulnerable and sad eyes that wouldn't look at him.

He brought her a bagel with cream cheese decorated with a clumsy happy face drawn in jelly. She only nibbled at it. In the car he played tapes, hoping they would relax her as they always did him. She curled up in the seat beside him and shut her eyes but she didn't speak. He reached into the back seat and pulled a worn afghan over her. Her eyes opened and she smiled dreamily up at him, but closed them again immediately. Time seemed suspended as he drove north on I-94. From time to time he glanced at her.

She needed to rest; too much emotion necessitated a reprieve from her thoughts. She would need all her strength once they reached The Lodge.

Before he would have believed possible, he pulled into his driveway and parked. The cessation of motion had her stirring and stretching.

"Don't tell me I slept the whole way?"

"We're at my house. I want to get my medical bag in case Penelope needs anything."

She let him unpack the car by himself, while she just stood at the window, staring across the lake. He wished he could keep her to himself for a few more hours. He would take her into his bedroom and make love to her over and over until the vacant look left her face and it was filled with the love and joy he had seen last night.

Almost as if she'd read his thoughts, she turned. A sweet smile lit her face. "We have to go to The Lodge, I know, but I love *this* house. I've dreamed about a house like this."

"It's yours." He said it without thinking, proving to himself how natural it seemed. Would she understand?

Apparently she did. But the effect on her was the opposite of what he wanted. Instead of reaching out to him, she withdrew. "That depends on what we find out, doesn't it?"

"No." He stalked her across the room, cornered her, and pulled her into his arms, holding her tightly to him. "It doesn't matter to me one tiny bit."

He could feel from the tension in her back and

shoulders that she still had doubts. He had to make her believe him. Staring down into her troubled eyes, he told the whole truth, *his* truth. "If a mistake has been made, there will be complications, there's no question about that. And lots of ramifications for other people. But not for me. Professionally, I followed every rule. You were identified by your aunt and uncle, the police, your belongings. If all of them were wrong, I can't take responsibility. Nor can you."

He kissed her eyes, her nose, her mouth. "What I'm trying to make you understand is that on the only important level it no longer matters who you were in the past. All that matters is who you are now."

"I believe you. I've always believed everything you've ever said to me. And last night it finally didn't matter to me either, because I don't want to be Tori or Amanda. *I'm not either of them anymore.* But I can't give up the fight to discover as much of the truth as can be found. It's too important for both of us." All the color left her face except for the blaze of blue shooting from her eyes. "I know now that I can't stop until I discover why someone would want to kill me."

He wasn't prepared for his reaction. In one breath, everything he'd ever believed was wiped away. He buried his face in her hair and held her fiercely, so she would know he'd never let her go. "I'll kill anyone who tries to hurt you."

SHE BELIEVED Jonathan implicitly. As his boat raced toward the island, she watched him. He was tense, closed in and tightly controlled. She didn't want to do this to him. She wanted them to love each other in sunshine and happiness, not darkness and fear.

The wind came up as they neared the island, and he turned to look behind them. A mist of rain seemed to follow them. They tied up at the main pier just as the waves increased in power, crashing onto the rocks and throwing spray into her face.

"Looks like we're in for another big one."

"Does it always storm so much up here?" They were the first words she'd spoken since he'd made his impassioned declaration. She hadn't known how to react except to love him even more. There really was nothing more to say until they heard from Detective Savage.

"Sometimes." He tied the boat up and helped her out before pulling over the canvas cover. "Here it comes. Let's make a run for the house."

Halfway across the lawn, she saw Lady at the edge of the woods. She stopped and called to her. "Here, girl. Come! You're going to get wet!"

The dog ran to her, licked her hand once and just as quickly ran away, back to the trees. Amanda started after her, but Jonathan called her back. "C'mon. Lady can take care of herself."

They made it to the porch only slightly dampened by the approaching storm. Behind them thunder rolled. The huge door to The Lodge opened into silence and heat. She hesitated in the hallway, a heavy feeling of being closed in descending on her.

"You came!" Margaret, a sweater draped around her shoulders, appeared at the doorway to the large parlor. "You look chilled. Go in and have some tea to warm you. I'll fetch Randall."

While she was gone, Jonathan sat her in a chair near the fire and poured her a steaming cup of tea. Before he could say anything to her, Margaret was back, Randall on her heels.

He looked relieved to see her. "We are so happy you decided to come, Amanda." His eyes drilled into her until she had to look away.

The sound of that name seemed to reverberate around the room. Her eyes flew to Jonathan's face, but he shook his head in warning. She said the first thing that came into her mind. "How is Mother Chambers?"

"Resting," Margaret answered somewhat testily. "I see Jonathan brought his medical bag. You can both see her when she wakes."

"Oh." She pressed her hands against the fragile china of her teacup, praying that the warmth of the tea would give her strength. "Actually, we have another reason for coming here today." She searched Randall's face. "We wanted to tell you the police have reopened the case."

Randall shook his head. "I wasn't aware they had ever closed it."

Margaret shrugged. "I assumed they'd come to the same conclusion I had. It was a random act of violence. You were simply in the wrong place at the wrong time."

"Margaret, that is unnecessarily harsh," Randall said, reproving her.

"In a way, she's right." Jonathan rose from his chair and moved to stand behind her. "*Someone* was in the wrong place at the wrong time that night. Now we're not so sure it was Amanda."

"Whatever are you talking about?" Margaret's voice rose slightly.

She had to be the one to tell them and quickly. What if they were like that family Detective Savage had told her about? They'd nursed her and loved her, but she might be the wrong person.

"I found a picture here on the island of a model named Tori Owens. We look amazingly alike. Is...is she a friend of the family?" Holding her breath, she waited for an answer.

"I can't recall anyone by that name." Randall looked quizzically at his wife.

She merely looked bored and shrugged. "Nonsense. All nonsense. What could a model have to do with us?"

"Just a minute, Mrs. Chambers," Jonathan began.

Margaret raised her hand and stopped him. "All right. For the sake of argument, where did you find this picture? In your room? Maybe she's a friend of yours that Randall and I don't know."

"Obviously I can't remember." Despite the tension building around her she refused to stop. The sooner it was said, the sooner she might get answers. "Something about her seemed familiar, so Jonathan and I found out where she lived and went there. We discovered from a message left on her recorder that she was supposed to be in the park the night of the attack, too. No one has seen her in weeks. It's..." She swallowed to soothe her dry throat. She'd said the words once before, and she could do it again. "There is a possibility Tori Owens was attacked in the park, not Amanda."

"How could that be possible?" Dazed, Randall's eyes went totally blank. "You had her ring!"

Margaret folded her arms across her chest, looking at her as if she were a willful child who needed guidance. "How could this *person* have been wearing your Medic Alert bracelet? Your mother's ring? How did she have your driver's license in her purse?" Her questions built in volume as they piled on top of one other. "And how could she have your blood type?"

"Maybe the things were given to her. Lots of people have the same blood type. Maybe mine is common. Or maybe someone changed the hospital records so the blood types would match." She'd given all these questions a lot of thought.

From behind her Jonathan sucked in a deep breath.

"That is preposterous." Randall sneered at Jonathan, as if blaming him for what she was saying.

"Now, Randall, think this through," Margaret said firmly. "It's possible that somehow Amanda's possessions got into the hands of this Tori Owens. I suppose it's possible someone could have altered the hospital medical records. Me. Or you. Or Jonathan." She smiled then, sweetly sarcastic. "We all had opportunity. Or it could be possible this is more of your reduplicative paranesia. Because there is no motive for any of this nonsense."

"I don't know why someone would have done all these things. I'm just trying to tell you as simply as possible that I might not be Amanda."

"Of course you are Amanda." Swathed in a purple robe, Penelope Chambers stood in the doorway, her braided white hair hanging over one shoulder like a schoolgirl's. She plunked her walking stick into the carpet as she purposely strode into the room.

Maybe the cat's eyes winked erratically. Or maybe it was intuition. In any case, Jonathan lunged around the chair and caught the old woman before she could collapse onto the floor.

CHAPTER THIRTEEN

PENELOPE FELT weightless in his arms. For the first time, Jonathan realized she wasn't the indomitable force he'd always thought her to be, but a fragile, lonely old lady.

"Put me down in my chair, young man. There's nothing wrong with me except my bad knee. I'm not helpless, you know."

He smiled at her response. She'd never give herself away. The color in her face was high, but her eyes were sharp. He wouldn't have to worry how she'd react to the news.

Making sure her robe remained tucked decorously around her, he placed her in the overstuffed chair.

"Please bring me my walking stick, Amanda."

He watched for her reaction. She flinched at the sound of the name, but obeyed. The woman he loved and the old woman who loved her, too, stared at each other wordlessly. The connection between them was almost palpable. Nothing would separate their very real feelings for each other.

It struck him suddenly that he didn't think of Amanda as the girl he'd known so long ago. Somewhere in the past few days he'd lost that image entirely. Yet he couldn't think of her as Tori, either, friendless and afraid. She had become a new Amanda, and whatever Detective Savage learned, her identity was uniquely forged. Randall and Margaret might be hurt by the truth, but they would weather it somehow. And he would make certain that she was never friendless again.

Mother Chambers took her hand. Either the cold from the soaking they'd received dashing through the storm or the emotions unleashed in this room caused her to tremble. He wanted to slide his fingers behind her slender neck and pull her back against his body to warm her, to reassure her, but he decided against such an obvious declaration.

She was determined to tell her version of the truth to her grandmother. Instinct told Jonathan not to interfere, because it was so important to her to have control of her life. She would have to play this scene out to the best of her ability.

Randall and Margaret stood on the other side of the room, as if they wished to be as far away from what was happening as possible. He walked toward them, more to give her the appearance of privacy as she talked to Mother Chambers than to support her aunt and uncle. He would still be able to hear every word spoken and to watch the older woman for signs of agitation.

"I heard everything you said, my dear." There was nothing weak in Penelope's voice, he realized with relief. But the possibility of a collapse existed, looming over the room with its potential for tragedy.

"Logic would dictate that the only reason this other young woman might be in possession of Amanda's belongings is that she was impersonating her. Why do you suppose she would be doing that?"

"I don't know. Unless…unless she was being used in some way."

Frowning now, the old woman pressed on. "Whoever hurt her wanted everyone to believe she was Amanda? That is what you think, isn't it? I can see it in your eyes. Oh, my dear, sweet girl, don't you understand whoever hurt her couldn't have depended on you developing amnesia. The whole plot, whatever its insidious intent, would have been unmasked at once."

"They weren't dependent on any outcome but death. They planned to kill her outright all along, but were interrupted by Officer Mahoney. If she hadn't stopped to rescue a little runaway dog, she…*I*… would be dead."

She walked away from the old woman in the chair, giving her time to digest her story. He had to admire her composure. She was dead-on so far. He had worked that much out himself. He wouldn't be surprised if Detective Savage had reached the same conclusions.

"Even though they failed to kill her, they were faceless—a random attack in the park. Really, it was an ideal cover. Even the police subscribed to it. The amnesia just bought them time."

All color drained from Mother Chambers's face. "Do you still feel you are in danger, my dear?"

"Yes."

Her strangled whisper somehow seemed more frightening than the storm outside. A calm before pandemonium broke loose.

"Stop it, both of you, right now!" Margaret found her voice first. "The way you're discussing Amanda in the third person is appalling! You've both been reading too many murder mysteries!"

"I agree." Randall stomped over to a table in the corner with a crystal decanter of amber liquid and glasses. He poured a liberal amount of bourbon and drank it straight. Jonathan understood his need.

"I'm starting to see little flashes of light in my mind. And I'm getting stronger. If there was a conspiracy, I'm still in danger. If I remember..."

Jonathan felt as if a hand was reaching out to choke him, and he stalked over to pour himself a glass of bourbon. She had opened the floodgates to a genuine horror story. He took a sip and let it burn down his throat.

"Let's be logical. We still don't have a viable motive for any of this. And we don't have any proof." They might all be pawns in this game, but he wasn't going to admit it.

"Impossible to think that someone could manipulate us like chess pieces in some sort of evil game." Penelope Chambers might seem old and weak, but her mind was as sharp as ever.

Randall pulled himself together enough to yank on the needlepoint bellpull behind him. "I will have Joe bring tea for you, Mother."

Joe appeared immediately, as if he'd been eaves-dropping just beyond the door. When Jonathan saw the tea tray, he knew his instincts had hit the mark. Joe had been waiting, wanting to know what was going on in this room.

"Thought you might need some more tea." He looked only at Mother Chambers, deliberately avoiding everyone else's eyes.

Imperiously, Penelope Chambers waved Joe away. "Where is this mysterious picture Amanda found? I wish to see it."

If he hadn't been watching carefully, Jonathan might have missed Joe's reaction. Joe's back arched, and a searing glare from his narrowed eyes swept the room before he ducked his head again. All the years of seeing Joe as a harmless ex-addict who had paid for his sins by relinquishing a part of his brain gave way to sudden suspicion. Joe? With his obsessive wall of photos? Could he somehow have cracked?

"Amanda, you look exhausted." Penelope broke into his speculation. "Besides being soaked to the skin. We all need to gather our thoughts before we discuss this further. Come now, help me back to my room."

Amanda immediately turned to obey the old woman's command, anxious to leave the turmoil in this room. Jonathan knew her so well, understood her needs. Actually it was amazing in its own way and further proof that she wasn't who they all thought. He'd never understood the real Amanda this way.

She glanced over her shoulder to meet his eyes, "Everything will be all right."

She gave *him* a promise, as if she wanted to protect him against whatever happened.

He couldn't resist showing her, showing all of them, exactly how he felt. He walked to her and brushed his mouth across her parted lips. "I know. Let me help you both upstairs."

"An excellent idea! Mother is right. We all need some time to digest this distressing news." Margaret began clearing the remains of the tea service. "I'll tell Joe to serve supper in our rooms. It will provide us some time to adjust. Perhaps then we can all begin thinking straight. Obviously, none of us are going anywhere tonight in this storm."

The house groaned as wind pounded against it, seeming to reinforce Margaret's words.

Penelope leaned heavily on Jonathan's arm as they climbed the stairs. She paused outside Amanda's ornately carved door. "Don't worry about me, my dear. I've weathered worse storms than this one. You go to your room and soak in a nice hot bath. It will make you feel better."

Amanda leaned forward and brushed the old woman's cheek with her lips. "You've been so kind to me. I don't know how to thank you." She gave both of them a small smile before disappearing into her room.

Penelope sagged against her door. "Such a sweet child." She straightened, striking the floorboard with her cane. "Come along, Jonathan. I think you and I should have a little chat right now."

It was a command he was happy to comply with. He would settle Penelope for the night before going back where he belonged. He knew Amanda would be waiting for him.

Mother Chambers's room was draped sumptuously in purple velvet even though the rest of the furnishings were simpler. An iron bedstead covered by an old quilt, an oversize mahogany wardrobe with a matching kneehole dressing table. She eased herself into a wing chair beside the cherub-carved limestone fireplace and lifted her left foot onto a needlepoint footstool. She must have noticed his appraisal of the room.

"It's exactly the way it was when my own dear husband was alive. The only change is the drapery, at Margaret's insistence. To keep the drafts out, she said."

She motioned him to the only other chair in the room, a wooden rocker. He pulled it over to sit directly across from her.

"Do you think she is Amanda?" Her eyes, glassy with emotion, pinned him awkwardly.

"I don't know. It seems she must be, but..."

"So you think she could be this other young woman? This Tori Owens?"

He could only shake his head and repeat himself. "I don't know."

"I see. The only thing you seem to know is that you love her, regardless."

His rueful laugh made her smile. "I always knew you were a shrewd lady."

"Not so shrewd. Simply old and experienced." Her thin fingers ran over and over the carved cat face on her walking stick. "We must get to the bottom of this. What is being done?"

Remembering Detective Savage's warning, Jonathan hesitated.

"Well, what is it?" Her restless fingers curled around the cat's throat and squeezed until her knuckles went white. "I want to know as soon as possible. My time is running out."

"The police are doing DNA testing on hair found in Tori Owens's apartment and...Amanda."

Her mouth pursed as she considered what he'd told her. "From what I've read, this might take several weeks to process. What can we do in the meantime to protect her?"

"Nothing will happen to her, I can promise you that. I just hope she regains her memory so she can tell us the truth herself. This is as difficult for her as it is for you." He saw an afghan folded on the dressing table chair and brought it to cover her. "I'm going to check on her now. Don't worry. Between us all, we'll keep her safe."

Randall waited in the hallway. He leaned against the wall, wringing his hands.

"What the hell do you think you're doing here?" Jonathan didn't like the thought of him lurking outside Amanda's door like some sort of stalker. He brought himself up short. Randall wasn't a threat to her. What was the matter with him?

Randall blinked, as if he were returning from some faraway time and place. "Oh. It's you. Obviously, I am concerned. I need to talk to Amanda."

"Not now. She's been through too much in the past twenty-four hours. Just let it go for now."

"Let it go? Are you mad? I never realized how deeply disturbed Amanda has become. If she has permanent brain damage, I will hold you, Dr. Johnson and the whole medical staff responsible. You doctors and your miracle drugs!"

He'd never realized just what a pompous ass Randall was. "Amanda is not brain damaged. As a matter of fact, her brain seems to be recovering from the trauma. She's reasoned through this whole situation a lot better than I have. Than you have. You must prepare yourself for the eventuality that a terrible mistake was made by all of us."

Randall shook his head, disbelief and doubt filling his face. "But if she isn't Amanda, then where is Amanda?"

AMANDA HEARD the hoarse question spoken outside her door and moved to confront whoever lurked there. Then the voices moved away, but the question lingered. *Where is Amanda?* And Tori, how had she become a part of all this? These questions haunted her, too. She realized she had to have been one of those women in the past. But which?

She turned to the mirror, the towel blocking her

body from sight. She studied the face in the mirror. The face of Amanda, or as close to it as Jonathan had been able to get. She'd looked at pictures of both women, noted their similarities. Actually, she didn't look like either one anymore. This was a whole new face, just as she felt she was a whole new woman.

She had had to tell the Chambers. They deserved the truth. All the opulence surrounding her, all the love they lavished on her, might be misplaced. She couldn't take advantage of them, prolong their agony if they found she wasn't Amanda.

Maybe she belonged in that squalid apartment instead, loved by no one, missed by no one. But regardless of what they discovered, she wouldn't be a part of either world again. She'd make her own future with Jonathan.

Her body warmed just thinking about him. She dropped the towel and turned her back on the mirror. It didn't matter what she looked like as much as who she was.

She reached for the body lotion that matched the scent she had used in the tub. While she rubbed down her body, she wondered if she had always done this. It certainly had become a part of her routine now, and she'd never really thought about it before. In fact, she realized, there were probably lots of things that she did unconsciously that would be revealing if she just stopped to think about them.

She shrugged into her robe and looked around the lavish bedroom as the thought came to her that many clues must be right here at her fingertips. If only she knew where to search.

She flipped the lock to her bedroom door for the first time. Maybe that instinctive need to lock doors should be explored. Why would she, no matter who she was, feel a need to lock a door inside her own home? She hadn't felt this way at Jonathan's or in the hospital.

She shivered and thought about everything that might make her feel unsafe. Joe's face when Mother Chambers mentioned the picture came to mind. There had been more than anger in his eyes.

Then she heard the faint sound of the knob turning. She shrank back, her heart beating wildly. The door held. The knob slipped back. She watched each movement, fascinated.

"Amanda."

The sexless, hollow whisper sounded unearthly... like the phone message on Tori's machine. Straining forward, she tried to identify it, but one word wasn't enough.

"Yes?" she answered, hoping to coax more from the other side.

But nothing else was said. Could she have imagined it?

She shivered and waited. When she thought enough time had passed, she rattled the knob herself.

Nothing.

Bracing herself, ready to flee, she slowly opened the door. The hall was empty. But she knew someone had been out there, someone who wanted to kill her.

She flew to the closet to pull out the first thing she could reach. A purple dress slid down her body, a breath of silk stopping midway down her calf. Like everything else in the closet, it hung loosely over her hips.

She had to find Jonathan, to tell him what had happened. To warn him they weren't safe in this house.

The flickering lights in the hallway weren't charming tonight. Shadows hid in every corner. She crept forward, straining to see or hear a menace before it could be upon her. The storm, which she'd forgotten about in her room, raged across the lake. The Lodge must be very old and not as well cared for as she'd thought. Windowpanes rattled and the house moaned and groaned around her like a living person in pain.

She knocked softly at Mother Chambers's door and opened it. Jonathan sat in a rocker by the side of the bed, a cup of coffee between his palms. The woman under the wedding ring quilt looked too small for the bed. With her fiery spirit hidden behind closed eyelids, she hardly looked alive. Her skin was too transparent, her bones too fragile to sustain life.

For a second her own heart skipped a beat. Then she saw the slight rise and fall of the quilt.

"She's fine." He reached out for her, and she took his hand eagerly, needing to feel his warmth, his strength. "Both Margaret and Randall sat with her for a while. Then I insisted she go to sleep. It's been quite a day for her. For all of us."

There was no condemnation in his voice. Just a statement of fact.

"Someone tried to come into my room." She tried to sound as matter-of-fact as he did. "But I had the door locked."

"Probably Randall. I know he wanted to talk to you." For some reason his nonchalant attitude made her feel less secure. "I think he's in shock. They need to prepare themselves for a long road ahead before we all find out the truth."

"No, Jonathan, you don't understand. Someone tried to force my door. And I heard the voice from the machine in Tori's apartment."

Pressing her palm to his warm lips, he gazed up at her. "You've been under stress, too. Don't you think maybe your imagination is working overtime?"

His logic worked. Or maybe it was his smile, the way his lips warmed her hand. She slid down onto his lap and buried her face in his throat, pressing her lips against the pulse beating there.

"The truth is locked in my head. But I can feel that it's getting closer. I really can."

"That's good." In an almost lazy gesture, he nuzzled her breasts, resting his cheek over her heart. "Until then, you'd better eat something. Joe brought food and a flashlight. This thunderstorm has been upgraded with tornado warnings. We'll need the light if we have to head to the basement."

She glanced at the sandwich he'd left on the tray. His soup bowl was empty, but although hers was covered, it was cold. Maybe all this was for nothing. Maybe her fright had just been someone bringing her something to eat.

"I'm not hungry. You go ahead and have my sandwich, too, if you want."

Blinking, he yawned. "Excuse me. I need more coffee."

"I'll get it." Brushing his hair out of his eyes, she pressed a kiss on his cheek and stood.

The silver coffeepot with matching creamer and sugar was on a table near the window. Through an opening in the heavy velvet curtains, she saw lightning illuminate the garden. A small movement caught her attention.

She pushed the curtains wider apart. The next flash lit the scene like a floodlight. Lady was at the edge of the yard, huddled under a bush.

"Lady's out in this."

Jonathan seemed surprised by her words but slow to react. "I'll get her." Then he yawned again.

"No, I'll take the flashlight and call her. It's pouring rain out there."

He nodded absently, gulping down the strong brew. "Hurry back."

She'd always thought this house was too quiet, but tonight it had a voice of its own as it murmured and grumbled against the storm. She reached the front door without seeing anyone. They all must be safe in their beds. The door blew out of her hands with the force of the wind, crashing back against the wall. She pulled it shut behind her so the floor wouldn't get wet.

Shivering against the cold, she stood on the top

step, below the porch overhang, and turned the flashlight beam into the darkness.

"Here, Lady! Here, Lady!"

The beam caught the dog, her eyes gleaming points of light. Lady ran toward her, then stopped, backing up.

"Come here, girl. It's raining. Come on in where it's safe."

The rain soaked her when she moved out from under the roof to coax Lady in. So she'd take another hot bath, she reasoned. She couldn't leave the dog outside in a tornado.

"Come here, Lady. Come on." She reached out her fingers in a coaxing motion.

Lady refused to come.

Wind plastered her dress to her body. So much for the silk. She moved a few steps closer to the dog. Lady whined.

"That's a good girl," she cooed. She'd almost grabbed the collar when Lady started to bark.

She froze, sensing something, someone, behind her. Hands grabbed at her and spun her around.

"I told you not to tell, Miss Amanda," Joe said softly. A streak of lightning half lit his face. The house was too far away. No one would hear her scream in this gale.

Instinct told her to run.

Twisting out of his grasp, she whirled. Lady was disappearing into the woods in front of her. She ran after the dog, ignoring Joe's hoarse shout, ignoring the fear that seemed hideously familiar.

She had tried to run away in the park, but she hadn't gotten very far. Almost, almost she could see that scene of herself struggling to get away, fighting off her attacker. But the image wouldn't come through clearly, and she couldn't decide if what she thought she remembered was real or manufactured from what the police had told her.

In any case, she knew her life depended on getting away.

The trail through the woods was slippery. A small rivulet ran where the path should have been. Off to the side, branches and rocks waited to trip her up. The rain felt like small shards of ice piercing her flimsy dress. She kicked off the sandals, hoping her footing would be more sure. But she never stopped and she never looked back.

Somehow she kept Lady in the flashlight's feeble beam as she stumbled through the darkness. Her breath came in short gasps, and the fury of the storm accentuated her fear for the dog and for herself.

Suddenly the wind and rain died away—a lull in the storm? She realized Lady had led her to the clearing where she had first lain in Jonathan's arms. The dog, panting hard, had flung herself in front of the door to the icehouse. Trying to regulate her breathing, she listened for the horrifying sounds of Joe's footsteps coming closer.

Overhead, as if the storm had gathered itself together for one last roar, lightning streaked across the dark sky. Thunder crashed around her. Even the thick overhang of branches couldn't protect her from this deluge.

Stumbling through the sodden grass, she reached the icehouse and pushed at the heavy wooden door. She could shelter inside, hide from Joe. It opened easily. Lady darted in.

She closed the door to block out the storm, content as long as she had the flashlight with her. There was a chill in the air, a chill that reached up to her from a path that sloped downward. An almost eerie silence fell around her.

"Lady, where are you?" Her voice echoed back from pitted stone walls as she shone the flashlight around.

A bark came from somewhere beneath her, and she saw a plunging wooden staircase. She could hear Lady whining down below.

"What is it, girl? Come on. Come up here and we'll get through the storm together."

But Lady wouldn't come. Amanda began to shake from the cold and the damp—not from fear, she told herself. She tried to see down into the darkness, but her flashlight wouldn't penetrate that far.

"Come back up here, Lady!"

Lady whined again, sounding so pathetic it tore at her heart. Maybe she had hurt herself and needed help. Amanda had to go down the stairs and find her.

The steps were narrow and well-worn. Frigid air enveloped her skin, turning her fingers numb where they gripped the narrow wooden railing. As she descended, the walls drew back from the stairway.

She was in a huge cavern, partly natural, partly man-made. The air seemed stale. It was too cold down here. Her teeth began to chatter. She needed to find Lady, get out of here and back to Jonathan.

"Lady, come!"

A low growl startled her. The dog was closer than she'd thought. She twisted around, trying to see behind the stairs. Her foot slipped. Fear shot through her, and she lost her hold on the railing and the flashlight. She plunged forward into an icy black void.

A sandy floor broke her fall. It couldn't have been more than one or two steps. She absorbed a hiss of frigid air that burned her lungs, and dragged herself up to her knees, assessing her condition. She seemed to be just fine. Except she couldn't see anything.

"Lady, where are you, girl?" Why was she whispering?

Awkwardly, she probed in the darkness for the flashlight, crawling in the sand.

"Lady?"

The dog was strangely silent now. Tears of frustration filled her eyes. Fighting for breath, she kept searching. When her hand brushed against metal, the tears started in earnest, icy drops on her cheeks.

For one moment she thought the flashlight had broken in the fall. Then she realized her fingers were numb. Carefully she found the right button and the light came on. Relief surged through her.

She saw Lady first, just a foot away from her, lying with her head down. She swung the flashlight in the dog's direction. It made a golden arc on the blocks of ice stored all around her.

And it lit a form between her and the dog. An unmistakable form. She focused the light on a face frozen in horror, sightless blue eyes gazing up at nothing.

The face of Amanda.

CHAPTER FOURTEEN

A SCREAM FILLED her throat, yet no sound broke the frozen silence. She could only crouch above Amanda Braithwaite's nude body, paralyzed by horror.

Gradually she became aware of herself and her surroundings again. Every grain of sand ground into her knees; her nostrils quivered at the musty smell assaulting them; the blood pumped through her body at a furious pace.

Not Amanda.

She was not Amanda. And even though she had suspected as much for quite some time, the reality was almost impossible to accept.

Her hand didn't tremble as she lifted the flashlight to illumine the face once again. She saw Amanda clearly, as if her body were lit by dozens of lights instead of one feeble beam.

Amanda's face was still quite beautiful, although her skin was tinged with blue. Her long fair hair was bleached white by frost. Blood had crusted in two patches of black under her breasts.

She barely understood why she began pulling at the skirt of her dress. But suddenly she was ripping the fragile purple material up to her thighs. Being very careful not to touch Amanda, she draped the cloth over the body to lend it some dignity. It seemed like a small thing to do for the woman whose life had become so entangled with her own.

That was when she noticed the gold Medic Alert bracelet identical to the silver one she wore, frozen to a block of ice where an arm rested. There was no question in her mind anymore.

Amanda had never left to go on one of her famous shopping sprees. Amanda had never been in the park. Amanda had died right here on the island.

Someone had planned to kill her, Tori, and make everyone believe she was Amanda.

Why?

And more to the point, that someone must still want her dead. She had to find out who before it was too late.

Lady had placed herself protectively near her mistress. Resting her head on her front paws, the dog watched over her. Had she been watching the day Amanda was murdered? Had she seen the murderer drag Amanda's body down these steps?

No wonder the dog prowled the woods and guarded the icehouse door. Lady had known the truth all along. She should have realized that the dog had bounded toward her because she was wearing Amanda's clothes that first day. But once close enough, the dog had sensed she was not her mistress and had seldom come to her again.

So many lies. So many clues. Could she unravel them all before the killer tried again?

The body was well-hidden down here among the ice blocks, where no one came anymore. The ice was probably only delivered once a season and then forgotten, since they must have a modern kitchen despite Mother Chambers's insistence that all remain as it had been seventy years before.

And everyone on the island knew the ice was here. But why wouldn't the murderer have buried the body to cover up the crime forever?

This was all too much for her to figure out on her own. She needed help. She decided to call the sheriff.

All the pieces began to fit together, forming a pattern she did her best to understand. Someone had seen her resemblance to Amanda and lured her into the park. Someone had beaten her beyond recognition and planted Amanda's identification on her so that when she was found...

Someone must have needed a body to cover up the fact that Amanda was already dead. Perhaps Amanda had been set upon here in her special place and the murderer had had to dispose of the body in a hurry. But why was the body naked?

The murder could not have been carefully planned, or the body would be long gone. It had to be a sudden thing—an act of rage or jealousy.

And then an insidious fear crept into her reasoning. Whoever had accomplished this grisly feat was on this island now, and Jonathan was alone in the house. She shot to her feet as the truth struck her. Jonathan was alone with the murderer, and totally unsuspecting! He was in danger and only she could save him.

Screaming his name, she scrambled back up the steps. A massive gust of wind tore the heavy door out of her hands and slammed it shut, locking the dog inside. She couldn't stop to think of Lady now. Jonathan needed her.

She ran across the clearing and into the woods. A root tripped her, and she pitched forward onto her knees. Panting, she sucked in air, trying to stop her head from spinning.

She sensed the presence as she had all those weeks ago. Again, there was nowhere to hide.

She had been found. With an irresistible need to learn the truth, she turned her head. Fear had no place in her mind, at least not fear for herself. At last she would know the face of her enemy.

"You really turned out to be more trouble than I'd ever believed possible, Tori." Margaret smiled down at her, a smile that froze her to the depths of her soul. Margaret had been so kind...the most loving of aunts. How could it be her?

A small gun aimed straight at Tori proved it not only could be, it was.

Instinct ordered her to act. She slammed the flashlight hard against the small bones in Margaret's wrist. Howling in pain, Margaret dropped the gun, and it spun away into the darkness.

"You little bitch!" Margaret raged, reaching out with curled fingers and bloodred nails.

Desperate, Tori head-butted her in the stomach, doubling her over. Then Tori slammed the flashlight against the exposed flesh at the back of her neck.

Without waiting to see the result, Tori sprinted back through the woods toward the house. Branches whipped her cheeks and tore at her clothes. Rain sluiced over her head, clouding her vision.

Menacing shadows reached for her with murderous intent. There was nowhere to turn, no one to believe in but Jonathan. Was Margaret alone? Or was her faithful servant, Joe, in league with her? And what about Randall; could she trust the husband and not the wife? Last, but not least, there was Mother Chambers. The old lady had loved Amanda. Surely it could not be her.

She swerved off the path in a straight course toward the house. Nothing would stop her until she reached Jonathan.

JONATHAN STRUGGLED AWAKE. Wave after wave of nauseating lethargy fought to hold him in some type of paralyzing grasp. He reached for the cup of coffee and found it empty.

He had just enough strength to push himself out of the chair and bend over Mrs. Chambers whose relaxed body and heavy breathing showed she had been claimed by a deep sleep.

What had awakened him? He could have sworn someone had called his name. But the old house only echoed the sounds of the storm.

He'd lost track of time. Hadn't Amanda been here with him? The dog. He remembered something about the dog. How long had she been gone?

He tried to read his watch, but it was nothing but

a blur. "Damn!" Shaking his head, he tried again. He could barely focus on the digital readout. Past eleven. Time seemed to have no meaning. He couldn't remember when Amanda had been with him or how long ago she'd left. Certainly she had to have found the dog and be back in the house by now. Maybe she'd looked in, found him sleeping and gone to her room. It seemed as if it had all happened hours ago.

His mind felt dull and his muscles wouldn't respond. He walked over to the coffeepot to pour himself another cup, but it tasted bitter, as it had earlier. An alarm went off in his head.

Drugged. Someone had drugged the coffee. And Amanda was out there, somewhere, without protection. She was alone. He'd promised her, promised himself, she'd never be alone again.

Adrenaline kicked in. He forced himself to stagger around the room to get his blood flowing faster. He found a wash basin and splashed water over his face. His instinct was to go straight to Amanda, but he was a doctor first.

He bent over the old woman again. Her pulse was strong and steady. If someone had drugged her, it wasn't enough to hurt her.

He had to find Amanda. Although, now, in his heart of hearts, he knew she couldn't be Amanda. Not if someone was dispensing drugs here at The Lodge.

She'd been right all along.

Tori. He rolled the name on his tongue, trying to get used to it. His body was coming back to life. He had to find her. He had to explain why he'd done what he'd done.

A part of him had recognized the truth the first time they made love. Amanda's skin had never been so soft. She had never groaned so sweetly in the back of her throat, driving him over the edge. He had never loved Amanda, or anyone, with the force that fed his feelings now. But he'd lied to her, and to himself. He hadn't wanted to know the truth, so he'd ignored it.

She'd been gone too long.

Fighting the seductive spell of whatever drug he'd ingested, he stumbled across the hall and into his bathroom. He turned the shower on full force. Then he forced himself to throw up.

The cure was nearly worse than the condition. Weakly he crawled into the shower fully clothed, letting the water's sting revive him.

He gargled with mouthwash, ridding his mouth of the disgusting taste. Pulling a towel around his clothes, he knew he didn't have another moment to waste. He had to find Amanda…Tori. He had to make sure she was safe. He had to warn her.

First he checked her room, starting with a knock that grew bolder when there was no response. He pushed the door open, and it was evident she wasn't there, hadn't been to bed.

She had gone downstairs for the dog. Logic drove him to the front of the house, even though the rain was coming down in buckets. She wasn't on the front porch, and he could see no sign of Lady outside. Rain slanted under the overhanging roof, soaking the wicker furniture. She wouldn't, she couldn't, be out in this storm.

He turned back into the house, not caring that he tracked puddles through the interior. The doors to the parlor stood open, and although the rooms were dark, at the back a faint light edged the door to Randall's office.

For some reason, he hated the thought of Randall being anywhere near her. But when he reached the office and pushed the door open, Randall was alone, sprawled in his desk chair, a half-empty glass of bourbon dangling in one hand.

"Where is she?"

Randall seemed surprised to see Jonathan standing in the doorway and squinted in his direction, without bothering to answer.

"You're drunk."

"Drunk? You mean this?" Randall held the glass up in a kind of salute. "Is it half empty or is it half full?"

"Pull yourself together and answer me. Have you seen her?"

"Her?" Randall's expression didn't alter, but his voice dropped to an insulting slur. "I noticed tonight you never called her by name. Amanda." He breathed her name on a sigh. "I have always loved her name. Just as I have always loved her."

Something in his face, the look in his eyes made nausea rise in Jonathan's throat. Throwing up the drugs he'd been given couldn't compare to the stomach-turning reality of what he read in Randall's eyes.

"I don't have time for this." He had to get out of here before he slammed his fist into Randall's face. "For the last time, have you seen her?"

"Her!" The roar came from deep inside Randall's chest. Surging to his feet, he hurled the crystal glass into the fireplace. The flames took on new life where the liquor fed them. "Say her name." He grabbed Jonathan by the collar. "She is Amanda. She has to be."

"Get your hands off me!" Relishing the opportunity, Jonathan knocked him away.

Randall stumbled back into his chair. It swiveled wildly and stopped on a half turn toward the desk. "I need another drink," he murmured, his chin sinking onto his chest.

Thoroughly disgusted, Jonathan left him reaching for the bottle. He ran back upstairs and searched every room, calling her name.

"Tori!"

He repeated the name over and over in his mind like a chant, until it became reality to him.

He combed through the house, room by over-crowded room, but there was no sign of her. No sign of the dog. No sign of Margaret. Finally, in the kitchen, he made himself stop and think. Logic had always saved him before. He would have to figure this out.

She wasn't in the house. Neither was Margaret. Or Joe.

Joe had the picture. He kept a shrine to Amanda

on his bedroom wall. And tonight he'd looked at them all with hatred in his eyes. Joe was the key.

Tori's survival depended on him as much as it had that first night. But this wouldn't be as simple. He couldn't rely on his knowledge, his skill as a surgeon. And when he told her the truth, how could she ever forgive him for not accepting it sooner?

A flash of lightning spurred him to action. He tore down the back steps, which were as slippery as a sheet of ice. The rain couldn't hurt him, for he was already wet. He'd go to Joe's before he tried the docks. He sprinted across the lawn and through the carefully tended garden. He knew a shortcut through the woods from that long-ago summer, but the storm made everything look different. He took a wrong turn and ended up having to backtrack.

By the time he reached Joe's cabin, he was frustrated and frightened. He kicked in the door when no one answered. One glance at the dry floors made it obvious that no one had been in the living room lately. He heard a crash from behind the bedroom door and dashed to fling it open.

But Joe's bedroom was empty, too. Rain poured through an open window, puddling on the hooked rug beneath it. He swung around and came face-to-face with the wall of pictures Tori had described. It was worse than he thought. Worse than she had described. The pictures showed Amanda all through the years she'd lived on the island. He recognized a few from that summer. And he saw something else. Something he'd never noticed before. A downward progression in Amanda's spirit as she grew older. A hardening in her eyes. A bleakness.

Maybe he was still too drugged to think straight. But none of this made sense. Why would anyone need to beat Tori? And where was Amanda?

The only answers he'd come up with were so far-fetched he refused to believe them.

He forgot to close Joe's door in his haste to find her. She'd gone after the dog. And he knew Lady loved the woods. Could she be lost or was she still chasing the dog to bring her in out of the storm? That would be like her, consistent with everything he knew or sensed of her. She didn't know she was on this island with the person who had tried to kill her. She didn't know the real danger she faced. He had to get to her in time.

"Lady!" He shouted over the storm, desperately trying to decide where to go next—the boathouse or the woods. And then he remembered. Lady haunted the clearing in the woods. It had been one of Amanda's favorite retreats. He'd try there next and hope he was right.

There was only one path through this part of the woods. He found it in the dark and started jogging, calling the dog's and Tori's names as he went.

There was no response, and after a while he decided he would be better off if his arrival was a surprise. He'd probably need a weapon, too. He hunkered down and searched the edge of the path for what he wanted—a stout branch. As he neared the clearing, he left the path and fought the underbrush.

The storm would cover any noise he was making, and whoever was out there would be shocked to see him come out of the woods.

An artificial flash of light alerted him. Someone *was* there. A flashlight beam bounced aimlessly off the trees.

He crept around the edge of the clearing until he could charge in from behind. Joe sat in the rain, bouncing the flashlight against one knee.

Moving swiftly, he reached for Joe's ponytail and yanked his head back with brutal force. Wrapping his forearm across Joe's windpipe, he glared down into eyes dulled by shock.

"Where is she? If you've hurt her, I'll kill you with my bare hands." Whatever needed to be done, he'd do it and pay the price later. "Tell me, damn it!" He tightened his arm.

"I was watching to make sure Amanda was safe. But she ran away from here. She came out of the icehouse and ran into the woods." Joe shook his head. "But, Dr. Jonathan, she's in there. Amanda is in the icehouse. How can that be?" Joe's choked whisper could barely be heard above the storm.

"You idiot—which is it?" Jonathan was almost beyond reason and ready to tear Joe apart.

"Both." Joe gasped.

It didn't make any sense. But the caretaker was shaking. Jonathan took the flashlight out of his limp hand and shone it in his face. He knew shock when he saw it. Force could do no good here.

"Where, Joe?" Somehow he gentled his voice.

Stroking his throat, Joe mutely pointed toward the icehouse.

"Stay here."

He pushed open the door. "Tori!" The frigid air crystallized the moisture on his skin. No one could last long in here after being out in this storm.

"Tori!" He called her name again. He heard a whine, and Lady came up the stairs. "Good girl," he said. "Is she down there, Lady? Is she all right?"

Who in their right mind would go down these broken-down stairs into that darkness?

"Tori!" He shouted her name as he descended, throwing the beam of light in front of him.

He'd seen his share of bodies, but this time he fell back in horror. He knew at first glance that it was Amanda, not Tori, stretched out on the floor of the icehouse. And even though he had begun to suspect the truth, the proof sickened him.

Then he noticed the purple fabric. Tori had been here and in her own way had paid tribute to the dead. But where was she now?

Driven by a blind panic, he raced back up the steps. Lady slipped out past him as he tore the door open and found Joe waiting for him.

He grabbed him by the shoulders and shook him. "Where did she go?"

"That way."

Joe pointed toward the house.

"Listen to me, Joe," He waited for Joe's eyes to focus on his face. "Take the boat and go get Sheriff Eller. Now!"

The storm had shifted, and for the moment only a thick mist hung overhead. Jonathan raced back toward the house, his deepest, darkest fears all-consuming. He had to find her. He had to protect her from the person who had tried to kill her in the park. For he knew without question that Margaret would try again.

CHAPTER FIFTEEN

CLOUDS SCUDDED ACROSS the sky, obscuring the moon and stars. The storm passed over, and with it the lightning that had helped her find her way. Her side ached from running. She was wet and cold and shivering.

She could only hope she was running in the right direction. She had to warn Jonathan. If she'd put him in danger, she wouldn't be able to stand it. If he got hurt, it would be all her fault. They never should have come back here. Why hadn't she seen the truth earlier? Why hadn't she connected Amanda's disappearance to these people on the island? They were too good at hiding their feelings; they had covered up their crimes brilliantly and put on such an act of concern and caring. But now she and Jonathan were in peril. She'd discovered the truth, and Margaret would do anything to stop her from telling.

She couldn't get two pictures out of her mind— Amanda lying in the cold and dark, all alone for months, and Margaret telling her she would have done anything for her sister's child. How could it have come to this? What had happened to this family?

Suddenly she heard a noise off to her right, as if

an animal were moving through the underbrush. She stopped dead in her tracks. A tiny light shone in the darkness of her mind; she remembered that night in the park, stopping and standing, feeling as if someone were stalking her. She hadn't been able to get away then. But this time she had to, this time there was more than her own life at stake. She couldn't, wouldn't, let fear take over.

She dropped down on her hands and knees to make less of a target. Mud squished between her fingers; dead leaves and twigs stuck to her clothes. She crouched very still, unwilling to give her position away. In the dark she had as much advantage as Margaret.

The scuffling noises grew nearer. Even the pungent woods couldn't overcome the scent of Margaret's perfume. Trapping her breath in her lungs, she froze, unwilling to breathe for fear Margaret would hear her. Her chest burned like fire.

And then it seemed the noises moved away. She drew in a sharp breath but held her position. Rain dripped off the overhanging branches and ran down her face. She stayed still, counting to one hundred mentally. She strained, every sense finely tuned, but didn't hear Margaret anywhere.

This cat-and-mouse game was making her crazy. She still had to warn Jonathan. Cautiously she raised her head and peered around.

For Jonathan's sake she had to take the chance. Springing up, she ran through the trees in a zigzag pattern. If Margaret was still close, she wouldn't give her an easy target.

She broke out of the trees and dashed onto the manicured lawn. She could just make out the house looming ahead of her—a massive shadow surrounded by greater darkness.

There was no visible light from the house. Jonathan was probably still in Mother Chambers's room, unaware of what was happening. Growing colder by the minute, she stopped at the bottom of the porch and searched the darkness behind her. Where was Margaret? She tiptoed up the slippery steps and inched the door open. The foyer was deserted. Just as silently, she closed the huge door behind her.

Was Margaret the only one who wanted her dead? She couldn't take a chance on Randall.

She ran lightly up the steps, cringing every time a floorboard creaked. The shadowed hallway seemed to stretch out forever in front of her. She felt as if she were moving in slow motion, like in a bad dream.

Finally she reached the door to Mother Chambers's room. There was no more time for caution or quiet. Boldly, she pushed the door open. The chair was empty. Penelope Chambers was alone in the quiet room, a fragile ghostlike figure in the center of the massive bed.

Where was he? She fought back an unreasoning tide of panic. She'd made it all the way back here, but he was gone. She began to shake, scalding tears cascading down her cheeks. She would never be warm and safe and dry again. She would never see him...

She forced herself down the hall to his room. The bed was still neatly made. So far, so good. At least they hadn't dragged him out of bed. But then, he wasn't waiting in her room, either.

She opened every door along the long hallway, praying for a miracle. He wasn't there. In fact, she guessed he wasn't in the house anywhere. Not for one second would she believe he'd deserted her. He must be out in the dark searching for her.

There was no point in leaving the house; she had no idea where Jonathan would go or how she could find him. She couldn't guess where Margaret was or how long it might take her to decide to come back to The Lodge. But she did know she needed help.

Without Jonathan, she'd have to find a way to help them both. Her first thought was the phone. She could call the mainland and demand that Sheriff Eller come out at once. If that failed, she could always call Detective Savage in Chicago.

But when she entered the library, she found Randall slumped over his desk, his usually impeccable appearance in complete disarray. He looked up at her, and his face blazed with a frightening intensity.

"Thank heavens you have come to me, Amanda."

With the ever-widening circle of light in her mind, she recognized an emotion she knew all too well in his eyes. She turned to run, but he lunged across the room and pulled her roughly against his chest.

"Amanda, my darling, I love you. You must remember that.'' His whisper washed across her face in a wave of bourbon. That smell, his large hands holding her tightly against his body—roaming down her back and over her bottom—his chest pushing against her breasts, invoked sick memories she didn't *want* to remember. The light expanded, and all the little pieces clicked into place.

She struggled in his overpowering embrace.

His face dissolved into her stepfather's swarthy countenance the night of her mother's funeral. Also drunk on bourbon, he'd come to her bedroom to declare his love and tried to paw her with his huge, sweaty hands. Sickened, she'd fought him off, lashing out at him with her nails until he'd stumbled from the room, bloodied.

She'd left the next day, only seventeen years old. She'd been on her own since then, with no family, lost in the big city, seeking anonymity to escape her past, trusting no one. Tori...*she* would be twenty-seven on 19 December. She was not Amanda, thirty on 9 August.

''Amanda, I love you.'' Randall's hoarse declaration broke through her memories to remind her of the present danger.

''I'm not Amanda.'' She said it calmly, firmly, hoping to break through his alcoholic haze. Using every bit of her strength, she shoved him away.

He stumbled, shaking his head in denial. ''You are confused, my darling. Let me help you remember everything about us.'' He reached out for her, his arms wide and welcoming. "Come back where you belong, Amanda."

She stepped away, trying to reach the door behind her without alerting him. Now that her mind was finally clear, she began to put all the pieces of Amanda's life together. Randall would never have hurt her or been a part of Margaret's scheme.

He seemed certain she would step into his arms, waiting in his inebriated haze for a scene to be played out that must have occurred over and over. Her stomach turned. He was Amanda's lover. And since Amanda had used the clearing by the icehouse for her trysts with Jonathan, she probably went there with Randall, too. She took another step back.

"I am not Amanda. Margaret killed Amanda when she found out about the two of you."

He seemed to turn into stone before her eyes.

"She's telling you the truth, Randall."

Margaret's voice came from the doorway behind her. She'd been so intent on getting away from Randall, she'd forgotten all about Margaret.

Now Margaret blocked any escape, holding the gun almost casually at her side. "How long had you been screwing my niece?"

He shook his head impotently, staring with stunned recognition into his wife's twisted face.

"I decided not to stay in town and came here to surprise you," she continued softly, as if they were enjoying a normal conversation. "I thought we'd have a romantic few days while Joe took Mother Chambers to the annual historical society symposium.

You were delayed by hospital business. Is this starting to ring a bell now?''

Randall gasped, shaking in fear and horror. Margaret just laughed. The sound froze Tori's blood.

"Yes, I can see it does, you bastard!"

"Please tell me this isn't true, Margaret.''

His pathetic plea made her laugh break into a high, keening wail. Goose bumps broke out on Tori's skin. Hoping Margaret had forgotten her in this ultimate confrontation with her husband, she inched toward the door.

"Don't you move!" Margaret leveled the gun at her chest.

Tori raised her hands, acquiescing completely. Her mind raced with possibilities. She had to stall Margaret somehow, had to keep her talking. Perhaps if she played up to Margaret's rage at Randall's betrayal, she could get all the answers and give Jonathan time to find her.

"Amanda was waiting for him in her favorite place that day, wasn't she?" Tori forced her voice not to quiver. "What did she say to you when you found her?"

Something in Margaret's face changed. A kind of relief softened her eyes. Tori knew she'd struck the right chord. Margaret *wanted* to tell. Wanted the ultimate vengeance on the husband she now hated.

"You were clever to figure out as much as you did. I think you deserve to hear the rest." Shifting her eyes between the two of them, Margaret smiled. "She tried to bluff me at first, Randall, even though she was lying there on the blanket naked. Hussy! She'd brought your favorite wine for your little picnic and got a real head start waiting for you."

"So she told you about them," Tori said, buying more time. Every second counted until Jonathan came for her.

"Yes! She told me their little plan." The response exploded out of her throat. "Randall was going to leave me when Amanda gained control of her inheritance on her birthday." Her eyes met Tori's, begging for understanding. "She laughed at me. Me! The aunt who had taken her into her home and given her everything. I loved her!"

Tori nodded. "She betrayed you. Then what did you do, Margaret?" She stepped toward the door, but Margaret was lost in her own world of pain and didn't try to stop her.

"I slapped her smirking face. But she only laughed at me again."

Randall aged in that moment, his skin sinking in on itself until he looked like a living skull. His mouth moved but no sound came out.

Margaret's face beamed with a warped sense of triumph, and Tori turned away, her stomach wrenching.

"So I picked up the bread knife and she stopped laughing."

She heard the insanity in Margaret's voice and instinctively took a step back.

Margaret whirled on her. "I told you not to move."

Again she made a gesture of surrender, which seemed to satisfy Margaret.

"Besides, you of all people should hear the rest." Her smile turned deadly.

A new danger swelled around them. She wasn't sure how much longer she could keep this madwoman from erupting into violence.

"Obviously I wasn't thinking straight. I foolishly thought Amanda could just disappear. But we couldn't use the money! When I called a lawyer, he said it would be seven years before a missing person could be declared dead. Then I realized I had to have a body. Your body."

Margaret caught her looking into the room beyond. "He won't come, you know." Margaret shrugged. "I drugged him."

So Margaret didn't know Jonathan wasn't upstairs. Tori stored that fact away as a last-ditch weapon. If only she could figure out how best to use it. *Keep buying time!* her instinct screamed. *He'll come.*

"Don't you think I deserve to know why you used me? I had never met you or Randall or Amanda before."

"How nice for you that your memory has returned. Lucky for me, it doesn't matter now." Her mouth curled in that mad little smile, which reminded Tori how close they were to disaster.

"Go on, Margaret, tell me everything," she urged, while she tried to scan the room for some kind of weapon.

"I was volunteering at the Wellness Clinic, and

one of the volunteers said my niece was there. I looked up and saw you.'' She laughed as if sharing a joke. ''For one awful moment I believed you were Amanda come back to haunt me. But then the light shifted and you really were someone else. In that instant, I realized I'd been saved. You were a perfect body double.''

Randall couldn't take it anymore. His knees gave way. With a groan, he sagged back into his chair and stared at his wife like a zombie.

''It was almost frightening how calmly I planned your murder. But once you've killed, the next time holds less horror. This had to be the perfect crime, and it took me a while to figure it all out. I had to get your records from the clinic and change Amanda's file at the hospital. I had to figure out a way to get you to the Majestic and to the park.'' Margaret gave a harsh bark of laughter. ''I couldn't kill you in that terrible neighborhood where you live! No one would believe for a moment that Amanda Braithwaite would be anywhere near that part of town. I knew you were poor and needed work, so I faked the call from your modeling agency. You obeyed my instructions perfectly, and I thought it was all too easy.'' She frowned at Tori. ''But you wouldn't die. You wouldn't stop fighting me off in the park. And each time I tried to finish it in the hospital, someone got in my way. Usually your devoted Jonathan. But not this time. There's no going back.''

Tori's thigh muscles bunched as she waited for just the right moment to leap for the gun.

"No more! No more killing!" Like the living dead, Randall rose from his chair and blocked his wife.

Tori turned to run, but the gun went off, the sound reverberating through the room. Tori whirled. A look of stunned disbelief crossed Randall's face; for one second he stared down at the red stain spreading across his chest, then he pitched forward at his wife's feet.

"Easier and easier," Margaret murmured, her expression never altering for a moment.

Tori fell to her knees and pressed her palms over the blood oozing from his chest. "We've got to help him." She knew if she didn't stop the bleeding, he would die. He'd tried to save her; she had to do something. "Margaret, for pity's sake, help him."

"It's too late for him. And for you." She grabbed Tori and jerked her to her feet.

Tori tried to break free, struggling as best she could, but Margaret's strength in her dementia was overpowering. Tori dug her heels into the thin oriental carpet, flailing her free arm wildly. "Jonathan!" She screamed out his name, pushing at Margaret with hands covered in Randall's blood.

No matter how hard she fought, Margaret wouldn't relinquish her hold. Then Margaret pushed the gun beneath her ribs and Tori quieted. They walked up the stairs side by side, as they had on many occasions, but Tori could feel the gun pressed against her. When they reached the top of the stairs, Mother Chambers was wandering toward them, a bewildered look on her face.

"What was that noise?"

"It's up to you whether she lives or dies."

Margaret's whisper was a threat Tori believed. She looked into eyes that glittered with madness and made a decision. No one else would die for her. Her hands balled into fists. When her chance came, they might be her only weapons but she would use them to full effect.

Mentally she called to Jonathan, just as she'd done in her darkest loneliness. Why didn't he come to her?

"Is something wrong?" The old woman's voice sounded feeble. Her hand gripped her cane as she stepped toward them with a heavy tread. "I thought I heard a gunshot."

"Everything's all right." Tori forced a smile across her tight face. "Go back to bed."

"Where are you going?" Her sharp eyes wavered back and forth between the two women.

"Amanda wants to see the stars from the widow's walk now that the storm has passed. We'll see you in the morning, Mother Chambers."

With the gun digging into her ribs and Margaret's threat to the kind old woman echoing in her head, Tori had no choice except to climb the narrow steps up to the widow's walk. She dragged her feet, making Margaret use her strength to push her along. Trying to suck extra oxygen into her body, she breathed very slowly and deeply. Once they reached the top, away from Mother Chambers, she would have to act fast.

"It won't do you any good, you know. I have the gun."

JONATHAN WAS GOING on pure adrenaline and gut instinct. He tore open the door to The Lodge, shouting her name.

"Tori, where are you?"

"Up here," came the weak response. "Hurry."

Penelope Chambers was at the far end of the hall, trying to go up the steep, winding staircase to the widow's walk.

"Up there. Margaret and Amanda. Something is wrong, something is terribly wrong. I can feel it."

Pushing past her, he took the steps two at a time.

There was no moon tonight, and the clouds made the sky seem even darker. He could barely make out two silhouettes on the bridge between the towers. The wooden planks sagged with his weight.

"Jonathan, thank heaven, you've come," Margaret called to him. She had one hand on Tori's arm and turned so he couldn't see the other.

All of his fears and panic drained away, leaving him deadly calm. He knew this woman, knew what she was capable of. He had to try to outsmart her. He got close enough to make out the expression in Tori's eyes. What he read there touched him, but he couldn't afford to be distracted now.

"She's gone mad, Jonathan," Margaret went on, unaware of the dementia in her voice. "She shot Randall in the library. Now she's trying to push me off the walk."

"I understand, Margaret. Let me take care of her now." He couldn't look at Tori or he'd blow it. He had to convince this madwoman that he believed her.

"She needs to be back under Dr. Newman's care. Turn her over to me so we can help her."

He took a step closer, almost near enough to reach Tori, but Margaret was faster. She stepped between them, her eyes narrowed, her nostrils flaring.

"Something smells rotten here." She laughed softly. "Rotten and musty."

Margaret's crazy laugh should have told him that he'd given himself away.

"You've been to the icehouse, haven't you? Now you have to die, too."

He had no time to react as she lifted the gun and fired.

CHAPTER SIXTEEN

EVERYTHING SEEMED to happen in slow motion, yet Tori could not make herself move fast enough. She saw the gun come up, heard the report, and only then managed to ram her shoulder against Margaret's arm.

Jonathan was hit. She watched as he grabbed his thigh and went down. Something inside her broke. She turned on Margaret, clawing at her face, fighting for his life and her own, fighting desperately as she had so long ago in the park. This time, she prevailed. Her assault sent the gun spinning down, down into the darkness.

"You bitch!" Margaret snarled, and slapped her across the face. "You should be dead!" Her hands closed around Tori's throat, forcing her back against the wooden railing.

The rough edge bit into her hips, but she'd learned how to survive on the streets. Focusing all her strength on her legs, she lifted her knee hard into Margaret's groin.

Even doubled over by pain, Margaret refused to let go of her neck. Thinking quickly, Tori used a reverse move. Instead of trying to pull away, she flung herself forward, toward Margaret.

Caught off balance, Margaret fell backward against the opposite railing, pulling Tori with her. The ancient wood gave way under their combined weight.

The bottom dropped out of the world. Tangled together, they crashed onto the roof and slid down the steep slope. Fighting for her life, Tori scrambled to catch at the rough shingles, trying to find something, anything, to break her fall.

Her foot caught on the gutter, slowing her down. Somehow she broke free of Margaret and concentrated on the gutter. Her hands found the edge and clung.

Screaming, Margaret slid past. She clawed out for the gutter but was moving too fast and went tumbling into the blackness.

Tori closed her eyes, but she couldn't keep from hearing the sound of Margaret's body hitting the ground far below her.

It was déjà vu. She hung helplessly in a black void knowing Jonathan was her only salvation. But he was injured and she was out of reach.

JONATHAN STRUGGLED to his feet, desperately stripping his belt out of his pants. He looped it around his thigh and tightened it, using just enough pressure to slow the bleeding. As he dragged himself to the edge of the walkway, the full horror of what had just taken place rocked through him. But he'd only heard one scream, one body hit the ground.

He saw miracles in the operating room every day.

He prayed for one now. "Tori! Tori, answer me," he demanded.

"Help me, Jonathan! I can't hold on for long."

His elation quickly gave way to fear. Stretching as far over the edge as he could, he saw her clinging to the gutter and dangling three stories above the ground.

There was no way he could reach her from here. There was no rope, no grappling hook; he couldn't even use the railing for fear it would break in her hand.

"I'm here." Mrs. Chambers crawled out onto the widow's walk, pushing her cane in front of her. "Where is she? Where is my Amanda?"

"Give me your cane."

She shoved it toward him. Jonathan's hand was sticky with blood. He wiped it on his pants before extending the cane down into the darkness.

"Don't be afraid, Tori! I've got Mrs. Chambers's cane. Grab hold and I'll pull you up."

TORI CLUNG TO the gutter bravely, but it was his voice in the darkness that gave her true courage. She couldn't see him. She couldn't see the cane. But she had to try. Using a final surge of strength, she let go of the gutter with one hand and reached out into the darkness. There was nothing.

"Jonathan." It was her last gasp of despair. She felt her hand slip. "I can't find it."

"Try again, Tori." He stretched a little farther. "It's directly above you. Try for us. I love you."

He loved her. That was enough—for however long her life lasted. She regripped the gutter and looked up into total darkness. She couldn't see his face, but she could hear him encouraging her. Then, out of the pitch-black nothingness, she saw a tiny glimmer. Then another.

Two gleaming cat's eyes winked at her.

She pulled upward, struggling to stretch the last few inches, and grabbed the cane at the indentation of the cat's throat.

"I've got you! Just hold on. Don't struggle."

Inch by inch, she moved upward, agonizingly slowly. At one point she had to give up her grip on the gutter and trust herself to him entirely. She couldn't say a word, she could only concentrate on clasping the cane. Then her foot gained a position on the gutter and she could lever herself toward him. It was a nightmare journey, as dark and terrifying as her recovery.

At last he put his arms around her and pulled her up onto the walkway. His breath came in huge gasps as he ran his hands over her, checking for any injury.

Then his mouth came down on hers. She drank in his strength and love. She poured all of her own love and hope into him.

She thought she would never let go. It felt so right to be in his embrace. His lips roamed over her face as he murmured endearments that were a balm to her soul. His hands roamed over her body, bringing it to life again. She rubbed her cheek against his. Her hands explored his arms, his back, his legs. Then she remembered.

"You were shot." Her hands came away sticky with blood from where she'd touched his leg.

"It's nothing. I felt the entrance and exit wounds, so the bullet's gone. It's just bleeding like hell."

"What can I do?" For a heartbeat, she thought of Randall's blood on her hands.

Jonathan's eyes glittered in the darkness. She couldn't tell if he was going into shock, but he'd lost a lot of blood.

"See if Randall has clean socks and a T-shirt in his room. By the way, where the hell is he?"

Somehow she held her anxiety in check. "In his office. Margaret shot him. I think he's dead."

"I've got to check." He tried to stand but couldn't. She gently pushed him down. "It's too late for Randall. I'm not going to let you die, too. I'll be right back."

She raced down the winding steps, tripping and falling down the last two. It didn't matter if she ached all over. Nothing mattered except Jonathan.

She paused in the doorway to Randall and Margaret's bedroom, feeling as if she were violating their privacy. But they were both gone, and she needed help for the living. She riffled through drawers until she found exactly what Jonathan had asked for.

It all looked so normal—a drawer full of neatly folded underwear. But the seeming normality of the house and the family was all a sham. Still, she felt a deep sense of loss. Amanda was gone forever. Poor little rich girl betrayed by those she should have been able to trust. And Randall. For all his obsession, he seemed to truly care for Amanda. That forbidden love had been his destruction. Even Margaret had been betrayed. In a way, Tori could understand how that ultimate treachery had deranged her.

She knew she was the one innocent in this mad game of betrayal and greed. A pawn. And yet that mad act had changed her life forever. It was all so sad. And she didn't feel hypocritical in the least. It was normal, healthy, to grieve. And someday she'd be able to forgive.

Standing in the quiet room, she relived the grief of her own mother's death. The consequences had been terrible, too much for the young girl she'd been then. The terror of her stepfather's actions had haunted her her whole life. But now, because of Jonathan, she recognized that she'd cut off all her emotions long ago. They had been too painful to handle until Jonathan had brought her back to the living.

EVERY MUSCLE IN his back was in agony. His thigh throbbed, but the flow of blood had slowed and he knew he was in no danger. And then he heard a rustling sound behind the door. Penelope Chambers! In his elation at Tori's rescue, he had completely put the older woman out of his mind. He levered himself up to go to her when he heard a measured tread mounting the steps toward him. These footfalls were far too loud to be Tori's.

A flashlight blinded him.

"What the devil's been going on here, Jonathan? I found Margaret Chambers's body on the front lawn. Randall's dead, too. I found him in the library." Sheriff Eller stepped out onto the widow's walk and looked around him. His face was gaunt with strain. "You've been bleeding, man." He fumbled in his pocket for a handkerchief and pressed it against Jonathan's leg. "Joe came to the office with some crazy story about Miss Braithwaite having two faces. I locked him up for the night and got my butt over here."

"Amanda's dead, too. She has been for months." Jonathan forced himself to go on. "Margaret killed them both. She would have killed me and Tori, too, but she fell. Over there, where the railing is broken."

The sheriff's eyes widened in disbelief. Then he heard the slight moan from behind the door. He unbuckled his holster before realizing who sat in the shadows.

Jonathan sank back down in relief, letting the sheriff ease Penelope to her feet. There was still a long night ahead for all of them. The sheriff would have to go to the icehouse. He felt suddenly very weary. Lack of blood...or lack of Tori. Without her near him, he knew he was only half alive.

AS TORI CLIMBED the stairs to the widow's walk, she heard voices. Who could Jonathan possibly be talking to? Joe! Was he somehow a part of this plot? Could he possibly want to harm Jonathan? She raced up the final steps, raising the glass of water she carried overhead.

"It's all right, Miss...?" Sheriff Eller turned, supporting Mother Chambers with one strong arm. "You don't need to throw water on me or club me with the glass. I'm on your side."

Relief made tears overflow as she held out her meager supplies to Jonathan.

"Perfect." He gave her a weak smile and placed one rolled-up sock at each wound, then wrapped the T-shirt around his thigh to hold them in place.

"Sheriff Eller found Margaret's body on the lawn. She's dead. So is Randall."

It could so easily have been her and they both knew it.

"Joe went for the sheriff while I came to find you." He cupped her face, kissing her. "He's very confused by all this. But he's the one who sent me to you. Thank God I got here in time."

"They're all gone, the whole family." The sheriff's hoarse whisper was incredulous.

"Not all," Jonathan reminded him.

Tori turned toward Mother Chambers, who looked very small as she leaned on the sheriff's arm. Even though she wasn't family, the old woman had had a profound effect on her life. She had to make some gesture, try to wipe the horror and loneliness out of her eyes. She pressed a kiss on Jonathan's lips and stooped to retrieve the cane that had saved her life. She handed it to the brave soul who had pulled herself up the winding staircase and been there when they needed her.

When Mother Chambers turned the cane around, the cat's eyes flashed. She placed it firmly on the walkway and let go of the sheriff. She straightened her back and stepped away. "Thank you, my dear," she said simply. "Now we must get Jonathan to the hospital in town."

HE FUSSED LIKE a bad patient and refused to allow the sheriff to help him down the steps, regretting it by the time he reached the bottom. His head was spinning, or was it the floor?

"Are you all right?" Tori came up beside him and placed her hand lightly on his arm. At once, everything righted itself.

"Now I am." He meant it. Without her, he never would have endured the pain of the long walk to the boat dock.

Before they could leave, the sheriff radioed for help, extra police and the county coroner. Jonathan had to describe how he'd found Amanda and exactly where she was located. Tori stayed very quiet, not volunteering any information. But she insisted that Lady be seen to before she got in the boat.

Jonathan was more worried about her state of mind than his injury, yet he didn't want to bring it up until she was ready to talk.

They huddled together in the police boat, wrapped in a single blanket. She rested her head, quite naturally, on his shoulder. Penelope Chambers sat across from them in her own blanket, a faraway look in her eyes. The island shrank to a black dot in the water behind the fast-moving boat. He hoped never to go back there again.

He knew he should be concentrating on what had happened, asking questions, trying to get the whole truth, but he was content to just hold Tori's hand. All the details could be handled later, when they felt up to it.

Never would he be able to forget those terrifying seconds when he didn't know if Tori was dead or alive. Nothing in his life had prepared him for that kind of anguish. He had so much to say to her. But now wasn't the time. She needed time to assimilate everything that had happened. It was only fair. She wasn't Amanda, and instinctively he knew she wasn't quite at ease being Tori, either. And even though he was perfectly certain of his feelings, he wanted to be fair.

He'd need a clear head when he convinced her they should spend the rest of their lives discovering each other, just in case she put up some flimsy argument.

The sheriff herded them into his car and turned on the siren. Its wail woke up half the citizens of the sleepy burg as they sped to the local hospital. Sheriff Eller drove with flair—screeching to a halt at the ER as two orderlies rushed out with a gurney.

"I don't need that," Jonathan started to protest, then stopped. Procedure was procedure. He'd better start acting like a patient. Resigned, he climbed onto the cart and let them wheel him in. As long as Tori stayed beside him, holding his hand, he could deal with anything.

As they passed through ER he noticed only one other cubicle with a patient, so he wasn't surprised when Dr. Madison arrived at once. He looked as if he had just completed his residency.

"Gunshot. Entrance and exit wound. I can move my toes and I can feel everything below my knees. I don't believe it nicked the bone."

The poor doctor looked at him as if he were mad.

"He's a surgeon," Tori whispered.

"You should X-ray to be sure. Antibiotics and a sterile dressing should be all I need."

The young doctor began to sweat when he removed the makeshift bandage and the bleeding started again.

Damn! He was out in the boonies. This could be a problem.

Mrs. Chambers was giving him a peculiar look. "What if you need a blood transfusion, Jonathan? I doubt they have any here with your rare blood antibody."

"How do you know about that?"

"Is it serious?" Tori asked at the same time.

"No." He wanted to reassure her. "It's nothing unless I need a blood transfusion. But I haven't lost enough blood." He smiled at her and turned to Mrs. Chambers. "Tell her it will be all right."

"Actually, my dear, it happened a long time ago. Appendicitis, I believe. He was in this hospital, but they had to fly some blood in from Chicago. His mother was beside herself, as you can well imagine."

"That incident was the start of my medical career."

"It most certainly was. The whole town kept track of young Dr. Johnnie's career." She banged her cane on the tile floor. "But your parents had the scare of a lifetime. I'm too old to have a repeat of such nonsense."

"We have to get you down to Chicago just in case."

There was a determined gleam in Tori's eyes, so he wisely kept his mouth shut.

"What kind of transportation is available?"

"In my opinion, a blood transfusion will not be necessary. But we do have a mobile intensive care unit that's not being used." Judging by the relief in his voice, it sounded as if Dr. Madison would be glad to be rid of them all.

"That's perfect. Mother Chambers and I will be accompanying Dr. Taylor." No one was able to withstand the fire in Tori's announcement.

"Fine. Now we need to take Dr. Taylor to X ray. You can see him again after his wound is dressed."

Allowing Dr. Madison some control in his own ER, Jonathan didn't protest when Penelope Chambers and Sheriff Eller filed out behind him.

At last he was alone with Tori. They'd run the gamut of emotions in the last few hours. He reached for her hand, only to find it right there by his side.

"I don't ever want you to leave me. Even for a minute." He pulled her down and took her mouth in a kiss. Even flat on his back, helpless to do anything about it, he burned for her.

"I wish we were alone," he moaned as he slid his mouth to her ear.

"We will be soon, I promise." The urgency he heard in her voice sent delight through his weakened body.

"Be gentle with me," he chuckled, nibbling on her throat. "They'll give me morphine for pain. I'll probably sleep all the way back to Chicago."

"I'll take care of you, no matter what." She pulled away, smiling. "I've recently discovered I'm a whole lot stronger than I thought."

He shook his head, wanting to soothe her. "When did you start remembering? I wish..."

Suddenly she pressed her mouth against his. "Not now." Their gazes locked. "I'll be there right beside you when you wake up. Then we'll talk this through, I promise."

She watched over him tenderly as the ambulance rushed through the night to Chicago. Hooked up to an IV, Jonathan looked young and adorably helpless. She brushed the heavy fall of dark hair off his forehead and pressed a kiss there. A wave of emotion more intense than she could have imagined brought tears to her eyes.

It seemed it had always been like this. At least since the last moment of her old life and the first of her new. He had been there for her. Perhaps it had started out because he cared for Amanda, but with time she had grown confident that it was her and not a ghost he was growing to love.

Nevertheless, there were still a lot of things to deal with. How would they ever untangle all the lies and misconceptions and mistakes? One of her tears dropped on his cheek, and she kissed it away.

"He will live. Don't worry. He comes from hardy stock."

Tori looked up and found Mother Chambers studying her. She tried to read the details in that strong face: the way she held her head with such proud grace, the purple shadows under her sharp eyes, the intensity of her gaze.

She knew what that proud old woman wanted to hear. With her newfound strength came the courage to face that impossible need.

"You know I'm not Amanda."

Mother Chambers stared at her as though she hadn't heard, but after a moment she said, "I know a terrible injustice has been done to you by my family. I am so deeply sorry."

Tori couldn't stop the rush of pity she felt for her. It combined with the admiration she'd always had for the old woman's strength.

"It's not your fault." She gathered the cold, age-spotted hands between her young warm ones. "None of this has anything to do with you. I won't let you blame yourself."

Mother Chambers's eyes overflowed with tears. "I know they were not perfect children. Randall. Margaret. My beautiful Amanda. But they were *mine*. Now I feel so alone.''

The mention of the one emotion that had tormented her childhood and plagued her life couldn't go unanswered. She touched the older woman's cheek. "You are not alone. Do you understand?''

Mother Chambers didn't respond. Tori let her free hand trail down to clasp the old woman's gently. "Horrible things have happened to both of us. There has been too much deceit and hatred. We've both lost so much. But we can win something out of the despair. For the first time in my life, I feel close to being the person I've always wanted to be. You helped me to do that. You made me understand I had to go out and seize life with both hands. And I did. Between you and Jonathan, I'm whole at last.''

Tori swallowed back the emotion, making her voice drop to a whisper. "I know I can't take the place of your family. But, please, can't I be part of your life?''

With a shuddering sigh, Penelope Chambers reached out and cradled Tori's head against her shoulder. They held each other as light began to overtake the dark night.

The ambulance sped on as a bond was forged between yesterday and tomorrow. And she hoped Penelope Chambers had found a measure of peace, at last.

CHAPTER SEVENTEEN

DAWN PAINTED the windows of Memorial Hospital pink as the ambulance pulled beneath the ER canopy. Penelope Chambers had fallen asleep about an hour before, but Tori couldn't rest. She ran her fingers lightly over Jonathan's face, checking, as she had every fifteen minutes, that he was still warm and breathing. A fine stubble covered his strong jawline. She decided she liked it.

The ambulance doors shot open, and light flooded the back of the vehicle. Tori blinked. Now she had to let him go. The staff was very efficient; surely they would take special care of one of their own.

Inside the emergency room there were at least two familiar faces. She wasn't surprised that Dr. Newman and Dr. Johnson were waiting for him—they were his friends.

"Couldn't go off duty without seeing how my buddy was doing." Dr. Johnson did a quick assessment and ordered, "Take him up to Two North." Then he turned to her. "Don't you worry. He'll be as good as new."

She was relieved when she saw him follow the gurney. She turned to find Penelope settled into a wheelchair, the ever-present cane tucked against her side. There were purple crescents of fatigue under her eyes, and one hand plucked nervously at the armrest.

Dr. Newman stepped forward, peering at her over the top of his glasses. "Tori?"

"That's right." She lifted her chin, finding the courage to tell him everything. "I remember, Doctor. Just like you said I would. Everything, except the actual attack. You were right. With time it all came back."

"I'm happy for you. However, you have been through a horrible ordeal." He seemed to be choosing his words with care. "If you want to talk about anything, anything at all, I'm available. But not tonight. I think you've been through enough, and there's someone else waiting to talk to you." He gestured to the far end of the hall, where Detective Savage waited in clothes that looked as if he'd been sleeping in them.

Her eyes full of torment, Penelope looked up at her. Impulsively Tori moved closer to her and patted her shoulder. The old woman let out a deep sigh. Tori straightened. This wasn't going to be easy for any of them.

"Good morning, ladies. The hospital has set aside a room so I can take your statements." Detective Savage reached for the wheelchair. "Let me help you here, Miss Owens."

"No." She would do this small service, hoping Penelope Chambers would derive some comfort from it.

During the ambulance ride, they had crossed some invisible barrier and come to a real understanding.

The detective led them down a long hall to a small conference room, where a recording clerk waited.

"Would you ladies like some coffee?"

Mrs. Chambers raised her head; she looked confused and frightened.

"Do we have to do this now, Detective Savage?" Tori asked. "Sheriff Eller has doubtless filled you in, so you know this has been a horrific night for both of us."

He patted her arm. "I understand, Miss Owens. And I know you're eager to see Dr. Taylor. But it's best to do this now when it's fresh in your mind."

"Fresh in my mind?" she echoed. "I won't ever forget it. Not one single second of it."

"Tell me, Miss Owens."

She stared into his kind brown eyes and started at the beginning. In a flat tone, she told him about Tori's life, how strangely enough it paralleled Amanda's. Betrayed by their male guardians, she had struck out on her own, a friendless, frightened girl, but Amanda had exploited her sexuality, using it to humiliate and torment the men around her.

Both girls had been lost in their own way.

Sometime during her recital, Penelope Chambers reached over and took her hand. She told how she'd been lured to the park, and why. She described finding Amanda. She ended up on the widow's walk, shaking her head at all the deaths, all the loss.

"Anything else, Miss Owens?" he asked quietly when she was finished.

"Yes. I want that report to state that Randall Chambers lost his life trying to save mine."

She could feel a tremor run through Penelope's body. Regardless of his sordid relationship with Amanda, in the end Randall had tried to save Tori.

Her face red from weeping, Randall's mother looked defiantly at the detective. "Do you have any questions for me? I was not aware of the situation until very late. Too late to do anything about it."

He frowned, loosening his tie to a lopsided position across his wrinkled blue shirt. "No, ma'am. Please accept my condolences on the loss of your son."

She inclined her head slightly. "Thank you."

He cleared his throat, "I believe there's a room here at the hospital for Mrs. Chambers. A doctor will be in to check on her, just in case. This has been a drainin' experience for all of you."

Tori insisted on seeing Mother Chambers to her room and making sure she was settled comfortably before she went to Jonathan. Detective Savage accompanied them. He seemed to want to say something to her, but was hesitant. As they walked through the hospital, she felt as if she'd come full circle. She recognized the sounds of all the morning activities—the clatter of meal trays and the whir of rubber wheels, the low hum of voices as staff exchanged information for the day.

The detective waited in the hall while she helped Penelope into a hospital gown and brushed her white hair, wishing all the while that someone would put her to bed, too. Every muscle in her body cried out for rest.

But she had to see Jonathan first.

"You need to get some rest, too, Tori."

It was the first time Penelope used her real name. She recognized in the sharp green eyes an offer to share as many of her tomorrows as possible. She smiled and stayed until the old woman finally closed her eyes.

As she went back into the hall, she caught sight of herself in a mirror. Blood was spattered all down her purple dress, and the hem was ripped in an uneven line. She looked as awful as she felt.

"He's two doors to your left. I checked," Detective Savage said quietly.

She longed for the moment when she could be private with Jonathan, but she couldn't put the detective off any longer. Clearly there was something on his mind. She stopped in the middle of the hall and crossed her arms over her chest.

"Let's get this over with. What is it you want to say to me, Detective Savage?"

"I'm sorry I didn't do a better job for you, Miss Owens. You had to save yourself and Dr. Taylor. You have my admiration."

She was surprised, but shrugged the compliment off. "It's over."

"I don't know about that. It seems to me there are a lot of loose ends that only you can tie up. I ordered your apartment sealed while we looked for evidence. Everything's still there for you."

She shuddered. No, it wasn't over yet. She didn't want to go back there, and they both knew it. But she had to. She nodded and turned away.

Quietly she entered Jonathan's room. The light had been dimmed so it wouldn't disturb the sleeping patient, who was curled up on his side. His eyes were closed, his face peaceful with that shock of dark hair falling across his forehead.

As if he sensed her presence, he sighed and stirred. He looked up at her with unfocused eyes. "Tori. I knew you'd be here."

"Go back to sleep," she whispered.

"Not without you." He reached out for her, to her, just as he had since the moment they met. It was comforting. It was irresistible.

She curled up next to him, pressing herself against his body, spoon fashion. Sliding her hand under the sheet, she slowly stroked the length of him until she reached the bandage on his thigh.

"Does it hurt much?" she whispered.

"That's not the part of my anatomy that aches when you're around." He rolled onto his back. Without warning, he pressed his lips against hers and sighed. His eyes drifted closed again.

That kiss offered her everything. She wrapped one arm around him and held him, careful not to press against his wound. Just for a little while, she promised herself, then she'd do what had to be done. It was safe and comfortable sharing Jonathan's bed. She slept.

When she woke, Bonnie was standing over her.

"I just took out his IV." Smiling, she bustled around the room, straightening things that didn't need it. "He'll be perfectly fine in less time than you'd imagine. Do you want to go get cleaned up? He'll be asleep for a few more hours."

"Yes, that's a good idea." Tori pressed a last kiss on his cheek before perching on the side of the bed. "Could you loan me cab fare?"

Bonnie was surprised, but Tori knew she had to be finished with the past before Jonathan woke up, before she faced him in the cold light of a new day.

He awakened to the scent of Tori's perfume. It clung to his skin and the pillow. He reached out to touch her, and found...nothing.

He opened his eyes and jerked up from the bed.

"Tori!"

"She's not here," Penelope said, and rose from the chair in the corner. Her cane beat a steady rhythm across the floor as she approached the bed. "You need a shave."

"A dressing change and a bath are also in order." Bonnie stood in the doorway, supplies in hand.

Didn't they realize the bottom had dropped out of his world? "Where is she?"

"I told her you'd be asleep awhile longer, so she went to change."

"Where?" His heart felt as if it would jump out of his chest.

"I'm not sure." Bonnie shrugged. "I loaned her cab fare. I knew you were good for it."

"I've got to get out of here." He flung back the sheet to discover the damn hospital gown was twisted around his waist. "Would you ladies leave so I can get the hell out of this bed."

"Do you know where's she gone, Jonathan?"

He could guess. "Back to her apartment." The thought of her there, alone with the past, made him crazy. "I need to be with her."

"Then do it, my boy, for both our sakes. She is quite a remarkable young woman."

"I will, Mrs. Chambers. Believe me, I know how lucky I am to have found her. I'm going to bring her back where she belongs. With me."

SHE BELONGED HERE—had belonged, Tori corrected herself. In this dingy hallway thick with the smell of cooking food. The super grinned at her and winked knowingly as he unlocked the door.

"That detective fella called and said to let ya in if ya showed up. Are ya gonna take all this junk away so I can let the place again? Think Tori is dead or something?"

She raised her chin, observing his reaction. "No. Tori Owens is very much alive."

She closed the door on him and leaned back against it. All her old ghosts were here, waiting. Yet this morning they seemed mere shadows. Deliberately she crossed the room and flung open the drapes to let the sunshine in. It felt good on her face.

The tiny bathroom shower sputtered water, sometimes too hot and then freezing cold. She didn't care. She reveled in it, letting it cascade over her until she felt clean and new.

The closet was small but it wasn't full. There didn't seem to be much to choose from. She pulled out the dress that was her uniform for modeling auditions, a basic black raw silk sheath. It fit perfectly. She slid her feet into her only remaining pair of black pumps. Her higher heels had been ruined in the park that night.

That night. A lifetime ago.

Her one good piece of jewelry was nestled in cotton in her top drawer. She slipped the gold chain over her head and examined the cameo her mother had given her on her sixteenth birthday.

"You'd be proud of me now, Mom," she said in a firm voice. "At last I'm the woman you would have wanted me to be."

She let the necklace fall between her breasts. There was really nothing else she wanted here. She could pack up some of the clothes, although she doubted she'd wear the drab colors again. The furniture and knickknacks held no sentimental value. It would be easy to walk away from her old life.

But would it be easy to start over?

With Jonathan anything was possible. There was a lot to tell him. She wanted him to see her as her new self, get to know her. It was a process she would be going through herself. But it wouldn't change the one unalterable fact of her life—her feelings for him.

She stared into the mirror—into eyes that were familiar, yet not the same. She remembered looking into her compact mirror beneath the Majestic Hotel marquee and vowing to change her life.

Her life was changed—irrevocably. Her face was different, like Tori's and like Amanda's, but new. And because of that, there existed a whole new set of possibilities.

The door opened and closed in the other room. She wasn't surprised to see Jonathan at all. She knew he'd find her, knew he'd understand her need to come back here. He wobbled a little on his crutches, frustrated by his clumsiness. She knew him so well—better than she knew herself.

She turned back to the mirror. His face was reflected directly behind hers.

"It will never be exactly the same." He watched her closely, waiting for a response.

"That doesn't seem important, Jonathan. I know who I am, who I want to be. That's what counts."

He searched her eyes. "I woke up and you weren't there. For a moment I panicked, but then Bonnie came in and explained. I knew you'd have to come here and say goodbye." He still watched her, reflected in the mirror. "I had to come here, too. To let you know I love you, Tori Owens."

Turning to him, she shook her head. "You fell in love with Amanda Braithwaite. You don't even know me."

"You're the only person I do know. You, yourself, not those other women, phantoms of the dark." He moved closer, dropping his crutches. His hair fell across his forehead as he reached for her. "In fact, I know you better than I know myself. I'm a whole new person now."

When she held back, he dropped his hands. "Do you think you love me because of gratitude? Because I helped to save your life that night?" He laughed, but it sounded hollow. "I guess I'm assuming a lot. You've never actually said the words to me."

He trapped her gaze and held it. As always, she could only tell him the truth. The truth about her feelings. "You don't really know anything about me. Everything between us has been based on misconceptions. We have to work through all that."

He stood so close to her she could smell the soap on his skin. "Once you told me you weren't going to look backward. I can't imagine looking forward without you." He kissed the tears sliding down her cheeks. "You are the strongest, most compassionate woman I've ever known. I need that. I need you. I'm alone without you."

Slowly, he stepped away, giving her space, time, if she needed it. He stared at her, and nothing on this earth could have wrenched her eyes from his face.

She had come here to face the past. She no longer belonged to it. She belonged with him.

She stepped into his arms, not seeking shelter or comfort. She was just a woman reaching out to the man she loved. She kissed his mouth, tasting him. He responded, kissing her back, holding her as close as she wanted to be.

"I love you," she said.

It was enough to last a lifetime.

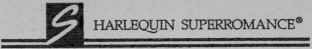

HARLEQUIN SUPERROMANCE®

THE MIRACLE BABY
by
Janice Kay Johnson

If having a baby with a stranger is what it'll take to save her eleven-year-old daughter's life...Beth McCabe is willing to have one.

Is the stranger?

Nate McCabe hasn't seen or spoken to his identical twin brother, Rob, for fifteen years. Now Rob is dead and Nate learns that Rob's widow, Beth, and her young daughter, Mandy, need him——but only because he's Rob's twin. Only because they need a miracle.

Mandy will die without a bone marrow transplant. When Nate's tissue fails to match, Beth persuades him to step into his brother's shoes and father a baby——Beth's baby, a child who has a one-in-four chance of saving Mandy's life.

Watch for *The Miracle Baby* by Janice Kay Johnson.

Available in April 1997,
wherever Harlequin books are sold.

9ML-497

LOVE *or* MONEY?
Why not Love *and* Money!
After all, millionaires
need love, too!

Suzanne Forster,
Muriel Jensen
and
Judith Arnold

bring you three original stories
about finding that one-in-a million man!

Harlequin also brings you
a million-dollar sweepstakes—enter
for your chance to win a fortune!

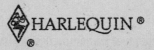

HARLEQUIN ®
®

HTMM

It's hot...and it's out of control!

Beginning this spring, Temptation turns up the
heat. Look for these bold, provocative,
*ultra*sexy books!

#629 OUTRAGEOUS
by Lori Foster (April 1997)

#639 RESTLESS NIGHTS
by Tiffany White (June 1997)

#649 NIGHT RHYTHMS
by Elda Minger (Sept. 1997)

BLAZE: Red-hot reads—only from

HARLEQUIN Temptation

and

HARLEQUIN

INTRIGUE®

Double Dare ya!

Identical twin authors Patricia Ryan and
Pamela Burford bring you a dynamic duo of
books that just happen to feature identical twins.

Meet Emma, the shy one, and her diva double,
Zara. Be prepared for twice the pleasure and
twice the excitement as they give two
unsuspecting men trouble times two!

In April, the scorching **Harlequin Temptation** novel
#631 **Twice the Spice** by Patricia Ryan

In May, the suspenseful **Harlequin Intrigue** novel
#420 **Twice Burned** by Pamela Burford

Pick up both—if you dare....

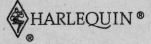

HARLEQUIN®

TWIN

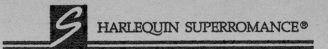

HARLEQUIN SUPERROMANCE®

WOMEN WHO *Dare*

NOBODY DOES IT BETTER
(#741, May 1997)
by Jan Freed

It took brains, independence and nerves of steel for Hope Manning to get where she is today, CEO of her own company. And *nobody does it better.*

Jared Austin teaches others to find the peace he himself discovered on a wilderness survival course. And *nobody does it better.*

Blackmailed into "chilling out," Hope reluctantly joins one of Jared's west Texas wilderness expeditions. And it's war between the sexes from the start! Then a sniper appears, gunning for Hope. To survive, she and Jared have to put aside their differences and work as a team....

And nobody *does it better!*

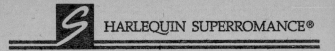